DIVINITY COMPLEX

Only God can grant life, but any man can impose death

P.H. FIGUR

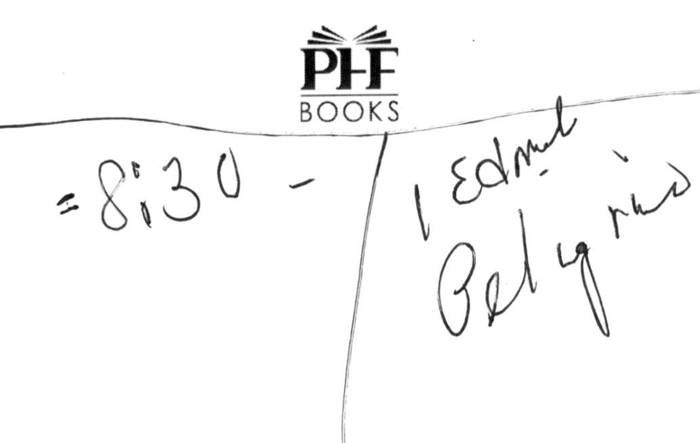

The Divinity Complex is a work of fiction. All depictions of characters and events are the products of the author's imagination. Any resemblance to actual persons or events is unintended and coincidental.

ASIN: B07FS3D91Z
ISBN-13: 978-17-1-949057-3

Other Books by P.H. Figur

The New America

Killen

Deathless

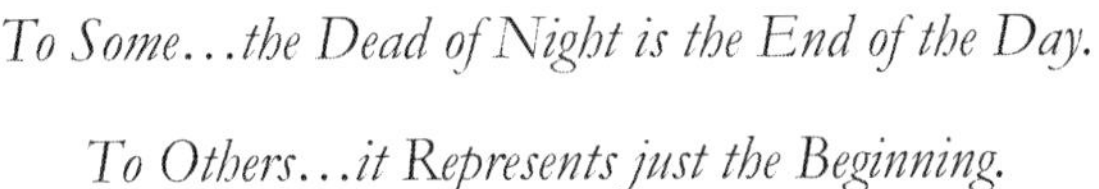

To Some…the Dead of Night is the End of the Day.

To Others…it Represents just the Beginning.

CHAPTER

1

Old Mustang

Sarasota, Florida

A FEW MINUTES BEFORE MIDNIGHT, Dominic Merino arrived at the Sarasota-Bradenton International Airport. As he pulled into the terminal, he parked his 1995 Ford Mustang in a restricted area typically reserved for law enforcement. Dominic glanced at his cell phone to check the time and watched in real-time as Saturday night turned into Sunday morning.

Dominic took a deep breath as his eyes surveyed the instrument panel. He grinned because the old Mustang had crossed an important milestone. The odometer reached the point where the display flipped forward to all zeros. Dominic sighed, ran his hands over the steering wheel, and patted the dashboard like a proud parent.

"You've been good, Mustang. Goin' on ten years, and you've never given me any problems," Dominic said aloud, as if the car had ears. "But age is catching up to you. I'm not sure how many more miles are left in your tank, but I'll promise to keep you running for as long as I can."

After working straight through the day, Dominic got a call from the office at 5:00 p.m. telling him to stop by the airport and then head to Longboat Key.

At the airport, Dominic turned the engine off, unholstered his Glock 19mm pistol, and hid the gun in the center console. The mid-summer night humidity was insufferable, causing beads of sweat to form on his forehead. Dominic rolled down the windows and reclined his seat as far as possible. A half an hour later, an odd sound awakened him from his unplanned nap.

Dominic opened his eyes and glanced at the passenger door window. His brother, Drake, smiled and then pointed towards the rear end of the Mustang.

Tap, Tap, Tap, Tap.

"Pop the trunk," Drake said as he threw in a duffle bag before climbing into the car. "Sorry, but they delayed my flight. Been waiting long?"

"About an hour, which is like a day in this car." Dominic straightened his seat and rubbed his eyes. "The air conditioning is on the fritz again."

"When are you gonna put her out to pasture?" Drake double-tapped the dashboard. "You've had this car for at least a decade. Brother, you need to move on."

"It's been nine years, seven months, and four days. But who's counting?" Dominic replied with a hint of sadness. "You're right. Maybe I should trade her in, but getting rid of her isn't easy. I can't let go. The old girl has given me some great memories."

"I get it, Dom. But the memories remain, with or without the car. Remember the happier times, not the years at the end of her useful life. Focus on the good memories and not the bad ones."

Dominic reluctantly agreed and nodded his head.

Drake was in Jacksonville with his fiancé, Taylor Brooks, when he got the call to return to Tampa. Drake and Taylor were both FBI Special Agents working on opposite sides of the state. They made the best of the situation, flying between the two cities every other weekend. But their situation was only temporary. Once they were married, Drake planned to transfer to Jacksonville so they could start their life as husband and wife.

"The office called four hours ago and told me to get here as soon as possible. They didn't give me a reason or explanation," Drake said. "I had to give up my Saturday night with Taylor. So, that makes you my date this evening. What are the plans? Dinner and a movie?"

"You think you're a comedian. But I got news for you. Stick to your day job," Dominic quipped. "We have a serious issue on our hands. There's a report of a murder in Longboat Key at Alden Moore's estate, and the details are disturbing."

"Wow, that's gonna be big news. Got any more information?"

"Someone called 911 from Alden's home. Everyone is on edge, so I suspect he may be the victim."

"You can't find anyone with a higher profile in Longboat Key. Who would want to kill him?"

"Not sure, but we'll find out."

"Dom, it's hot in here. How do you travel around in this thing without air conditioning?"

"The old Mustang has a backup system."

Dominic floored the Mustang, going from 0 to 60 mph in a mere five seconds. He then rolled down Drake's window as the wind rushed into the car. Dominic then turned to his brother and smiled.

"There's your air conditioning."

The Merino brothers were part of a proud family, many with long, distinguished careers in law enforcement. Their father was Sonny Merino, a well-known and respected director in the FBI's Criminal Investigative Division.

When Sonny retired, the plan was for his sons to follow in his footsteps. But as Drake and Dominic entered high school, they showed little interest. So, after their freshman year, Sonny put on a full-court press and introduced the boys to law enforcement. He started force-feeding Drake and Dominic information to change their minds. Afterward, if his sons went in another direction, then at least he could look in the mirror and say he tried.

Sonny began the dissemination process with Drake and Dominic at the beginning of their sophomore year. He started with FBI academics and then mixed in operational skills as they got older. By their senior year, they were well versed in the basics of conducting criminal investigations, disarming, and apprehending subjects, and defending themselves against different threats.

However, during his career, Sonny experienced things not found in textbooks or training videos. He referred to those learnings as "Sonny's Maxims." His wisdom wasn't just for his sons to use as FBI Special Agents. He encouraged them to incorporate his insight into everyday life. Four of the maxims stood out amongst the others.

- The obvious question sometimes can be the key to the ambiguous answer;
- For decisions, the head is adept, the heart is ardent, but the gut is absolute;
- The weak always have a chance to win the battle, but the strong always win the war; and,
- Always be there for your brother, because your brother will always be there for you.

By the time they graduated high school, Drake and Dominic finally came to appreciate the honor of serving in law enforcement and understood what it meant to their extended family. If you talked to Sonny over a few beers, he'd tell you those years instructing his sons wasn't so much a master class but a slow-paced indoctrination.

From an outsider's viewpoint, it looked as if Sonny put his thumb on the scale and steered the outcome in one direction, but ultimately, Drake and Dominic had to make their own decision if they wanted to pursue careers in the FBI. Sonny breathed a sigh of relief. The Merino family tradition continued for another generation.

~

The Merino brothers arrived at Longboat Key within half an hour. Representatives from the Sarasota and Bradenton Police Departments greeted them with both an update and a warning.

"Sorry to pull you boys away from family, but it's for a good reason. This is no ordinary crime scene," Officer Phillips said. "We're trying to get information and gather evidence as fast as possible before the media gets a hold of this story. This case is going to take on a life of its own."

"Was Alden Moore the victim?" Drake asked.

"Yes, he was," Officer Phillips responded. "But prepare yourself for what you're about to see. I've seen nothing like this in my lifetime. Whoever did this wanted to send a message."

"We've dealt with some horrid crime scenes over the years," Dominic said. "But to be honest, this job never gets any easier. Everyone has their breaking point. They just don't know where it is. Then when they find out, it's too late. The psychological damage has been done."

Drake and Dominic left the officers and walked towards the front of Alden's home. From a distance, they noticed a gleam of light emanating from a pair of oversized mahogany doors. Light usually represents a sign of hope, but this time, it meant something more ominous. With every step, the radiance became brighter, as if the light were daring anyone to enter.

When the Merino brothers reached the door, a bloody message greeted them.

YOU MAY ARRIVE A VISITOR,

BUT YOU MAY LEAVE A VICTIM—JACK

"Phillips was right. This is no ordinary crime scene." Dominic said as he walked through the doorway. Drake remained on the other side as if his shoes were stuck in cement. "Are you coming in?" Dominic saw his brother was contemplating something.

"Yeah," Drake responded as he glanced at the bloody message a second time. He looked into Dominic's eyes. "But something tells me this is no ordinary investigation."

CHAPTER

2

Crown Royal

Longboat Key, Florida

ALDEN MOORE was a 40-year-old self-made millionaire. He bought his 5,100-sq.-ft. estate two years prior for $3.9 Million. The sprawling, luxurious mansion overlooked Sarasota Bay and was one of the most sought-after properties in Longboat Key.

Over the years, Alden's residence became famous for its traditional private dinners and wild after-hour parties. Ask anyone in town, and they would tell you the many politicians, celebrities, and socialites who graced the walls of Alden's home was a "Who's Who" amongst the power elite.

The Merinos walked into a large reception area inside the home. They were greeted by a double-sided wood-burning fireplace, which split the room in half. On the left side was a chef's kitchen with a granite-topped island and top-of-the-line luxury appliances. On the right side was a formal dining room accompanied by a combination home office and library.

"Sure is nice to have some coin," Drake said with a hint of jealousy.

"Just remember, nothing in life is free," Dominic said. "If you want all this,"—Dominic stretched out his arms for dramatic effect—"you'll take the baggage that goes along with it."

"I'll take my chances and let you know how it turns out," Drake replied.

Dominic turned towards his brother, narrowed his eyes, and shook his head.

The Merinos walked to the back of the residence, where they came upon the home's most impressive feature. A series of twenty-foot-high windows stretching from floor to ceiling. Opposite the windows was an oversized leather couch angled to provide the quintessential view of Sarasota Bay.

They stopped short as their hearts became stuck in their throats.

In front of them was Alden Moore sitting comfortably on the leather couch. He was relaxed, with legs crossed and arms outstretched. Alden's right hand was clutching a half-empty glass of Crown Royal Canadian Whisky, his drink of choice after a long day of negotiating multi-million-dollar deals.

"Alden's ice melted sooner than he expected," Dominic noted. "He should have freshened his drink before we got here."

Alden couldn't top off his Canadian Whisky because something important was *missing*. Well, that wasn't entirely true. It's hard to make the case something is missing when it's in plain sight. A better descriptor would have been *misplaced*.

The item in question was perched on a large rectangular coffee table in front of the couch. In the middle, propped up on display, was Alden's severed head with a single bullet hole in the left temple. His eyes were wide open and pointed towards his own corpse.

Behind Alden's body on the wall, someone removed a large oil painting. In its place were words scribbled by a madman. The killer didn't need a palette of colors as preferred by most artists. He needed only the dark crimson siphoned from Alden's body. It was another cryptic message. This one was more haunting than the front door.

I WALK THE EARTH, SECOND IN COMMAND.

THOSE WHO DOUBT, WILL DIE BY MY HAND—JACK

Alden always thought he would go out in a blaze of glory.

In his mind, he envisioned his life would play out like a movie scene. The end would occur in a large conference room with greedy investment bankers, briefcases of unmarked bills, and concealed handguns. A civil discussion would turn into an argument. Shots would ring out, and he would meet his fate. But the reality was his demise was pure fantasy because Alden Moore was just another statistic in a long line of unsolved murders.

Death for Alden was swift and violent.

In the moment of truth, there was no time for him to be afraid. What surprised him was his final emotion was one of anger, not because his life ended abruptly. Instead, it was because he couldn't fulfill his dying wish. Alden Moore was angry because he never finished his Canadian Whisky.

~

Drake panned the room and changed his mind. "If this is the baggage that comes with success, then I'm not going to be taking any chances anytime soon."

"Wise choice," Dominic said.

Off to the side, Tyler Woods was busy taking crime scene pictures. They noticed a glazed look in Tyler's eyes as he peered through the viewfinder and clicked the camera shutter.

"Tyler, are you okay?" Dominic asked.

Tyler knelt and put the camera on the ground for a second to wipe away tears. He stood up after a few seconds.

"Sorry guys, but this is tough for me. Alden and my older sister were a couple at one point. They saw each other off and on for five years. During that time, he took me under his wing and treated me like family. To Alden, it didn't matter if you were an investment banker or some snot-nosed kid. When Alden talked, you could tell he cared. He invested his time to get to know you. To see him like this is horrible."

"Didn't the office realize where they were sending you?" Drake asked.

"It's not their fault. I didn't tell anyone about my connection to Alden. They just told me to come here and take pictures. I didn't realize this was Alden's home until it was too late."

"Go on home. We'll send for someone else," Dominic said. "You need to stay away from the crime scene. Remember Alden in happier times, not what you see here at the end of his life. Focus on the good memories and not the bad ones."

"Thanks, Dominic," Tyler said as he left the room. "Don't worry. I'll be okay."

Once Tyler was out of sight, he heard Drake behind him in a sarcastic tone. "Sound advice. Seems like I've heard something like that somewhere else." Dominic turned around and stared at Drake. "Now isn't the time." Drake smiled at his brother. He always liked to inject light humor to distract himself from the carnage.

The Merinos returned their attention to Alden Moore, spending three straight hours taking notes and collecting evidence. Before leaving, Dominic caught Drake staring at the wall again, reading the message aloud one more time.

I Walk the Earth, Second in Command.
Those who Doubt, Will Die by my Hand—Jack

"Drake, let's go. We'll return in the morning."

Drake didn't respond, transfixed by the bloody message.

"This isn't a one and done," Drake muttered. He continued to stare straight ahead. "This problem is bigger than we thought."

"What makes you say that?"

"This is the work of a serial killer," Drake said.

"Well then. It sounds like we'll be traveling around the state looking for this guy. Are you gonna be up for a road trip?"

"I'll join you, but I have one request," Drake said.

"What would that be?"

"Get the damn air conditioning fixed," Drake said with a smile.

On Monday, Drake woke right before dawn. He brewed a pot of coffee and sat on his backyard deck until the sun peeked through the clouds. He always looked forward to watching the sunrise. Partly because it represented the gift of another day, but also because it was a temporary distraction from the images in his mind of Alden Moore.

Drake walked down to the lake behind his house. In the distance, he saw an older man in a small fishing boat. It was Kurt Schwartz, Drake's friend, and longtime next-door neighbor, along with his fishing buddy, the infamous Jacques Catsteau.

Kurt was a retired investment banker and a man of many talents. At the crack of dawn on weekday mornings, he was an avid fisherman. But by the afternoon, he turned into a talented craftsman. Kurt spent hours in the garage building everything from coffee tables to small fishing boats.

On top of all his skills, Kurt was also a closet sage. He knew something about everything. He could talk to you about replacing car engines, balancing retirement accounts, or making crab cakes. It was easy to see why everyone respected his opinion on almost any topic.

After Drake's friendly wave, Kurt reeled in his fishing pole and headed back to the dock. Drake walked over to say hello. Jacques jumped from the boat and trotted over to brush up against Drake's leg. He returned the welcome gesture with a quick scratch behind the cat's ears.

"Mornin' Kurt," Drake said. "You better put a ball and chain on your cat. He keeps coming by and visiting me every night."

"He visits you only because you keep leaving food outside for him," Kurt replied.

Jacques grabbed onto Drake's pant leg, trying to get his attention.

"Maybe not," Drake said. "Face it, accept the fact he likes me."

Kurt flashed a stern but playful look at the feline.

"Jacques, stick with daddy, or your fishing days are over."

"Short fishing trip this morning?" Drake asked.

"Yeah," Kurt responded. "I can't stand fishing when clouds are in the way."

"You're in the minority," Drake said. "Most people look forward to a beautiful day like this."

"When you're retired, just waking up is a gift," Kurt said. "What are you up to today?"

"It's Monday. Time to head to the office," Drake said.

"Today is Monday?" Kurt asked as he tilted his head.

"Yeah, it's the start of a new week," Drake replied. "What day did you think it was?"

"I could have sworn it was Tuesday," Kurt responded as he scratched his chin. "I forgot the other thing about retirement."

"What would that be?" Drake asked.

"Every day seems the same," Kurt said with a chuckle.

Drake made a few stops before going to the office. But it wasn't the usual morning. It was the Monday morning after the Alden Moore murder. The whole city was on edge. So, Drake braced himself for the myriad of questions that were about to come his way.

His first stop was at the Race Trac to fill his gas tank and grab a newspaper. He walked in, picked up a Tampa Bay Times, and made his way to the cashier.

"Mornin' Brian," Drake said. "$30 on #10 and the paper."

"Looks like someone has been up all night," Brian said. "I bet it's because of what happened to Alden Moore."

"How would you know?"

"The bags under your eyes are a dead giveaway."

"Yeah. I guess," Drake admitted. "I haven't got much sleep lately."

"Any idea what happened to Alden?"

"Brian, I can't divulge details. It's an ongoing investigation."

"Someone told me he was dismembered from head to toe."

"Brian, don't believe everything you hear."

"Was it true?"

"Brian, I can't"—Drake was cut off mid-sentence.

"I know," Brian said, "It's an ongoing investigation."

"Now you're catching on," Drake said. "You'll find out what happened when the public does and not a day sooner."

"I understand," Brian said. "But do yourself a favor and go to bed early tonight. Those bags make you look ten years older."

Drake chuckled and then turned towards his car. As he was walking away, he said, "Guess I'll have to start dating older women."

~

The next stop was Designer Cleaners to drop off and pick up dry cleaning. He flung a bag on the counter filled with shirts and pants.

"Hello, Mr. Drake!" Luis said as he turned to get Drake's clothes. "How are you his morning?"

"Okay, Luis," Drake said. "A lot is going on right now."

"Did you hear about Alden Moore?" Luis asked. "The story was on the news this morning. They said someone murdered Alden. But they didn't give out any other information. Do you know anything about it?"

"Luis, I can't divulge details. It's an ongoing investigation."

"I'm sorry for putting you on the spot," Luis said. "Cable news is reporting that there's a serial killer in the bay area. You need to catch him quick!"

"Are you going to catch the bad guy?" asked Christopher, Luis' eight-year-old son, who appeared from behind the counter.

"He knows?" Drake asked as he looked at Luis.

"The story is all over the television," Luis said. "It's hard not to know."

"I know how to catch the bad guy," Christopher said.

"How?" Drake asked, as he leaned over towards Christopher.

"Dudley Do-Right can catch him," Christopher said. "He always gets his man."

"Christopher, Dudley Do-Right is in Canada," Drake said. "He's busy trying to track down Snidely Whiplash. But don't worry, we'll get the bad guy soon. I promise."

"Luis, make sure your son sticks to Rocky and Bullwinkle cartoons and lays off the cable news," Drake said with a smile. Luis nodded in agreement.

~

The last stop of the morning was Political Donuts, Drake's favorite breakfast spot. It was a trendy shop with a catchy slogan:

Political Donuts—We serve donuts left and right.

Behind the counter was Nikki. She was a tall, thin brunette who always greeted Drake with a smile. Nikki had a big crush on Drake but kept her feelings to herself because she knew he was engaged. But that didn't stop her excitement whenever Drake walked into the shop.

"Well, look what the cat dragged in," Nikki said with a smile.

"Hey Nikki," Drake asked. "What's in the bag from both sides of the aisle today?"

"The conservative donut choice for today is a traditional glazed. On the progressive side, we've got a raised yeast donut covered in vanilla frosting and topped with Frosted Flakes. We call it—The Cereal Killer. Get it?"

Drake loved when Nikki laughed, but for once, he thought her joke wasn't so funny. He forced a smile for Nikki and paid for his breakfast. On the way out, Drake chucked the Cereal Killer into the trash because all it did was remind him of Alden Moore's murder.

One of Nikki's co-workers asked why Drake threw away the progressive donut of the day.

"I guess he doesn't think Frosted Flakes are so Gr-r-reat after all," Nikki said.

CHAPTER

3

That's Life

Tampa, Florida

DANNY NOLAN pulled into the parking garage at the Henley Street Condominiums on Saturday at 1:00 a.m. He jumped out of his BMW 7-Series Sedan and flipped the keys to the attendant. He couldn't wait for his head to hit the pillow.

"Hey, Henry, can you park her for me?" Danny asked. "I need to go to bed as soon as possible. It's time to crash. I'm dog-tired."

"Sure thing, Mr. Nolan," Henry responded. "No worries."

Henry hopped in the car and saw Danny's phone on the dashboard. A huge smile came across his face, and in a soft voice, he said, "Cha-Ching."

"Hey, Mr. Nolan," Henry yelled. "You forgot your cell phone again."

Danny stopped in his tracks, dropped his head in disgust, and turned around. He was mad at himself, not for leaving his phone in the car, but because his mistake cost him ten dollars.

"I knew you'd forget your cell phone again. That's why I saved a place in my pocket for your ten spot."

Danny made a bet with Henry to have some fun at the attendant's expense. But it wasn't the primary reason for the wager. Danny hoped the risk of losing $10 to a twenty-year-old kid would force him to remember to take his phone. It didn't.

"Here you go," Danny said as he grudgingly passed an Alexander Hamilton to Henry.

Bringgg, Bringgg, Buzzz, Bringgg, Bringgg, Buzzz

"Hold on. This may be the President calling to offer you his heartfelt congratulations."

Danny's iPhone displayed a familiar number. It was Stephanie from the club.

"Hi. What's up, Steph?"

"Hey Danny, sorry to bother you, but the back door is still broken, and we can't close up shop. I thought someone took care of this."

"Yes, Brent Adams fixed it last week. The lock worked last night when I left. Not sure what happened. Let me call Brent. I'll have him come out in the morning. Don't worry, I'll be there in an hour, so you guys can go home."

"No need to come out here, Danny. I'm here with Paul and Gina. We can secure the door from the inside and crash in the office. Everything is under control."

"Are you sure? You guys are sitting on at least ten grand. I don't feel comfortable leaving you all alone."

"Danny, when was the last time someone reported a robbery in this neighborhood?"

"Um...uh...never?"

"*Ding, ding, ding*...correct answer," Stephanie said. "Nothing to worry about here. We'll secure the door, the money will be in the safe, and we'll be sleeping with our friends Glock and SIG Sauer."

"All right, but text me to let me know everything is okay."

"You got it, boss. Good night."

Danny stared at his phone for a few seconds and wondered if he should go back to the club.

"Are you okay, Mr. Nolan?" Henry asked.

Danny shook the cobwebs from his head.

"Yeah, I'm fine, Henry. I just need some rest. I may need to leave at a moment's notice. Park her close by and have her ready to go."

"Will do," Henry responded.

Danny Nolan lived in Palm Harbor, an upscale community located west of Tampa on the Gulf of Mexico. After graduating from the University of Florida, he partnered with his father in a new chain of family-oriented restaurants, making the Nolans a lot of money.

Ten years later, Danny broke away from his father and started his own business. Danny's Dinner Club opened in downtown Tampa on Channelside Drive. The club was an upscale restaurant that also had a small concert venue for live performances. At first, Danny spent a lot of time there. But after three months, he ceded control to his team.

Stephanie Powell ran the day-to-day operations as the Restaurant and Club Manager. She had two assistants, Paul Knight, and Gina Richards. Danny's stayed open to the early hours on weekends. So, it wasn't unusual for the managers to crash in the office and spend the night.

A few hours later, at 6:45 a.m., Danny woke up and stumbled downstairs to grab breakfast. He looked at his phone and realized he never received a text message from Stephanie. Danny tried to contact her, but the phone went straight to voicemail. His muscles tightened, and his heart raced. His gut told him something was wrong.

Danny skipped breakfast and drove to the club. He stared out the front window of the BMW as a million thoughts went through his head. Suddenly, his phone rang, and his heart raced again.

Bringgg, Bringgg, Buzzz, Bringgg, Bringgg, Buzzz

Danny swallowed hard. He picked up his cell phone as sweat poured down the side of his face.

"Mr. Nolan?" Officer O'Neil asked. "Is this Mr. Nolan?"

"Yes, it is," Danny responded.

"We have some troubling news. Someone reported a disturbance at your club overnight, and we're on-site investigating. When can you get here?"

"Already on my way. Be there within 45 minutes."

Danny got a sick feeling in the pit of his stomach.

Something was very wrong.

The marquee at *Danny's Dinner Club* hadn't changed since the night before. It still read "This Weekend - The Rockin' Keys Featuring the Dueling Pianos." The marquee changed later in the day, replaced with another signboard to accommodate a longer running act called "Closed Until Further Notice."

A black Cadillac Escalade with tinted windows parked across the street from Danny's. The Merino brothers and Tyler Woods got out and entered the club through the back door. They weren't prepared for what they were about to experience.

Later, they'd say they felt like a group of scared teenagers in a Halloween house of horrors waiting for an actor to jump out of the darkness and yell "Boo." But at Danny's, they didn't have to worry about a soul jumping out from anywhere. That's because nothing was moving at Danny's…nothing at all.

Tyler pointed his video camera towards the stage where two Yamaha baby grand pianos faced one another. On each piano bench was a victim, slumped over their respective keyboard, with a single bullet to the temple. On top of the piano was sheet music for "That's Life" by Frank Sinatra. At first, it seemed to be a strange coincidence, but more likely, it was an intentional cruel joke of a madman.

The group worked its way to Danny's office. As the three men entered, they noticed blood splattered everywhere. Towards the backside of the room was a built-in wall safe, which held cash and credit card receipts. It was wide open and cleaned out. Someone took the time to stack everything on Danny's desk. The money was in neat piles, denominated by face value.

Meanwhile, Stephanie's body was propped up at the desk, positioned as if she were still reconciling the night receipts and preparing the bank deposit. Not a penny was missing. The killer wanted to emphasize that the motive behind the murders wasn't financial. In fact, there didn't seem to be a motive at all. On the wall in front of Stephanie was a short message written in blood:

WHAT YOU REAP IS WHAT YOU SOW.
AS LONG AS YOU LIVE, THAT'S HOW IT GOES—JACK

When Danny's BMW pulled into the parking lot, the police were in full force, with half a dozen squad cars and three ambulances. The authorities roped off the back entrance of the club. Danny's heart got caught in his throat as he ran towards the officers.

"I'm Danny Nolan, the owner. What happened?"

"Mr. Nolan, we have multiple homicides inside the club," Officer O'Neil said. "We have to notify next of kin before we can make any formal announcements."

Danny fell to the ground as a river of tears rolled down his face.

"Let me in. I know who's in there," Danny said as he got up and took two steps towards the back door.

"I'm sorry, Mr. Nolan," Officer O'Neil said. "This is an active crime scene, and unauthorized individuals can't go inside."

Danny moved forward again, but this time, two officers stepped in and brought him to an ambulance. When the door opened, Danny saw a man sitting with an oxygen mask. Once he climbed inside, an officer closed the door behind him.

"Brent, you okay?" Danny asked.

"I think so," Brent replied. "I fell and hit my head, and when I woke up, I was sitting right here."

"What happened?"

Brent stared at the floor. He couldn't look Danny in the eyes.

"I got here early to fix the lock," Brent said. "When I got out of my truck, I saw the back door of the club was open. The lock seemed fine, but I made a few adjustments anyway to make sure."

"Why was the door open?"

"Not sure. I went inside to investigate. The reception area and restaurant looked normal. I then went to the other side, and when I saw the carnage on the stage, I fell and hit my head. I must've passed out."

"Danny, I've seen nothing like this in my life. There are no words to describe it. Someone murdered Stephanie, Paul, and Gina and butchered them from head to toe. I've come across some gruesome scenes overseas in the army, but this is different. This is the work of a madman."

Danny's body froze, and he couldn't utter a single word. Brent finally got the courage to look into Danny's eyes.

"Please make me a promise, Danny. Don't go inside. The scene isn't for human eyes. You need to remember Stephanie, Paul, and

Gina in the best of times with smiles on their faces. If you go in, it'll haunt you forever. I made that mistake already, and I'll pay for it. Don't go inside. You'll be sorry if you do."

Danny rested his head in his hands and wept again. Brent put his hand on Danny's shoulders for support, and the two men embraced. The ambulance door opened. A paramedic came by to check on them.

"Brent, are you feeling better?" the paramedic asked.

"Other than this bump on my head, I'm okay."

"Good, the FBI arrived and wants to speak to you. Up for it?"

"Yeah, I can talk to them now."

Danny wanted out too, but the paramedic blocked him.

"Sorry Danny, you need to stay here longer. Those were my orders from the officers. Don't worry. You'll be out soon."

As Brent got out of the ambulance, he told Danny to stay strong. They would get through this together. Before the door closed, Brent turned around and noticed something about Danny. He looked like someone about to jump off the deep end.

Little did Brent know…Danny had already jumped.

Twenty minutes later, the Merino brothers and Tyler stepped outside the club for some fresh air. Tyler laid his camera on the ground and pointed it in their direction to capture thoughts and reactions to the crime scene. They all took deep breaths and wiped away the sweat from their faces. It was a troubling experience.

"This is no ordinary run-of-the-mill murder scene," Dominic said. "Someone planned and carried this out with precision. Whoever did this didn't leave many clues."

Dominic took a drink of water and continued.

"Individuals who carry out crimes like these have deep-seated mental issues from their childhood. But what they don't realize is that they can't continue with their murder spree forever."

"Whoever Jack is, he is just playing with us," Drake said. "That's why he poses the bodies and leaves cryptic messages. You can sense the arrogance in his words."

"We'll see about that," Dominic responded. "These lunatics always make mistakes, and they always get caught."

"Jack will kill again," Drake said as Dominic's eyes widened. "He believes he has the right to do so. Jack is driven by something few people possess."

"What would that be?" Dominic asked.

"Divinity," Drake responded.

Drake's response caused Dominic to run his hands through his hair and shake his head. He asked his brother to elaborate.

"After Alden Moore's murder, I wondered why someone would want to kill him in such a brutal fashion. I kept thinking about the first line of the bloody message on the wall. Jack said he 'walked the earth second in command.' I did some research and discovered the phrase had something to do with divinity."

Dominic couldn't figure out what direction his brother was going.

"Divinity has a few meanings," Drake said. "But one definition is 'someone who ranks below God but above all humans.' The divine think they're superior to everyone else. Jack believes he has the power to decide if someone should live or die.

"When did you figure all this out?" Dominic asked.

"Within the past week. Just a theory I'm kicking around. I wasn't going to mention anything until I finished my research. But now that we've seen another message from Jack, I had to tell you."

"Interesting, but your theory isn't based on reality," Dominic said. "We need to focus on someone that has the prototypical characteristics of a serial killer. A middle-aged man with a troubled past, a power junkie who manipulates people, a loner with shallow emotions, or someone who is impulsive and can't show remorse or guilt. I could go on for a while, but you get my point."

"Most likely, you're right, but my gut tells me otherwise," Drake said. "I'm concerned because the power of divinity is something we've never dealt with. Divinity doesn't grow on trees. It's usually given to someone and is in good hands. However, if it falls into the wrong hands, it becomes extremely dangerous."

Dominic and Drake both looked at each other. They were far apart in their theories. But they agreed on one thing. They hadn't heard the last from Jack. Not by a long shot.

CHAPTER

4

Mount Washburn

Cody, Wyoming

HARRISON BRADFORD sat at a small round table in a large corner office, staring out the window. In front of him was a breathtaking view of Mount Washburn and Yellowstone National Park. He was waiting for an 11:00 a.m. meeting to start. Ten minutes later, a head poked through the door.

"Harry, Jameson is running late. He said to sit tight," Lilly said.

"Do I have a choice?" Harrison responded, "I'm waiting for the CEO of Pharmatech. If I got up and left, that would be grounds for dismissal."

"Don't be silly," Lilly said with a smile. "I have a better chance of winning the Mega Millions lottery tonight all by myself before you ever get fired."

"Well, if you win, call me," Harrison responded with a wink and a smile. "I'll leave here and be your personal financial advisor."

Another ten minutes passed, and still no Jameson. Lilly poked her head in once more.

"Sorry Harry, he just messaged me and said he was pulling into the parking lot."

"No worries," Harrison turned his chair. "I'll just look out the window and enjoy the majestic landscape."

Once he graduated from the University of California in San Francisco, Harrison accepted a position at Pharmatech. The company was a national pharmaceutical business based in Cody, Wyoming. It would be the only company he would ever work for his entire life.

A few of the older employees were jealous of Harrison's rise to become the Chief Financial Officer. The rumors were that he curried favor with executive management. But the truth was, Harrison was a skilled tactician who knew accounting and finance like the back of his hand.

Half an hour later, Jameson Bradford walked into the room with a huge smile on his face. He was more than the founder, CEO, and President of Pharmatech; he was also Harrison's father. They met on the fifth day of every month to review Pharmatech's financial performance. Jameson was aware of everything going on at Pharmatech, but he still liked to hear the good news straight from his son.

"Hello Harry," Jameson said. "Today is a blessed day, isn't it?"

"Dad, you're so predictable," Harrison said. "You've been saying the same thing every quarter of every year for the past five years."

"Well, have I ever been wrong? I think not. Nothing makes me happier than seeing all the hard work translate into good results. Now hit me with some more good news."

Harrison handed Jameson the most recent financial statements and long-term revenue projections. The elder Bradford looked at the information for a minute and grinned from ear to ear.

"As of today, Pharmatech is one of the richest companies in the world with annual revenues of $400 billion," Harrison said. "Projections show in the next five years revenues will be close to $1 trillion per year. At this rate, we're printing money. Nothing can stop us."

"What did you expect, son? When Pharmatech eradicated neurological disease, the company reaped all the benefits."

Harrison looked out the window and wondered if his father's ego was getting to be bigger than Mount Washburn. The mountain came in first, but Jameson wasn't too far behind and was gaining ground.

Wealth and success gave Jameson the power to do whatever he wanted. He never worried because he knew he could dictate any outcome, solve any problem, or overcome any obstacle. As far as Jameson was concerned, if he had a problem, all he had to do was to throw money at the situation. And he had more than almost anyone else in the country.

To many people, Jameson came across as a shrewd businessman who cared for others. But those closest to him knew of a different side. Behind closed doors, Jameson was a cutthroat who believed he was above all others. As Harrison looked at the landscape outside the window one more time, Mount Washburn didn't seem to be all that big anymore.

A decade earlier, Pharmatech was one of many struggling pharmaceutical companies. Neurological disease had reached a critical phase of epidemic proportion. After a worldwide call to action, a coalition of countries raised billions of dollars for research to find a solution.

Jameson jumped at the opportunity and instructed Pharmatech to invest in a new project called "Reverse & Restore." He was passionate about the project because degenerative neurological disease affected the Bradford family tree. That's where the commitment came from to develop a miracle drug to reverse the effects and restore lives to normal.

The project focused on understanding how the brain kept and processed information. Studies showed when humans are born, the brain is working at its peak efficiency. Billions of neurons wait to receive, process, and share information with each other. Synapses function as bridges to connect one neuron to the next. But over time, the synapses weaken and become frayed or broken. The data stored in each neuron becomes stale and outdated, which is the genesis of many neurological diseases, including dementia, Parkinson's disease, seizures, stroke, and even headaches.

A few years later, Reverse & Restore had a significant breakthrough. Pharmatech discovered a new miracle drug called Restorex, which paired an inhibitor called Mendaryl with Dopamine. Restorex visited every neuron in the brain, and when the drug came across a non-functioning neuron, two things happened.

First, Mendaryl repaired the synapses between neurons and made the connections as good as new.

Second, each neuron received an infusion of dopamine to reverse the effects of the disease.

In layman's terms, it was akin to replacing the wires in an automobile engine and filling the tank to the brim with premium gasoline. The only thing missing was a free car wash.

Once Restorex was approved, it went to market within three months. The goal was to gain worldwide distribution at an affordable price so that any country that needed the drug had equal access. Pharmatech's breakthrough cured neurological disease and made the company one of the largest pharmaceutical companies in the world.

~

Jameson clasped his hands and placed them behind his head. He reclined in his chair. He had big plans for Pharmatech, and he wanted to share them with Harrison.

"Harry, what are your thoughts about the future?" Jameson asked.

"Dad, I can't think of anything else Pharmatech can do," Harrison replied. "With Restorex, there's no need for research or market, and we have no competition. The drug sells itself. All we need to do is manufacture, distribute, and watch our bank accounts grow.

I never thought I'd say this about any product, but we're at the point where we don't even need a long-term strategy."

Jameson stood, put his hands in his pants pockets, and looked out the window.

"Harry, what do you see?" Jameson asked.

"Mount Washburn," Harrison replied.

"Look closer, son. What do you see?"

Harrison panned the landscape again.

"A large majestic mountain overlooking everything within its domain."

"Precisely, son, the mountain is Pharmatech, and our domain is the world."

Harrison's concerns about Jameson's ego were becoming a reality.

"Harry, you may think we can't do something, but we can."

"What would that be, dad?" Jameson turned to his son with a big smile. "You'll find out in a few minutes."

CHAPTER

5

Hoodwinked

Cody, Wyoming

AFTER A KNOCK ON THE DOOR, two large men walked into Jameson's office. Both were over six feet tall and looked more like football players. However, the expensive suits, pocket squares, and oversized briefcases were a dead giveaway. The two men weren't playing a game. They were there to conduct business.

"Harry, let me introduce you," Jameson said. "This is Benjamin Franklin Pierce and John Francis McIntyre."

As the men shook hands, Harrison was in a temporary state of disbelief. His face had an expression people have when they sign a long-term agreement for a timeshare property. Usually, once they have a moment of clarity, they realize they've been hoodwinked.

Harrison wasn't expecting others to join his meeting with Jameson. He always met one-on-one with his father to discuss business results. Something was going on, and he was about to find out what it was.

"These two men have been working with me on another project," Jameson said.

Harrison wasn't in a state of disbelief for long. He reoriented himself and rejoined the conversation.

"What's the project?" Harrison asked.

"Harry, at Pharmatech, we've accomplished what many would say was the impossible by eradicating neurological disease. We have shown the world that no one else has our knowledge and resources. Now we can take the next step for the greater good."

"I guess I'm not following. What other diseases or conditions can we cure?"

Jameson and the two mysterious men chuckled.

"Harry, our future isn't to find another cure. Our vision is much bigger. We want to develop something that has a significant impact on the world."

Jameson walked around the office. He liked to stroll around whenever he pontificated and stood in one spot when he wanted to make a point.

"What we plan to do is rid the world of its greatest threat. But it's not what you think. The threat isn't a country, person, or ideology. This may be a surprise, but the biggest threat to mankind is addiction."

Jameson stopped at the head of the table and continued.

"Let me explain. Addiction enslaves us. It masks our thoughts and feelings and overtakes our mind and body. Addiction replaces truth and reality with lies and fairy tales. Over time addiction isolates us from everyone and everything."

Jameson looked straight into Harrison's eyes.

"That's until the day we realize everything we said and done was all a big mistake. When the moment of clarity arrives, it's usually too late."

Jameson sat at the table.

"We're all addicted to something. Some addictions are positive, and we can live with them. But other addictions have the potential to overwhelm us. Those are the addictions we must eradicate."

"Pharmatech has the resources, capital, and knowledge to do anything it wants," Harrison said. "Why is solving addiction so important?"

"I've never told you this, Harry, but in my life, I had multiple addictions. Primarily alcohol, drugs, and gambling. But to be truthful, I was addicted to everything I came in contact with."

"I did not know," Harrison said as he looked his father in the eyes.

"The devil was in my house and came close to destroying me. It took years of rehabilitation to summon the courage to confront my demons and return to a normal life."

"Well, I'm glad you beat it."

"Harry, no one ever beats addiction. The struggle never ends because the devil never goes away. He is always right outside your house, waiting for an opportunity to get inside again."

"But what can Pharmatech do about addiction? How does the company fit into all this?"

"Great question, Harry. After hitting rock bottom, I made myself a promise. If I ever had the money and resources, I'd do something about addiction. I wanted to make sure no one went through hell as I did. Pharmatech's success has put me in a position to do just that. I'm going to take on the challenge."

"How are you going to do it?"

"What we've learned from our initial research is that once someone reaches the point of addiction, it's too late. So to answer your question, we're going to develop a drug to attack the precursors to addiction. To understand the theory and logic, we need to understand three things."

Jameson walked over to a whiteboard next to the conference room table and wrote three lines.

- Behaviors are an accumulation of responses.
- Habits are an accumulation of behaviors.
- Addiction is an accumulation of habits.

"These three theoretical statements represent the framework that explains how we're going to do this," Jameson said as he strolled around the room again.

"Let us start with the first statement. When something stimulates us, it initiates a response. If we repeat our responses over time, it becomes a behavior."

Jameson pointed at the whiteboard.

"Next, we have the second statement. Let's use the same logic. If we repeat our behaviors over time, it turns into a habit."

Jameson pointed at the whiteboard one last time.

"Last, we have the third statement. This is where things get dangerous because if we lose control over a bad habit and it's repeated over time, it becomes an addiction. This is the point where, where the horse is out of the barn, there is no turning back."

"So, what do we do?" Harrison asked.

"We have to address the issue much earlier," Jameson responded.

"I see where you're going with this," Harrison said. "If you can change people's behavior, then the behavior can never become a habit. Therefore, the habit never turns into an addiction."

"Correct, son. Our focus will be on how humans develop behaviors. Once we understand the triggers for behavior, we can develop a drug to alter the mind's modus operandi. This drug won't affect decision-making but will change behavior. It will make addiction impossible."

"So, once this drug is available to the public, what do you think the impact will be?" Harrison asked.

"Son, ask yourself the following. What if we lived in a world with less crime and violence? What if we got rid of substance abuse, health issues, or neurological disorders? What if we had no negative behaviors, compulsions, or obsessions?"

Harrison took a moment and looked at his father.

What if you didn't have an ego as big as Mount Washburn?

After his thought, he provided a politically correct answer.

"Everyone would live happily ever after."

"Correct, son. That's what the project is all about."

Harrison opened his mouth to speak, collected his thoughts, and continued.

"I'm wondering if we are playing in the wrong sandbox?" Harrison asked. "Curing people of a disease is one thing, but altering the way people think is another. It sounds like we're forcing people to respond in the same way. I'm not sure we should go there."

Jameson became agitated and bit his lower lip.

"Harry, I assure you that's not the case. Remember what we talked about at the outset. This project is for the greater good."

Harrison nodded in agreement but did so only to appease his father. He knew Jameson had an ulterior motive, but Harrison wanted to appear cooperative so he could stay involved and see where this was going.

"What's the name of the project?" Harrison asked.

"It's called 'Project Diablo,' which is an acronym that stands for 'Development of Individual Attitudes and Behaviors for Long-term Oversight.' If you can change your attitude and behavior, then you can gain control over your life."

Harrison looked at the two mysterious men and realized they hadn't said a word in the entire meeting. Jameson watched as

Harrison made eye contact with them. After an awkward moment of silence, Jameson sensed he needed to break the ice.

"You're wondering what roles Benjamin Franklin Pierce and John Francis McIntyre are playing in Project Diablo. They have led the charge for Phases I and II. They built and populated a secret test environment away from the public eye. It's a prefabricated town filled with people who have enlisted to take part in the project. Each volunteer has a unique story that includes addiction, compulsion, or some other issue. We'll track and observe the volunteers in the town from a distance to get the information needed to help us develop a solution."

"Phases I and II sound like other projects," Harrison said. "I'll be in contact with these men to make sure we stay on track. I'll set up…"—Jameson stopped his son in mid-sentence.

"Harry, you can't be involved in the project. When we enter Phase III, you'll take more of a leadership role. I'm telling you this for two reasons. First, you're Pharmatech's CFO, and second, you're my only son. You need to know what's going on because you're next in line to run this company. This will all be yours someday."

Franklin and John sat still and displayed no emotion. Harrison wondered if the two men were androids.

"Can I keep in contact with them so I can stay in the loop?" Harrison asked.

"Harry, you must abide by one simple rule. You can't contact or communicate with them. In fact, for security purposes, I can't even tell you their real names. Franklin and John refer to two fictional doctors from MASH, a 1970s sitcom."

Harrison looked over at the two android-like men. They both had huge grins on their faces. They were human, after all. Harrison wanted to kick himself because he should have known androids couldn't smile.

"You can call them Hawkeye and Trapper John if you like," Jameson said. "Those were Franklin and John's nicknames. MASH was before your time, son. That's why we could pull off our little joke."

Harrison took in a deep breath and exhaled. But after a few minutes, his gut told him something was wrong. He'd been hoodwinked once again.

CHAPTER

6

The End

Kingsland, Georgia

TAYLOR BROOKS left Winston-Salem in her BMW 325i and jumped on I-95, headed south towards Jacksonville. She was driving home with a full tank of gas, an ice-cold Coca-Cola, a loud car stereo, and not a worry in the world.

Buzzz, Buzzz, Buzzz, Buzzz.

Taylor answered her speakerphone as music bounced off the windows. Whoever was on the other end of the line was unintentionally greeted with an earful of The Beatles. Taylor fumbled around with the radio knobs for a few seconds and lowered the volume.

"Sorry about that," Taylor said, hoping the caller was someone she knew well.

"Looks like someone is having a good time tonight," Drake said in jest.

"Hey, cut me some slack. The only time I have time to listen to music is in the car. Besides, it's keeping me awake until the next service area. I need to get some caffeine. Can't make it through seven hours on just music alone."

"The song sounded familiar. Was that 'The End' by The Beatles?" Drake asked.

"Uh...um...yes."

Drake pretended to be outraged. "What's going on here? You make fun of me for being a big Beatles fan, and now I find out you're listening to them behind my back?"

"Cool the jets, Drake. I'm about to make a confession. When we're apart for an extended period, listening to The Beatles reminds me of you. It warms my heart like comfort food."

"That's the nicest thing you've ever said, or the best lie you've ever told," Drake said.

Taylor laughed, "I assure you it's the former. I'm not a great liar, especially under pressure."

"Did you know that song came from *Abbey Road*? It was the last song The Beatles ever recorded together," Drake noted.

"Interesting but useless information," Taylor replied.

"Taylor, have you told your parents the news?"

"Yes, I did. Mom wanted to know why you waited eight years to ask me to marry you. All kidding aside, she was ecstatic. As far as dad, he got emotional because he realized he was losing his little girl. But I can tell he's happy. I'll give you a detailed play-by-play when I see you."

"Where are you now?" Drake asked.

"Somewhere in South Carolina," Taylor replied. "Still have a couple of hours to go."

"Okay, just call me later, so I know you're okay."

"Will do," Taylor said. "Can't wait to see you."

~~

About an hour outside Jacksonville, Taylor stopped at Jimmie's Travel Center. On her way inside, she passed by a Blue Chevy Impala and noticed something odd. An older woman was in the passenger seat, facing forward, praying with her eyes closed. Behind the woman in the backseat was someone dressed in a black hoodie, leaning forward at an unusual angle. The person turned their head to the right and stared straight at Taylor. She froze for a moment, transfixed by a pair of dark, soulless eyes. It sent chills up her spine.

Taylor turned toward the front entrance of the store and bumped into another patron. As she gathered herself, she noticed the man was shivering and sweating. His face was emotionless.

"Excuse me, I wasn't looking where I was going," Taylor said.

The man didn't say a word. Instead, he opened the front door and motioned for Taylor to go ahead of him. As she passed by, he nodded and pointed his eyes toward the Blue Chevy Impala. Taylor was convinced he was trying to send a message.

Inside the store, Taylor stopped in front of the beverage coolers and tried to decide between an energy drink and an iced coffee. That was when she observed a nervous customer having an awkward interaction with the attendant at the cash register. It was the same man she bumped into a minute earlier. When the customer left, Taylor went to the register to pay for her items.

"Hey, did you notice something odd about the last customer?"

"Sure did," Randy replied. "He was trying to tell me something. He acted as if someone had a gun in his back. Probably in some sort of trouble. I'm gonna call the police and give them the license plate number."

"No need to," Taylor said as she flashed her badge. "I'm with the FBI. I can get someone to run the tag."

"Yeah, and I'm a Senior Vice President at Apple," Randy claimed as he pointed to a crate filled with McIntosh and Granny Smiths. He couldn't believe such a beautiful young girl could be an FBI special agent.

"You shouldn't judge a book by its cover," Taylor said as she raised her sweater, exposing a SIG Sauer 9 mm handgun. "You might get more than you bargained for."

Randy let out a nervous laugh as he handed Taylor the vehicle description and plate number. He was at a loss for words as he searched for his jaw, which had fallen on the floor.

"I know what you're thinking. Not the typical FBI profile," Taylor retorted. "Here's the short story. Every generation in my family served in the FBI. When I was born, my dad steered me away from law enforcement. But I felt obligated to follow in his footsteps. After a couple of years, I developed a passion for the FBI and realized that's what I wanted to do."

"I'm sorry, ma'am, forgive me," Randy replied. "Pretty girls rarely walk in the store at this time of night. Especially pretty girls with FBI badges packing heat."

"Thanks, don't worry," Taylor said. "I'll check the tag on the vehicle." She winked at Randy and walked out the door with an energy drink and a bag of Fritos.

Randy couldn't wipe the smile off his face. But someone else close could. Teri, playing the dual role of night manager and jealous girlfriend, emerged from the back office, observed what was happening, and made her way to the front of the store. Randy turned around and was startled. Teri's eyes were shooting daggers.

"Uh, when I said...uh pretty girls...I was talking about...only the customers," Randy babbled as he tripped over his own words.

"Keep digging that hole you're in," Teri grumbled. "You're not quite six feet under, but you're getting close."

Once Taylor got her car on the interstate, she cracked open the bag of Fritos and called Drake to check-in.

"Hello again, honey," Taylor said. "Just checking in as you asked me to."

"Hi, I'm mentally exhausted," Drake replied. "Dominic and I have been running around in circles trying to find Alden Moore's killer. Every lead turns up dry. It's like getting the 'Go to Jail Card' in Monopoly over and over again. We keep returning to square one."

"Remember, when you go to jail, you don't collect $200," Taylor responded. "But don't worry, I'll get you out. I have connections in law enforcement."

After a few more minutes, Taylor remembered the couple in the Blue Chevy Impala.

"Can you run a plate for me?" Taylor asked.

"I love when you talk about work late at night. It's so...sexy," Drake said. "Where are you now?"

"I'm close to Jacksonville. I'll be home within an hour."

"When are you coming to Tampa?"

"Wednesday. I have to wrap up a case first, and then I'm off for the rest of the week. Enough with the chit-chat. Just run the plate for me."

"Yes ma'am, just give me a second," Drake said. "Why the rush?"

"When I was at the travel center getting gas, I saw a couple who looked to be in distress. I want to make sure they're not in danger."

Taylor waited as Drake plugged away on his computer.

"Well, this is interesting," Drake said and then paused. "Looks like your subject is Chris Martinez of West Dallas, Texas. Someone reported him and his wife Becky missing a week ago. I guess you found them—Where are they now?"

"The car left the travel center before me. I just got back on the interstate."

"I'll call the plate in and have state troopers look out for them," Drake said. "Be careful. Don't do anything stupid."

"Yes sir," Taylor responded. "I won't engage without backup."

"So now we need special agents to join our engagement?" Drake asked in mock anger.

"Very cute, Drake. I love when you talk about work late at night. It's so...sexy."

CHAPTER

7

Collateral Damage

Kingsland, Georgia

TAYLOR ENDED THE CALL and continued south on the interstate. About twenty minutes from home, she came across an abandoned Blue Chevy Impala parked on the grass on the side of the road. It was the same vehicle she saw at Jimmie's Travel Center. Her instincts and training told her to stop. Someone might need help. It was a reflexive action she would end up regretting.

She pulled her BMW off the road and parked thirty yards behind the Impala. Taylor got out with her hand on her service revolver. As she got closer, she heard Drake's voice inside her head. "Be careful. Don't do anything stupid." Those words seemed to be good advice an hour earlier, but now that Taylor was in the heat of the moment, they didn't mean as much because lives were in the balance.

As Taylor got within a few feet of the Impala, she peered inside, and her heart broke. She saw a male and female slumped over the center console, each with a single gunshot wound to the temple. Taylor assumed it was Chris and Becky Martinez. She raised her gun but suddenly stopped.

At that moment, another chill traveled along her spine, similar to the shiver she experienced at Jimmie's. This time the chill was real, emanating from cold, hardened steel pressed into the back of her head. Taylor closed her eyes as her heart raced and held her breath, waiting for the gun to discharge. But a few seconds passed, and she was still alive. Taylor opened her eyes, and a voice spoke.

"Don't even think about it. Grab the barrel of your gun like you're shaking hands with someone, keep your fingers off the trigger, keep facing forward, and hand it to me…slowly."

"Who are you?" Taylor asked as she handed over her gun.

"I'm Officer Watson. What did you do to these two people?"

Taylor took a deep breath, comforted because law enforcement was at the other end of the handgun. But she didn't understand why she was being considered a suspect in the murder of Chris and Becky Martinez.

"You got this all wrong," Taylor said calmy. "I'm with the FBI. I thought these folks were in trouble and only stopped to check on them. I'm telling you the truth. You can inspect my credentials."

"Keep your hands where I can see them. Stay facing forward and hand over your identification," Officer Watson barked.

Taylor pulled out her FBI badge and handed it to Watson without turning her head.

"Let's see what we have here."—there was a brief pause—"This says your name is Taylor Brooks, Federal Bureau of Investigation, Special Agent based in Jacksonville, Florida."

There was another pause. This one was longer and uncomfortable.

"Well, what do you know? I found myself an FBI special agent. I never killed someone in law enforcement. I guess there's a first time for everything."

Tears welled up in Taylor's eyes, and her heart raced again. She had to remain composed and try to convince the officer they both played for the same team.

"Why would you want...to kill somebody...one of your own?" Taylor asked as her arms trembled.

"Typically, I only kill people who deserve to die," Watson said. "But on this Sunday morning, I'm going to make an exception."

"What makes me so special?" Taylor pleaded. "I'm in law enforcement, just like you."

"Forgive me, Special Agent Brooks, but I haven't been truthful with you. My name isn't Watson, and I'm not an officer of the law. But thanks for the compliment."

"Who are you?" Taylor asked.

"Well, it depends on who is in my presence. I go by different names, but most people know me as Jack."

"What do you want from me?" Taylor said, hoping to figure out a way to escape the situation.

"Nothing, Special Agent Brooks. I wish something could change the outcome, but there isn't. The decision is final."

Taylor thought of Drake and her extended family and friends. She didn't want to die. Tears cascaded down both cheeks.

"Why do you want to kill me?" Taylor asked, fearing the end was near. She tried her best to keep the conversation going. Taylor figured as long as her questions were answered, she had hope.

"Great question," Jack responded. "They taught you well in FBI school. The short answer is in my pocket. I have a list of people, all of which have something in common."

"What do they all have in common?"

"Each one of them will meet the same fate. They will all die by my hand."

"How did I...get on the list?"

"Don't be silly, Special Agent Brooks. Your name isn't on the list," Jack said. "If it were, we wouldn't be having this conversation right now."

"I guess I'm not following you. If my name isn't on the list, then why must I die?"

"You're what we call in the business 'collateral damage,'" Jack said. "Chalk it up to a case of being in the wrong place at the wrong time. When you left Jimmie's, you could've gone home. Instead, you stopped on the side of the road and tried to be a hero."

"That's not true," Taylor said. "I think…"—Jack interrupted and yelled—"I don't care what you think."

"Once we saw each other in the parking lot at Jimmie's, I couldn't take any chances. I parked the car on the side of the road so you wouldn't miss it. I knew you would stop."

"Why must I die?" Taylor asked again.

"Because you're guilty."

"Guilty of what?" Taylor asked. "I've done nothing wrong."

"Oh, yes you have. Special Agent Brooks, you are guilty of being a witness to a crime. Your sentence is death. But don't fret because I have good news."

"What…would…that be?"

"The good news is you don't have to wait years on death row awaiting your fate. I have the responsibility of being judge, jury, and executioner."

After a brief period of silence, Taylor closed her eyes tight and prayed. She wanted it to be over with, but something unexpected happened. The pressure on the back of her head eased.

"Do you believe in God, Special Agent Brooks?" Jack asked.

Taylor thought it was a strange question, considering the circumstances. The question threw Taylor off guard for a few seconds.

"Yes, I believe in God."

"Do you think God controls who lives and dies?" Jack asked.

"Yes. God has the power to do anything."

"Bullshit," Jack yelled.

"Don't you believe in God?" Taylor asked as she cried and trembled.

"I believe there is a Lord, but he isn't a savior. He doesn't make those decisions. We're on our own in this world," Jack said. "Our journey through life is like a book. In the beginning, God constructs the outline of the story and writes the script. But when the end comes, we decide our fate. It's up to man, and only man, to pen the final chapter."

"How do you know that to be true?"

Jack didn't respond.

"How...do you know...it's true?" Taylor asked a second time. The silence was damning.

Jack took a deep breath and said in a calm voice, "Only God can grant life, but any man can impose death."

Taylor whispered her last words as the gun pressed against her head once again.

"Drake, if you can hear me, I will always love you. No one can break our bond. My spirit will remain with you forever."

Without another word, Jack pulled the trigger, sending a bullet through the back of Taylor's head and straight through the middle of her forehead. Taylor's body fell to the ground in a pool of blood.

"Sorry, Special Agent Brooks. Don't worry. This isn't personal. This is just business."

Jack looked at Taylor's left hand, saw a large engagement ring, and tried to remove it. No matter how hard Jack twisted and pulled, the ring wouldn't budge.

"Why do I always do things the hard way?"

Jack got out a Bowie knife, hacked off Taylor's finger, and slipped the ring off.

"Now that's more like it. I knew there was an easier solution."

Tampa, Florida

At 4:00 a.m., Drake woke up in a cold sweat. He laid in bed for two more hours with eyes wide open until his restless legs forced him out of bed. Before getting up, Drake made a quick call to Taylor to make sure she got home. But her cell phone went straight to voicemail.

Drake had no worries and carried on with his usual morning routine. He brewed a pot of coffee and sat on his backyard deck, and saw Kurt in the backyard. He walked over, coffee cup in hand.

"You seem to be in a good mood this Sunday morning," Kurt said.

"I had a fantastic dream last night about Taylor."

"Just give me the PG version," Kurt said. "It's too early in the morning for anything else."

"Don't worry, the entire dream was PG," Drake said as he laughed. "The dream was like a 'Best Of' or 'Greatest Hits' version of our entire relationship. It spanned everything from when we first met in high school all the way through to when I proposed to her. I recalled every birthday present and holiday meal, meeting her family for the first time, and all the vacations we took together."

"Sounds great, but something doesn't sound right."

"What do you mean by that?" Drake asked.

"Dreams are never normal. Usually, something strange occurs which has a deeper meaning."

"Now that you mention it, something was odd," Drake responded. "The dream ended with a picture of Taylor's smiling face and Paul McCartney singing about someone being in his dreams tonight. The lyric is from a Beatles song, 'The End,' which I heard playing in her car over her cell phone. That's when I woke up in a cold sweat."

"Something still doesn't make sense," Kurt said.

"Why makes you feel that way?" Drake asked.

"You would only wake up in a cold sweat if you were under some kind of stress while dreaming," Kurt said.

"You're a philosopher and a sage." Drake said as he started back towards his house.

"All in a day's work, son," Kurt yelled as Drake walked away.

Drake had nothing planned for the rest of the day and took an unplanned nap on the deck. Within five minutes, his eyes closed, and he was completely asleep. He only needed a half-hour power nap, but his mind and body wanted more. A thirty-minute rest turned into two hours. When Drake woke up, he saw someone sitting in a chair across from him. It took him a minute to clear the cobwebs from his head and see who it was.

"Dominic? Is that you?" Drake asked.

His brother sat silent, like a stone.

"How long have you been watching me?"

"I...uh...have been sitting here for about twenty minutes," Dominic said.

"Why didn't you wake me?"

"You looked so peaceful. I didn't want to disturb you."

Tears welled up in Dominic's eyes. Drake knew something was wrong and ran over to his brother. He hugged him tightly and grabbed his face.

"What's wrong, Dominic? Tell me, what's wrong?" Drake screamed.

Dominic was crying and could barely get the words out.

"Taylor...is...dead."

CHAPTER

8

Concealed Evidence

Tampa, Florida

MID-MORNING ON A SUNDAY in South Georgia, State Troopers found a Blue Chevy Impala on the side of the interstate with three bodies inside. When word reached the FBI Tampa Field Office, Dominic was the first to find out one of those bodies belonged to Taylor Brooks. Once he broke the news to Drake, he called immediate family members and disseminated the tragic information.

Dominic remained by Drake's side until family members showed. Mom and Dad were the first to arrive by mid-afternoon, followed by other close relatives and fellow special agents. The bevy of supporters presented the perfect smokescreen, enabling Dominic to sneak out with no one noticing. As he walked through the front door, he crossed paths with Kurt, who stopped by to pay his respects.

"Dominic, how's Drake?" Kurt asked.

"He's still in a state of shock and knee-deep in the denial stage. Drake can't comprehend how in just a few hours he went from having a casual conversation to making her funeral arrangements."

"Everyone goes through the same stages of grief," Kurt said. "But we all deal with those stages in our own way."

"Yeah, but I'm not looking forward to the pain and anger stages."

"What happened to Taylor?" Kurt asked.

"Initial reports were that she stopped to help another couple. Someone murdered them and then killed Taylor in cold blood."

"Oh, my lord." Kurt's eyes bulged as he shook his head.

"I was the first to find out. I wanted to be the one to tell Drake and the rest of the family."

"There's no easy way to tell someone that a lunatic murdered their fiancé and best friend in cold blood." Kurt shook his head again.

"It was the hardest thing I will ever do in my entire life. I wanted to pull the bandage off the wound as fast as possible. The hurt was beyond belief, but necessary to start the healing process."

"Can I see him?"

"Sure, go ahead. Kurt, I'm headed to the crime scene in South Georgia. I couldn't go until other family and friends arrived. I didn't tell Drake."

"What if he asks for you?"

"I'll call him later. At that point, he won't be able to do anything about it."

"I'll help him as much as possible," Kurt said.

"Thanks Kurt, much appreciated," Dominic said as he got into his car.

Kingsland, Georgia

Dominic took the first flight he could get from Tampa to Jacksonville. After landing, he exited the jet bridge and noticed a middle-aged man with tears in his eyes. Dominic walked up with his hand extended.

"Agent Garrison?" Dominic asked. Mark Garrison nodded his head as the two shook hands while walking towards the exit.

"How's Drake?" Mark asked.

"Still in shock, but he's in good hands. Sonny and Mary were the first to arrive. Friends, neighbors, and agents trickled in over two hours. By the time I left, twenty people were in Drake's living room. What about you? Are you okay?"

Mark choked up as he took a deep breath.

"Taylor walked into the office every day with a smile. She was a special person. Most people wouldn't stop to help a stranger, but Taylor wasn't most people. I've been in the FBI for 30 years and have seen my share of senseless murders. I can't tell you how many times someone asked me why someone would take another person's life. There's no good answer. Now I'm the one asking the same question."

The two FBI agents drove north of the city for half an hour to Kingsland, Georgia. On the southbound side of I-95, they saw two stranded vehicles within a roped-off area, half a dozen police cars, and three local news trucks. Mark drove to the next exit to get on the south side of the interstate. They got out of the vehicle with the same thought in mind. They knew this was going to be tough.

Mark walked Dominic to the crime scene and introduced him to Detective Roberts out of the Jacksonville office.

"Dominic, we roped off the area and secured the boundaries," Roberts explained. "We also performed a preliminary survey of the crime scene."

"Can I view your notes?" Dominic asked. Roberts handed over a pad with bullet points and a timeline, which was a chronological walkthrough of what he observed.

- 0800 Hrs - Received communication of a situation with multiple homicides.

- 0900 Hrs - Arrived south of Kingsland, Georgia, on the southbound side of Interstate I-95 at mile marker 52.

- 0920 Hrs - Found red 2002 BMW 328i parked on the shoulder of the road. No one was inside the vehicle. We found a women's pocketbook with wallet untouched, a half-empty bottle of Red Bull, a half-eaten bag of Fritos, and various credit card receipts. The luggage in the truck was untouched. No signs of struggle in and around the vehicle. The license plate tag ISL-151. Later, determined car registered to Taylor Brooks of Jacksonville, Florida.

- 0930 Hrs - Found blue 1997 Chevy Impala roadside on the grass and obscured by brush. The Impala is about 50 yards from the BMW. Vehicle license plate tag XLP-473 registered to Mr. Chris Martinez of West Dallas in Texas.

- 0935 Hrs - Approached the Impala, looked inside, and discovered two bodies. In the driver's seat was a white male, approximately age 43 years old. In the passenger seat was a female, approximate age 39 years old. Confirmed victims were Chris and Becky Martinez. The cause of death for both victims was a single gunshot wound to the left temple. The Male still had a wallet in his pocket. On the floor of the vehicle on the passenger side was a woman's pocketbook. Robbery was eliminated as a potential motive. Need forensics for fingerprints and other evidence.

- 0930 Hrs - In the backseat, discovered a deceased female 25 years old with a single gunshot wound in the back of the head. The Female was sitting upright with hands tied. The victim was missing left ring finger.

"What have you done so far with the victims?" Dominic asked.

"We conducted a second walkthrough, took photographs and video, and collected physical and forensic evidence," Roberts said. "We haven't moved the bodies yet. Do you want to take a walk through the crime scene?"

"No, I don't," Dominic replied. "But I have to for Drake's sake."

Mark walked with Dominic towards the Blue Chevy Impala. Dominic turned around and asked Mark to stay behind.

"This was my brother's future wife and my sister-in-law," Dominic said. "Taylor was family. I need to do this by myself."

"I understand," Mark said. "Go pay your respects. I'll be right here when you return."

Dominic resumed his walk towards the Impala. He stopped a few feet from the vehicle and stared straight ahead. He didn't want to look, but he had to. Dominic didn't want Taylor's last day on earth spent in the arms of strangers. He wanted to make sure a family member was with her in the final hours.

Three more steps put Dominic in front of the driver's side window. He glanced inside and saw Chris and Becky Martinez. Dominic took a deep breath and peered into the backseat. Dominic's eyes welled up with tears. He bowed his head and said the following words.

"Taylor, I know you can't hear me, but I feel like your spirit can. Everyone is devastated by your loss, especially Drake. He loved you very much. He couldn't be here today, so I came today in his absence. I wanted to let you know your entire family will never forget you. I promise we'll sort this out and serve justice. Rest in peace."

Dominic raised his head and walked through the crime scene. He switched out his "brother-in-law hat" to his "FBI cap." He didn't want to miss the slightest piece of evidence to point him in the right direction. Dominic noticed a small piece of paper protruding from Taylor's shirt pocket. It was a handwritten note written in red ink.

I Haven't Killed in Quite a While

Three Tonight Made me Smile—Jack

Dominic felt sick in the pit of his stomach. Drake was right. Jack killing Alden Moore wasn't a 'one and done.' Dominic knew Jack would strike again but never thought someone he knew would be one of Jack's victims.

Dominic folded the piece of paper, put it in his pocket, and walked over to Mark and Detective Roberts.

"Are you okay?" Mark asked. "I can't imagine how difficult that must've been."

"I'm...all right," Dominic replied with a shaky voice. "I said my peace. I went over the whole crime scene. Did you get a good look at the bodies?"

"We didn't touch the bodies yet. That was our next step. We were waiting for you to arrive first."

"Have you removed anything from the victims?" Dominic asked.

"Not yet, but we will."

Dominic realized he had an important piece of evidence in his right hip pocket. He knew the killer. But he wasn't sure how Drake would react when he found out Jack murdered Taylor, so he kept it as a secret for the time being.

If anyone at the FBI found out Jack was the suspect in Taylor's murder, someone would have instantly taken both Merino brothers off the Alden Moore case. Bringing Jack to justice was more important than ever. The stakes were a lot higher now. Finding Jack was no longer a part of everyday business. It was now becoming personal.

CHAPTER

9

Nightmares

Tampa, Florida

EACH MORNING AT THE BREAK OF DAWN, there was a test of wills. A battle between a worn-out old man and a stubborn cat. It was a classic confrontation pitting sleep deprivation against clinical starvation.

In one corner was Kurt Schwartz, pushing 225 pounds at 70 years old, needing as much sleep as possible. In the opposite corner was Jacques Catsteau, weighing in at 15 pounds and 6 years old, expecting to be fed on time.

Jacques always landed the first blow during the 5:00 a.m. hour. Around that time, Jacques jumped on the bed and strategically placed his weight on Kurt's chest. That was always followed up with a combination of head butts while purring like a runaway freight train.

On most days, Kurt weathered the storm and waited for an opportunity to fight back. No matter how hard Kurt pushed him away, Jacques returned to the battle. They went at it until either Kurt fed the little monster or Jacques walked away. Being fifteen times bigger than Jacques, Kurt felt he had a distinct advantage. But ask Jacques, and he'd tell the match was even. As far as who won, it depended on who you talked to.

One morning, the daily battle in the Schwartz household was preempted by the sound of footsteps. Kurt kept his eyes closed, thinking Jacques had found a new way to wake him up.

"I know that's you, Jacques," Kurt said from under the covers. "Make as much noise as you want. I'm not falling for it."

A minute later, more footsteps. Kurt sat up in bed at full attention and saw Jacques at the top of the stairs, looking down towards the first floor. The curious cat glanced at Kurt and headed downstairs to investigate. Kurt grabbed a flashlight and followed close behind.

No one had breached the house. The alarm showed all the doors and windows were still locked shut. Then came the mysterious sounds again. There were footsteps followed by broken branches. Before Kurt opened the front door, he stopped in his tracks. He heard a voice. Someone was having a conversation with themselves.

Then came the scream.

The sound curled Kurt's toes and arched Jacques back like a Halloween decoration. Someone or something was in the bushes in front of the house. Kurt grabbed his sawed-off shotgun, walked out onto the deck, and walked around to the front of the house, not realizing Jacques was behind him.

The last thing he wanted to do was shoot someone, but if he was ready to defend his home. As Kurt peered around the corner, the bushes moved. Jacques ran past and straight into harm's way. Kurt had no choice but to protect his furry son.

"Who's in there?" Kurt yelled as he stared down the barrel of a shotgun. After more rustling amongst the bushes, Jacques emerged, purring as if he had found a long-lost friend. A shivering man crawled out wearing nothing but boxer shorts. It was Drake Merino from next door. Kurt laid the shotgun on the ground and helped Drake up.

"You need to speak up, son," Kurt said. "If it hadn't been for Jacques, I would've plugged you a couple of times. What the hell happened to you?" Drake was disoriented and confused. "Let's get you inside and get some coffee." Kurt put his arm around Drake and helped him back home.

They climbed onto Drake's deck and entered the house through the back door. When Kurt stepped inside, he was surprised at what he saw. The kitchen looked like a war zone with dirty plates, utensils, and half-eaten meals scattered from one end to the other. As they walked through the living room, cushions were thrown off the couch, and the wide-screen television had a big crack in the middle.

The second floor wasn't much better. The hallways were littered with junk, unopened mail, and dirty clothes. The bathrooms looked as if they hadn't been cleaned in weeks.

Kurt realized this was no way for anyone to live. Something was wrong, and he needed to find out what it was. He took Drake over to his house, sat him in the kitchen, and brewed a double espresso. Once the caffeine took effect, Drake came to his senses.

"Where...am I?" Drake asked while still half asleep.

"Drake, this is Kurt. You're at my house next door. Are you okay, son?"

"I'm...I'm not sure."

Drake looked around Kurt's kitchen and then at himself. He was wearing only a pair of boxers, and dirt was on his arms and legs. Drake looked up at Kurt with a confused look on his face.

"What the hell is going on?"

"Everything will be okay, Drake," Kurt said. "You were in my bushes talking to yourself. Do you remember anything at all?"

"No, I don't. I had a horrible dream, and the next thing I remember is sitting here with you. Everything else between is a complete blank."

"What was the dream about?" Kurt asked.

"It was based on something that happened when I was ten years old. I was on summer vacation with my family. We stayed at a resort along the coastline. One day, I found myself at the bottom of a pool and couldn't swim. I lost both consciousness and hope. My spirit was fading away and floating to the heavens. Death was on my doorstep, waiting to place a shroud over me. It felt like the beginning of the end."

Drake took another drink of his double espresso and continued.

"As I passed out, someone tugged on my right arm. Something grabbed my limp body and brought me to the surface. After I regained consciousness, I opened my eyes to see someone. It was the person who saved my ten-year-old life."

"Well, that sounds far from a nightmare. Seems like a happy ending. Someone saved your life."

"I've had the same recurring dream for almost thirty years," Drake said. "But tonight, the dream had a different ending. When I got to the surface, I opened my eyes and saw my savior…the headless body of Alden Moore. Taylor was a few feet away, with a huge gash on her forehead. Blood was everywhere. She was trying to reach out to me, but a throng of strangers held her back. I couldn't move and was forced to watch. That's when the screaming started."

"It looks like an old dream has now become a new nightmare," Kurt said.

Drake rubbed his eyes until they were raw. He was hoping to wring out the vision burned into his memory. But he couldn't. Because when a person sees the face of death, it can't be unseen. For Drake, the vision was going to remain with him for the rest of his lifetime.

Kurt let Drake crash on his couch for three hours. He couldn't send him home to live in squalor. While Drake slept, Kurt went to Drake's house to get clothes and personal items, including his cell phone.

Bringgg, Bringgg, Buzzz, Bringgg, Bringgg, Buzzz

"Mornin' Drake, how are you doing today?"

Dominic never called his brother before heading to the office. Kurt had leaked the information. He hated to go behind Drake's back, but this was an issue that had to be addressed.

"I'm okay," Drake said. "Why are you calling me?"

"Do you know what time it is? You missed our morning staff meeting."

"Sorry, I wasn't feeling well and planned to take a personal day. I forgot to call in. Can you tell the front desk I'm at home today?"

"No, you can't take off. Save the day for next week. Get your lazy ass in here. We have some new leads on the Alden Moore case."

"Um...I'm not going to make it in today," Drake said. "I have some issues to deal with."

Dominic hesitated for a few seconds before continuing.

"Okay…I'll stop by later and check on you. Get some sleep," Dominic said.

Once Drake ended the call, Kurt was grinning at him like a Cheshire cat.

"Looks like you have a free day, and I have the perfect elixir to clear your head," Kurt said. "If you want to forget your worries, there's no better way than spending a few hours on the lake."

Drake wasn't into fishing, but the thought of relaxing on the water and getting away from everything seemed like a good idea. Within the hour, the two neighbors were sitting on Kurt's boat with their fishing rods in the water. The lake was calm, and no one was around. Add in a light breeze on a beautiful day, and Drake found nirvana.

"I got one rule on this boat. Just relax and forget about everything else. We can talk about the other stuff later when you're awake and rested."

"Okay, Kurt," Drake said.

Drake wanted to talk about Taylor. The wound hadn't healed, and he was close to entering the depression phase. But, he didn't want to ruin Kurt's day, so he abided by the rules.

"Kurt, something's been bugging me," Drake said. "How do you always home with a bucket full of fish, and I can't catch one? What's your secret?"

Kurt chuckled and flashed a huge smile on his face.

"See this fishing pole?" Kurt pointed at his rod. "I've had it maybe for thirty years. I've been an honest fisherman my whole life. Never needed a new rod or one of those electronic fish finders. Fishing isn't supposed to be easy. So, I don't have any secrets, but I have some advice."

Drake was all ears.

"You don't need a fancy fishing pole or lessons on how to cast like a professional angler. Catching fish comes down to the bait," Kurt proclaimed, as if he was grabbing the ear of an apprentice.

"People don't realize all you need is one fish," Kurt said. " Lure the bugger in with something he can't resist. Then you wait a while. At some point, the fish will return to his school and brag to his classmates what he found, and before you know it—jackpot."

Drake nodded as Kurt continued.

"The key is to do your research," Kurt said. "Understand your environment, get an accurate weather forecast, note the time of day and the season, and decide what you're going after. Throw all of your information into Google, and you'll get the secret sauce."

"Sounds pretty straightforward," Drake said.

"I always tell everyone. Fishing isn't rocket science."—Kurt paused for a few seconds—"But do you know what is like rocket science?"

Drake shook his head from side to side.

"Rocket science," Kurt responded. "Everything else in life is easy. You can do anything if you put your mind to it."

Drake let out a big laugh but realized Kurt was right. He learned over the years to never doubt his neighbor. Kurt always knew what he was talking about.

"I'll tell you something else," Kurt said. "My advice applies to almost anything in life. Look at your line of work. If you're trying to catch a criminal, all you have to do is draw them in close and set a trap. But I'm sure you knew that already from special agent school."

"They never taught us about the fundamentals of fishing," Drake replied with a slight chuckle.

"Well, remember what I told you. If you want to catch something or someone, make sure you use the right bait. You'll catch them every time."

Drake agreed and then had a thought

Sometimes old fisherman can be the wisest men on earth.

CHAPTER

10

Desk Duty

Tampa, Florida

DOMINIC WAS ON DRAKE'S FRONT PORCH at 7:30 a.m. He rang the doorbell three times with no response, then pounded his fists on the front door, sending reverberations throughout the house.

Bang, Bang, Bang, Bang.

If anyone was inside, they were on notice a visitor was at the door.

Bang, Bang, Bang, Bang.

Still no response.

Dominic walked around the side of the house and, in the distance, saw his brother talking to a neighbor.

"Look, Drake, it's your brother," Kurt said as he pointed behind him.

Drake turned around and looked like a little kid who got caught cutting class. Dominic never stopped by his house before work at such an early hour.

"I told you I was going to pick you up this morning. We have an important meeting," Dominic said.

"Are you sure? I didn't receive an invitation."

"You are now," Dominic said. "Special Agent Gordon wants to meet with us."

Kurt turned to Drake's brother.

"Hey Dominic, we've met before. Kurt Schwartz from next door."

"Hi Kurt, I remember you," Dominic said. "Drake tells me you're quite the fisherman."

Jacques waltzed by and brushed up against Dominic's leg.

"Who is this?" Dominic asked as he picked up the feline. "Somebody sure wants attention."

"The infamous Jacques Catsteau," Kurt said. "Jacques is my fishing buddy. Never go out on the lake without him."

"Drake, get ready. We can't be late."

"Okay, give me fifteen minutes," Drake said as he walked back to the house.

"Dominic, I'm worried about him," Kurt said. "His house is a war zone. He doesn't care about his appearance or the conditions under which he is living. He looks like someone who has given up on life. What could have caused this?"

"The crime scenes we've seen recently have been disturbing. No amount of training prepares us. Everyone has a different reaction. We just have to learn how to deal with it.

Drake is having a difficult time right now.

"So, how can we help him?"

"I'll talk to him. Do me a favor, monitor him and if you see anything, call me."

"Will do," Kurt said. "I'll also make sure Jacques pays him regular visits."

Dominic and Kurt continued to talk until Drake emerged from the house. He motioned with his arms and yelled from a distance. "Let's go."

~~~

The Merino brothers made their meeting with a minute to spare and walked straight to see Richard Gordon, the Special Agent in Charge.

"Mornin' boys," Richard said." Thanks for coming in on short notice. I wanted to talk to both of you together."

Dominic and Drake didn't know what Richard would tell them, but they both expected bad news. Over the past year, Dominic spent most of his time pursuing Jack, and Drake was still fighting the after-effects of losing Taylor. Both underperformed but for different reasons. Change was in the air, and the Merino brothers felt it coming.

"I guess you're wondering why I called you here this morning," Richard said. "I'm going to make adjustments affecting both of you. The first order of business is Jack. We need to turn up the heat. Over the past year, we haven't provided adequate resources to support the investigation. But that's about to change."

"Why now?" Dominic asked.

"We've gotten word the media plans to publish pictures from Jack's crime scenes. We have a leak somewhere, but that's a fight for another day."

"When will the pictures be published?" Drake asked.

"This evening. The public will learn these cases we're investigating are all linked by a common thread. They will demand a call to action, and we need to get out ahead of the curve."

Richard pulled out a folder and handed a piece of paper to both Dominic and Drake. It was an organizational chart for the Jack investigative team. At the top was the name Dominic Merino, Lead National Investigator.

"Well, this is a surprise," Dominic said. "What does this mean?"
~~~

"We're expanding our scope to neighboring states, and Dominic, you'll be the lead investigator," Richard said. "Your primary responsibility will be to coordinate investigative efforts across state lines. You'll have the full support of the FBI and resources at your disposal. You're the right person to lead the team."

Dominic was only half listening to Richard. He was excited to be promoted and appreciated the added support, but something was missing on the organizational chart. Dominic didn't see Drake's name. He looked over at his brother, and he could tell by Drake's body language he didn't see his name either.

"What about Drake?" Dominic asked. "Why is his name not on the organization chart?"

"I said these changes would affect both of you," Richard said. "Drake, you've had a tough year with your loss, and it's affected your performance. The best thing to do at this point is to give you some added time to heal. We're assigning you to desk duty for three months. We'll shift your caseload to other agents. Afterward, if everything checks out, we can put you on the team. It's the best for all the parties involved."

Dominic remained quiet, bit his lip, and waited for his brother's response. Drake slumped in his chair, but sat upright to respond.

"I'm not going to lie to you. I'm disappointed," Drake said. "Being an FBI special agent is all I've ever known. I realize my performance has suffered, and I take responsibility. I'll work hard to get back to where I was."

"I'm confident you will," Richard said.

"What does desk duty mean?" Drake asked.

"That is subject to interpretation. The short definition is no fieldwork. You won't be able to travel. Anything else is fair game. We'll conduct internal discussions this week and contact you with more details next Friday. In the meantime, stay home over the next couple of days and relax. We'll talk next week with clear heads. Drake, we don't do this for everyone. But you're a special case, and we care about you. We want the old Drake back."

"Thanks," Drake said. "I appreciate your support."

After a few more minutes of discussion, the three men shook hands, and the Merino brothers left the office. During the car ride home, Dominic had a heart-to-heart with Drake. He was honest and held nothing back.

"Drake, I'm proud of how you responded," Dominic said. "I wasn't sure how you were going to react."

"Richard made his decision, so no use fighting it. The only option was to take the high road."

"This is a critical time for you and your career," Dominic said. "Everyone has had their eyes on you the past couple of months. I covered for you whenever I could. The reason we haven't discussed this sooner is that I expected you would be back to normal by now."

"I knew of the scrutiny and chose not to do anything," Drake said. "As long as a paycheck was coming in, I didn't care what others thought."

"But you started coming in late to the office or sometimes not at all," Dominic said. "Your appearance and health changed. Something didn't seem right. I could only do so much."

Drake cowered his head in embarrassment.

"After your sleepwalking incident," Dominic said. "The FBI wanted to relieve you of your duties. But I convinced them to keep you. So, this is where we are. You've got three months to work hard and save your career."

"I plan to do just that, but let's be honest. It's not going to be good for me to sit around for three months and do nothing." Drake said. "I need to keep busy to take my mind off of Taylor. The best thing for me is to stay on the team and be part of this investigation."

"I understand, Drake. I want you to be part of the team, too. This is what I'll do. While the FBI is figuring out what your responsibilities will be over the next week, I'll talk with Richard again and try to work out a compromise."

"Thanks, Dominic," Drake said.

"You're my brother," Dominic said. "I have to take care of you. If I didn't, dad would kick me in the ass.

For the first time since Taylor's murder, there was light at the end of the tunnel. He just hoped it wasn't an oncoming train.

~

Over a couple of months, Drake gained 15 pounds. The cause of the sudden weight gain was a lethal combination of a poor diet and lack of exercise. It wasn't a coincidence his health went downhill when Richard assigned him to desk duty. Because Drake wasn't traveling, he found himself in Political Donuts almost every day.

Drake was walking around with a lot of guilt. It wasn't just because he was eating donuts every day. Instead, it was because Drake started to look at other women again. He loved Taylor, but it had been some time since her death, and he was sure she wouldn't want him to be miserable for the rest of his life.

Nikki noticed the changes in Drake. She became a bit more aggressive and more friendly towards him every morning.

"Mornin' Drake," Nikki said.

Drake usually matched Nikki's smile. However, on one Friday morning, she noticed he didn't.

"Drake, it's Friday," Nikki said. "Where is your Friday smile?"

"I'm not feeling too well today," Drake said. "I've been coming here every morning for the past three weeks, and your donuts have resulted in this."

Drake pointed towards his protruding belly.

"What are you talking about?" Nikki asked. "You look the same as always."

Nikki was lying. She would say anything to get on Drake's good side.

"It's about time I show a little willpower," Drake said. "Let's just go with one donut today instead of the usual two. I got to start somewhere."

Nikki got Drake a plain donut and put it in a bag.

"Why did you give me a plain donut?" Drake asked.

"I'm just trying to help you," Nikki said. "I want to see that smile again on your face."

Drake did smile as he paid for his donut and coffee. Nikki grabbed the receipt, wrote something on the back, and put it in the bag.

"See you on Monday, Nikki," Drake said as he walked out.

"Have a nice weekend, Drake," Nikki exclaimed.

When Drake got to his car, he took a sip of coffee and a bite of his plain donut. He saw that Nikki wrote her number on the receipt.

Drake picked his head up and saw Nikki smiling through the window. He waved at her as she pulled out of the parking lot. Drake showed some willpower when it came to donuts. However, he wasn't sure he could do the same when it came to Nikki.

After a long Monday, Drake crashed on his living room couch and was out like a light. An hour later, at 7:30 p.m., he woke up to the sound of footsteps on the deck. Drake got up from the couch and looked out the kitchen window, and saw Jacques running around after a small red toy in the shape of a mouse. On the right side of the deck, sitting on the steps, was Dominic. Drake went outside to find out what was going on.

"What are you doing here this late?" Drake asked.

Dominic threw the red toy again, this time farther into the backyard grass. Jacques leaped with excitement and went on the hunt.

"We're going to Chicago," Dominic said. "There's a report of a homicide similar to the Tampa murders. We need to check it out."

"What do you mean by 'we'?"

"Pack your bags, Drake. We're going on a road trip. You're going to the Windy City."

"But I'm not allowed to travel...I...I can't travel."

"You can go, and you will go. I received clearance from Richard. I need help to make sense of all this. I trust no one more than you."

Drake didn't have a ready-made excuse available. He turned around and walked into the house to pack for the short trip. Ten minutes later, Drake reappeared with a large duffle bag with two wheels on the bottom, making it easier to maneuver through the airport. He flipped the bag on its side. Jacques jumped on top, dropped the red toy, and reached out to Drake to ask for a goodbye hug. It was a small sign from Jacques that there were no worries.

"The cat has taken a liking to you," Dominic said. "Jacques is a good influence. Whenever he's around, you seem like your old self."

Drake smiled at his brother. He indeed felt better when Jacques was around. The cat gave him something to look forward to when he returned from the short trip to Chicago.

Across the way, Kurt watched from a distance. He sensed Jacques knew Drake needed emotional support, so he didn't mind the cat jumping ship. Kurt was confident that Jacques would return home once Drake worked through his issues. At least, he hoped that was the case. The last thing Kurt wanted to do was find a new fishing buddy.

CHAPTER

11

Bloody Mary

Chicago, Illinois

IN THE EARLY HOURS OF SATURDAY MORNING in the stockroom of Madison Street Sports, a trail of blood led to the selling floor. A video camera picked up the blood trail and the hand-painted red arrows on the walls. The first-person perspective from the camera lens gave the viewer the impression of someone walking through a museum. But at the end of the bloody trail, one thing was clear. Madison Street Sports wasn't a museum. It was more like a house of horrors.

In the first exhibit, over in the fitness section, lay a lifeless young man on an Olympic bench press. His arms dangled at his side, touching the floor while a plateless barbell straddled his neck. Next to him was a half-empty bottle of Gatorade, a new wallet, and car keys. The man also had a personal workout schedule, which showed he was in the middle of his last set of exercises. The bullet hole in his head made sure it was the last set of his life.

The next exhibit was by a row of treadmills, running slowly and angled at a slight incline. Someone tied a middle-aged woman's hands to the handrails as the rest of her limp body laid on the rotating belt. The heart rate monitor on the treadmill registered zero. Behind the two bodies on a wall was a message written in blood:

THERE IS NO DESTINY. THERE IS NO CONTROL

LEAVE IT TO FATE TO TAKE CARE OF YOUR SOUL—JACK

The group finished watching an unedited version of the Rosemont murders from two nights earlier. The video cut off, and the lights turned on in the conference room. Dominic spun around to elicit Drake's response. But he did a double-take because the seat behind him was empty. The meeting wasn't even a half-hour old, and Drake picked the worst time to disappear.

"Sorry, I'm not sure what happened to my brother," Dominic said to Chicago FBI special agents Frank Howell and Greg Carton. "Let me go find him. I'll be back in a few minutes."

Dominic checked the nearby restrooms, the employee cafeteria, and various hallways. He couldn't find a trace of Drake anywhere. Dominic walked to the front entrance and asked security if they saw Drake. They told Dominic someone who looked like him left the building ten minutes earlier. Outside in the distance, Dominic found Drake sitting underneath an oak tree on the front lawn. He walked up to Drake and stayed calm, as if nothing was wrong.

"Hey, Drake. Are you all right?" Dominic asked.

"I'm...not sure," Drake replied. "Something is wrong with me. No one knows what I'm going through."

"What are you going through?"

"They're haunting me," Drake trembled. "All of them are in my thoughts during the day and in my dreams at night. They want something from me, but I'm not sure what it is."

"Who are you talking about? Who is haunting you?"

"The headless body of Alden Moore, the victims at Danny's, and even Taylor," Drake said as he held back tears. "They're all inside me. I can see, hear, and feel them. This is more profound than your everyday nightmare. I'm reliving the entire experience over again in my mind."

"From what you describe, there doesn't seem to be anything to worry about," Dominic said. "If you ask me, Alden Moore is trying to save you. He wants you to live. All the others feel the same way. They're just trying to help."

"Why do a bunch of dead people care whether I live or die?" Drake asked.

"They want you to live so you can find their killer. You're their only chance for justice. They want you to find Jack," Dominic said.

"I'm not so sure," Drake said. "Each night, I wake up from the nightmare screaming. That's not a sign of help. It's a warning to be careful, or I could end up dead."

Drake closed his eyes and rubbed his temples, trying to get the images to go away. He would have no such luck.

"Coming to Chicago to investigate the Rosemont murders was a mistake. I can't handle seeing the carnage anymore. It's making the nightmares worse."

Dominic sat down next to his brother and put his arm around his shoulder.

"I understand what you're going through," Dominic said, even though he didn't. "If you don't want to take part in fieldwork operations, so be it."

Drake looked up at his brother as if someone had lifted a tremendous weight off his shoulders.

"I'll continue to push Richard regarding your status. Maybe we can create a hybrid position where you split your time between desk duty and helping me catch Jack."

Drake appreciated the offer but wondered what the catch was. He asked, "What do you want in return?"

"Just be the best special agent you can be," Dominic said. "You're still one of our smartest agents. No one knows how to put together a puzzle and solve a mystery better than you."

Drake raised his head with a hint of a smile.

"We're a team," Dominic said. "I'll feed you the facts and clues, and you can interrogate suspects and interview witnesses in the office. If we travel, I'll limit what you're exposed to. Don't worry. You'll remain an important part of the investigative process."

Dominic was getting ahead of himself by making promises he couldn't keep. He had to sell his idea to Richard first. But he thought persuading Richard was easier than trying to get Drake to snap out of his funk.

"Seems like a good idea," Drake said. "Don't worry, I'll get over this, and things will return to normal."

Dominic wasn't so sure but patted Drake on the back to provide comfort.

"I'm sorry for all the trouble. I've thought a lot over the past two weeks about disappearing. Going somewhere else far away and starting over. Everybody would be better off with me out of the picture."

"Don't talk like that, Drake," Dominic said. "I need you around. I can't function without you. Also, don't forget Jacques needs his evening belly rubs. Get those thoughts out of your head."

Drake felt better after coming clean with his brother.

"Okay, let's go inside," Drake said. "We have a killer to catch."

The Merino brothers returned to the office to discuss the Rosemont murders with Frank and Greg. The four special agents went over every aspect of the crime scene with a fine-tooth comb. During the discussion, Drake excused himself twice. Each time Dominic was nervous, but it was only nature calling. After three intense hours, everyone agreed there were similarities between the cases. The facts were obvious:

- The murders were well-planned and premeditated. The killer targeted the victims.

- The killer showed no motive for the murders. The killer removed nothing of value from the crime scene.

- The cause of death was a single gunshot wound to the head. The killer inflicted other injuries after the murders.

- The killer posed the bodies after the victims were deceased to get maximum shock value.

- A bloody cryptic message was at each crime scene. The same killer wrote the messages.

- There were no fingerprints, and other evidence was minimal.

What started as a local Tampa murder turned into a regional investigation. But after the Rosemont murders, the case went nationwide.

Drake and Dominic drove to O'Hare International Airport. They found a tavern on the way and stopped for steaks and adult beverages. Drake ordered a Grey Goose Collins to settle his nerves, and Dominic got a Bloody Mary. Drake gave his brother a dirty look.

"Out of all the things," Drake observed, "You had to get a Bloody Mary?"

"Sure, why not. Tomatoes are full of Vitamin C and E, and they improve blood flow and circulation. Plus, Bloody Marys taste damn good. What's the problem?"

"I thought, based on what we've seen, you would stay away from the color red."

"Don't be silly. A Bloody Mary is the ultimate in tomato deliciousness, for crying out loud."

Drake dropped a hint the drink bothered him. But what he didn't know was Dominic ordered it on purpose. He was trying to toughen his brother up. If Sonny were sitting at the table, he would've done the same thing.

"What's next?" Drake asked. "The killing will continue. How can we get ahead of this?"

"The killer craves publicity and shock value," Dominic said. "He won't kill in some random town in North Dakota because he prefers to work near large cities. Let's get the message out to our other FBI offices."

"What do you want me to do in the meantime?"

"Review all leads and keep going over the evidence until you find something. Remember, you know how to solve a puzzle better than anyone."

Tampa, Florida

Every few months after Taylor's death, Drake tried to get himself to read the investigative report. He couldn't do it because, for the longest time, he was afraid of his reaction. Drake wasn't sure if he wanted to know the details. He got chills every time just thinking of the events leading up to her murder.

Two years after Taylor's murder, Drake felt he was ready. The only way for him to gain closure was to find out what happened. One early Monday morning, he drove to the FBI Tampa field office and locked himself in the office. Drake retrieved the report from the FBI database and scrolled through the pages, skipping the checkboxes and other supporting documentation. He took a deep breath and headed straight to the narrative.

Afterward, Drake found himself somewhere between denial and acceptance. He wanted to believe it was a bad dream. However, with few clues and even fewer leads, Drake had to accept the possibility Jack would never face justice for the murder of Taylor Brooks.

As Drake sat in his chair staring into space, someone knocked on the door. It was his brother.

"I finally did it," Drake said.

"Did what, Drake?" Dominic asked.

"Read the whole report," Drake responded. "But I skipped the graphic evidence. The only thing I want to remember is the image of Taylor's smile.

Dominic saw Drake's misty eyes. A single tear rolled down his face.

"I read you were at the crime scene," Drake said. "Thanks for being there for her."

"No worries," Dominic said. "Someone needed to be there for her. Remember what dad taught us. 'Brothers have to be there for each other.' Hey, are you okay?"

"I'm…not so sure," Drake said. "In the report, it says the killer took her engagement ring. Is it true?"

"Yes, it is," Dominic said as he looked towards the floor.

"Why didn't anyone tell me?" Drake asked. "I was under the assumption the ring was lost. I can't believe the bastard chopped off her finger and took it."

"Look Drake. I'm sorry we didn't tell you," Dominic said as he put his arm around his brother. "Everyone felt it was better if you didn't know. I hope you understand."

"At least Taylor died trying to help someone else," Drake said. "She had a good heart. I told her not to do anything stupid, but Taylor didn't listen. That's who she was. She was always thinking about others before herself. I'm so proud of her."

The two Merino brothers got up to leave the office. There was a staff meeting to attend.

"Do you think we'll ever find Jack?" Drake asked.

"We will, Drake," Dominic responded. "But between you and me, when we do, the son-of-a-bitch will suffer."

"Monsters can't run around choosing their victims," Drake said. "They can't be the one who decides if people live or die."

"Don't worry about it," Dominic said as a slight grin appeared on his face. "As far as Jack goes, we'll be the ones deciding between life and death.

CHAPTER

12

Jacobson's Ladder

St. Louis, Missouri

FOUR HOURS before the ball made its annual descent in the middle of Times Square, Norman's cell phone rang. The incoming call was from an unknown number. Norman activated the speakerphone and heard the words of a troubled soul.

"Dr. Jacobson, I need…I need…to talk to you tonight. If I don't, there's a chance…I mean a real chance…I won't see the new year. I'll be outside your office…waiting."

The caller took a deep breath and cried.

"I'm on my way," Norman responded.

An hour later, Norman was in his office, sitting at his desk with a lukewarm cup of coffee. His patient sat opposite him in an oversized leather chair. Cushions supported the patient's head, and their eyes were wide open, focused straight ahead.

"So, what brings you here?" Norman asked.

The patient hesitated for a moment and then responded.

"When I was growing up, I always heard Christmastime was the most wonderful time of the year."

"You mean like the song? You know there'll be parties for hosting and marshmallows for toasting." Norman joked. He always injected humor to gain trust.

"Bullshit…it's not true," the patient yelled. "For some people, the holiday season is an unfortunate reminder of a past they want to forget. To them, Christmastime is far from wonderful. Instead, it's a time of severe depression."

"Now, calm down. You're with a friend, someone who cares for you," Norman said in a soothing voice. "Don't you trust me?"

The patient blinked their eyes and held the last blink for five seconds. While under hypnosis, Norman established blinking as a form of communication. A long blink meant 'Yes' while two quick blinks meant 'No.'

"Let's get back to what you were saying," Norman said as he stirred his coffee. "You were talking about the unfortunate people around the holidays. Are you one of them?"

"Yes...I...I am. This time of the year has always been difficult for me. Most people have a list of presents to buy, but I have a list of people to kill. I'm a loner. No family or friends and no one to talk to. Sometimes, the pain of hanging myself or slitting my wrists seems more desirable than life."

Norman was well versed in dealing with suicidal patients. When someone cried for help, he made sure he listened. Norman made himself available to his patients every day and at any hour. Even at the stroke of midnight on New Year's Eve.

"Let's delve deeper," Norman said. "I sense something is bottled up inside of you. A story no one knows. If you get it out in the open, you'll feel better. You've got nothing to be ashamed of. You are safe within these walls."

After a minute of silence, Norman sat in his chair and clasped his hands behind his head. Norman sensed the patient was ready to tell their story.

"Dr. Jacobson, you're one of the few people I trust. You're right. There's a story buried deep inside me. But you don't want to hear it.

"Now, let me be the judge," Norman said.

"The burden on your soul will be too great. I must warn you. If you uncover my past, you may not survive."

~

After 50 years as a clinical psychologist, Dr. Norman Jacobson looked forward to retiring and spending his golden years with his wife. The Jacobson's planned to start the next stage of their lives in style with a cruise around the world. The Queen Elizabeth 2 set sail on a five-month journey to 45 ports in 25 countries.

Norman informed his patients of his impending retirement. Most took the news well, but a handful didn't. To them, Dr. Jacobson was the only person they felt comfortable talking to concerning their problems.

In his younger days, Norman published six books on mind control and had a short stint as a television celebrity. But in his later years, he shunned the spotlight and focused on helping as many people as possible. Patients traveled from across the country to see Dr. Jacobson. It wasn't because of his novels or his television appearances. They had one specific reason.

They wanted to experience Jacobson's Ladder.

~

Two decades earlier, Norman didn't understand why he couldn't heal every patient. It was because patients buried the answers to their problems in the deepest recesses of their minds. However, Norman knew a solution existed somewhere. He just had to find the key to unlock the door. That's when Norman started performing research and conducting clinical trials. Five years later, his hard work culminated in an extreme form of neuron-hypnotherapy called Jacobson's Ladder.

The name "Jacobson's Ladder" was loosely based on the story of Jacob's Ladder from the Book of Genesis. In the Bible, a ladder appears in Jacob's dream. The ladder symbolized a relationship between earth and the heavens, and the steps represent the sequence of kingdoms that ruled the world.

But Norman, in his research, stumbled upon an alternative theory that stated the ladder symbolized the lessons learned in life, which, if properly used, brought them higher and higher in knowledge; however, if lessons were forgotten, there was a danger of falling.

In Jacobson's Ladder, the rungs represent the years in a patient's life. Sometimes the rungs are missing or may appear brittle. These years hold secrets, memories, and information that could be the key to unlocking the most complex psychological wounds.

What Norman's therapy did was help rebuild or repair the missing or broken rungs, enabling someone to uncover a forgotten past. After climbing the ladder, patients returned to consciousness with no recollection of where they were or what they had done. Patients relied on Norman's notes to understand what they experienced.

Norman only used the Ladder in extreme cases. He had strict requirements before agreeing to administer the therapy. First, patients committed to see Norman for one year. Then they submitted to an in-depth interview and a myriad of comprehensive tests. He couldn't cut corners because the radical therapy brought people to a difficult time, and there was a severe risk that uncovering the events would affect their lives.

Norman glanced at the digital clock on his desk. It read 12:30 a.m.. He texted a quick, "I love you, Vivian, Happy New Year. Be home in two hours" to his wife. Before his eyes left the phone, a text appeared, "Love you too, honey. Happy New Year. See you soon." Vivian had been waiting for her husband's message.

He wiped away a tear from his eye. For the first time in 45 years, the Jacobsons were spending New Year's Eve apart. They didn't seem to mind because retirement and a trip around the world were in their immediate future. It was going to be the trip of a lifetime, but what they didn't know was it was going to be in more ways than they could imagine.

CHAPTER

13

Test of Faith

St. Louis, Missouri

NORMAN AND HIS PATIENT met at the foot of Jacobson's Ladder.

"We'll start now. Grasp the first rung of the ladder and tell me the year."

"It was 2002 when we started, but now it's 2003," the patient said.

"Correct. Now, as you look at the ladder, what do you see?" Norman asked.

"The past, a troubled past."

"Grab the next rung and tell me the year again," Norman said.

"No. I...I can't."

"Don't worry, no one can do anything to you as long as I'm right by your side," Norman said.

The patient was unsettled but moved backward in time.

"2001."

"Grab the next rung," Norman said.

"2000."

"Good, keep going until you reach the year where your story begins."

The patient grabbed each rung, spoke the year, and kept retreating to the year 1975. Then there was silence.

The patient waited a minute and said in a higher-pitched childlike voice, "We have arrived."

"Don't worry, I'm right here next to you," Norman said. "Now, let's rebuild the rung. Do you know where you are?"

"Yes, I'm home in Shrewsbury, Massachusetts."

"How old are you, and what is the date?"

"I'm only ten years old, and the date is December 31, 1975."

"Okay, now I'll turn it over to you," Norman said. "You're about to relive the events of December 31, 1975. What you see in your mind's eye will appear real to you, but it's your recollection of what happened that day. If you wish to stop the therapy, just raise your right hand. Understand?"

"Yes, I understand."

Doctor and patient climbed through three decades. Now together, they were about to uncover the patient's story.

"Remember to tell me what you see and hear. Leave nothing out. Make me feel as if I'm right by your side," Norman said. "The floor is yours. You may now begin."

There was a moment of silence, and the patient swallowed hard.

"The day is New Year's Eve 1975, and the time is 11:00 p.m. I was ten years old, and it was way past my bedtime. My parents were in the living room watching television. I wasn't tired and snuck out of my bedroom to peek around the corner. Mommy was curled up in a blanket with the cat, and Daddy was in a recliner with his eyes barely open. They were both struggling to stay awake to see the ball drop. Then—"

"What happened?

"I heard a loud 'bang,' and three masked men broke into the house. They rushed in through the back door and went straight to the living room. I was scared and ran to my room and hid under the bed."

Beads of sweat cascaded down the patient's face.

"Then what?"

"One thug ordered Daddy to go to his office to open the safe. Somehow, they knew that was where Daddy kept lots of money. He kept money at home because he thought the government and banks were evil."

"Were you still under the bed?"

"Yes, I was under the bed and heard the thugs yelling and asking for money. Daddy told them he had none because he bought Christmas presents. They didn't believe him and pushed Daddy into the living room. Mommy couldn't talk, and I couldn't breathe."

The patient acted out the scene and tried to make the dialogue as authentic as possible.

Thug: I'm gonna give you one more chance to tell me where the money is, old man.

Daddy prayed out loud,

Thug: What are you doing?

Daddy: I have no money here, and I don't want to die. So, I'm praying to God for you to let us go.

Thug: Do you think your God can save you?

The three men laughed.

Daddy: Yes, He is my Lord and Savior.

The Thug chuckled.

Thug: Look, old man, I'm a fair person. I'll give you ten minutes with your Lord, and we'll see if he can work a miracle.

There was silence. Then I heard a countdown.

Thug: Five minutes left...Three minutes to go...One minute and counting.

I was crying under my bed.

Thug: Ten seconds.

I panicked and ran out to the living room. I turned the corner and watched.

Thug: Time is up, old man. What does your Lord have to say?

Daddy: He has a message for you. He says if you leave, he'll forgive you for your sins.

Thug: I have a message for you.

Daddy picked his head up.

Daddy: What is it?

Daddy cried and pleaded for his life. He knew what was going to happen.

Thug: I am your Lord...but not your Savior.

"Those were the last words my parents heard on this earth. Two bullets went through their heads. The thug turned, stared straight at me, and smiled. He pointed his gun at my head. I closed my eyes, waiting to die like Mommy and Daddy. But it never happened. I was still alive.

"The thug smiled and said, 'It's your lucky day, kid.' He paused for a second and continued, 'Remember, only God can grant life, but any man can impose death.'"

The patient broke down in tears and trembled.

"It's okay. Let it all out," Norman said in a comforting voice. "Cry as much as you need to. I'm here with you. You're not alone."

The patient continued through tears, "He should have killed me. He let me live, knowing I'd carry the burden of watching my parents die for the rest of my life. God had no say in who lived and died that night, but there was one man who did."

After a few minutes, the tears dried, and the patient calmed down.

"Once the men left, what happened?" Norman asked.

"I'm not sure. The next thing I remember was waking up in the hospital. At first, it all seemed like a bad dream. But then I opened my eyes and saw my grandparents. They had fake smiles on their faces. I could tell they were sad."

"What did they say to you?"

"They told me I was in the hospital, and the doctor was making sure I was okay. They bowed their heads and cried. They were trying their best to be strong. I had a question for them."

"What was the question?"

"I asked if God exists. Grandpa said God watches over everyone. I didn't understand. I then asked why God didn't protect Mommy and Daddy."

"What was his answer?"

"Grandpa didn't know. But he told me everything in life happens for a reason. Daddy and Mommy didn't die in vain. He said one day, God's plan would become clear. We'll find out the answer."

"They told me the thug that killed my parents was evil. I asked them why evil gets to choose? Why does evil win?"

"Did they have an answer?"

"Grandma said during our lifetime, sometimes evil wins. It's just a test of our faith. Evil may sometimes win the battle, but God always wins the war."

"How do you feel right now?"

"Confused and upset. The experience changed my perception of life and death. I can't tell anymore where one starts and the other ends. There are so many unanswered questions in my head, including the biggest one of them all."

"What is the question?"

"Can man have the power to decide who lives and dies?"

CHAPTER

14

Sick Seven

St. Louis, Missouri

AFTER THREE WEEKS OF INTENSE THERAPY, Norman took another run up Jacobson's Ladder with his patient. He revisited his notes before starting the session and saw the patient had skipped rungs on the ladder. Norman figured that repairing the rungs would shed light on the patient's ongoing psychological issues.

"We've re-established some of your repressed memories. Now how do you feel?" Norman asked.

The patient took a measured tone and said, "Better."

"Good. Today we'll start where we left off," Norman said. "I noticed you bypassed some rungs. We need to find out why."

Together, Norman and the patient crawled back to New Year's Day in 1976. The day after, a man thug killed the patient's parents. From there, they worked forward and stopped in the year 1981. The patient had broken the rung.

"Okay, let's see. By my calculation, those were your high school years. Any traumatic events, turning points, or discoveries in school?" Norman asked.

"My father was a well-respected psychologist," the patient said with pride. "He graduated from the Johns Hopkins School of Medicine near the top of his class. Dad specialized in criminal behavior. He spent years studying real-life murderers and killers; the more twisted and fucked up they were, the better."

"I'm aware of his work. I sat in on one of his lectures once. He was a brilliant man."

"He was an even better father. It was hard those first few years. I still miss him."

The patient stopped for a moment to reflect on something before returning to the conversation.

"After Dad died, I'd sit in his office every day after school. One day I stared at the bottom right-hand drawer in his desk. The drawer always intrigued me. When I was younger, I tried to open it but was unsuccessful. Dad always kept it locked. Something important was in the drawer. I had to find out what it was. So, I broke the lock."

"What was inside the drawer?"

"A few different folders. But one caught my eye. On the front, in bold letters written in thick red magic marker, were the words 'The Sick Seven.' The folder contained handwritten notes and articles on the seven most notorious serial killers in American history. Dad chose them based on the uniqueness of their criminal cases, not based on the body count."

"So, who were The Sick Seven?"

"Ted Bundy, Jeffrey Dahmer, Edmund Kemper, Dennis Raider, Leonard Lake, Ed Gein, and John Wayne Gacy."

"Did the folder and its contents hold significance?" Norman asked.

"Yes. I became obsessed with learning about serial killers. It was important to my father, so it became important to me."

"Why was that?"

"Life is precious," the patient said. "But the Sick Seven didn't care. Something drove them to kill strangers in cold blood. Dad always said nothing happens by accident. There was a reason for everything. The Sick Seven had their reasons, and I wanted to find out what they were."

The patient paused and took a deep breath.

"As I thumbed through the folder, I thought again about the words from the night my parents died."

ONLY GOD CAN GRANT LIFE,
BUT ANY MAN CAN IMPOSE DEATH.

"The thought of having such power was intriguing. I wanted to experience it myself and be the one to make the ultimate decision between life and death."

The patient's tone turned serious.

"I went through the folder and came across a theory Dad had. He categorized all killers into one of three types: Those who need to kill, those who want to kill, and those who enjoy the kill."

Norman sensed something big was going to happen and tried his best to maintain momentum.

"Let's stay with your high school years," Norman said. "Something needs to be fleshed out."

The patient became tense and angry.

"High school...was...it was...a terrible experience," the patient said. "Everyone referred to me as 'The Loner' for obvious reasons. Most of the kids treated me like a stranger, while the bullies viewed me as an easy target."

"Did you do something about it?"

"I told teachers and counselors," the patient said. "But they all turned a blind eye. 'They're picking on you because they like you,' they all said. That was a load of crap."

The patient's voice rose, on the verge of yelling.

"If they liked me so much, then why did I eat lunch by myself every day? Why was there always an empty seat next to me on the bus? Why did I have bruises on my upper arms? Fuck them all."

The patient was shaking with rage. A few minutes passed.

"I...I...concluded the only way to stop the physical and mental abuse was to take matters into my own hands. That's when I came up with...the list."

"You were doing the right thing by sticking up for yourself," Norman offered encouragement. "Ronald Reagan once said, 'If no one amongst us is capable, then who amongst us has the capacity?' Sometimes the 'who' is us. Tell me about this list."

"The list comprised 13 kids who picked on me and made my life miserable. I printed their names on a small piece of paper and kept it in my wallet. I swore to myself one day I'd get revenge. I wasn't sure when or where, but someday they would all pay, dearly."

Norman noticed a smile came to the patient's face.

"Why the huge grin? Did something good happen?" Norman asked.

The patient responded with a more prominent grin, "Yes...something wonderful happened."

"In June, my grandparents sent me to summer camp with all the other kids. I didn't want to go, but they insisted. Grandpa and Grandma kicked me out of the house and told me to find friends. Easier said than done. If they spent one day with me in school, they know it was a bad idea."

"Why? Kids enjoy summer camp."

"One weekend, the counselors took the kids upstate to go hiking in the mountains. Everyone paired off in twos. Sean Burke took me by default. I could tell he wasn't happy. But guess what? Neither was I."

"Sean pretended to be my friend that day because he had no other choice. He talked a little, and at first, I was cordial. But the thought of him feigning friendship made my fucking blood boil. Hatred ran through my veins. Bad thoughts were raging in my head."

"What happened next?"

"The two of us were standing on a hill overlooking a deep ravine. Sean was blabbering about the awesome view. That's when I heard those words again in my head."

ONLY GOD CAN GRANT LIFE,
BUT ANY MAN CAN IMPOSE DEATH.

"Something came over me; a warm feeling spread throughout my body. I took a quick look and saw no one was around. Sean was on the side of the ravine with his back to me. I didn't hesitate and pushed him over the edge. He fell head over heels, hitting a dozen jagged rocks on the way down. Sean was a bloody, tangled mess at the bottom. I stared at his lifeless body from a distance."

"How did it feel to be responsible for someone's death?" Norman asked.

"It didn't bother me in the least bit. I decided that was Sean's last day on earth. I pulled the list from my pocket and crossed off #11 - Sean Burke."

The patient smiled as if they recalled opening their favorite childhood Christmas present.

"I was only 15, and it was my first kill," the patient said.

Then came a chilling admission.

"It wouldn't be my last."

CHAPTER

15

Crazy Train

St. Louis, Missouri

NORMAN ENCOUNTERED A DOZEN INSTANCES where patients confessed to murder while under hypnosis. In each instance, Norman performed therapy under "physician-patient privilege" to put their minds at ease. Most of the time, patients exaggerated their crimes, but sometimes patients told the truth. Norman never once came close to turning in a patient to the authorities. But that was about to change.

It had been two weeks since Norman and his patient were at the foot of Jacobson's Ladder. They made considerable progress, but he noticed the patient had avoided some rungs. His gut told him those years held a pivotal piece to the puzzle. If Norman was going to uncover those repressed memories, he needed a different approach.

Instead of staying in the present and relying on the patient's first-person account, Norman would travel to the past and join in the experience. This was a radical and reckless idea, one which Norman had contemplated throughout the years. But now, he was nearing retirement, and this could be his last opportunity if he wanted to climb the ladder with one of his patients.

Norman started the therapy session by putting his patient in a deep, hypnotic state. He then told his patient to wait at the bottom rung of the ladder for further instructions. Norman needed time to hypnotize himself. He turned on a hidden video camera, locked his office door, and closed the window blinds. Norman then positioned his recliner opposite his patient and began hypnotizing himself. He waited until he was in a relaxed and focused state.

~

Twenty minutes later, Norman was standing on the first rung on the ladder.

"Doctor Jacobson, what are you doing here?" the patient asked.

"I'm here to observe. It's a much more efficient and effective way to gather information from patients. We're close to a breakthrough, and I want to see what happens first-hand."

"But don't forget Dr. Jacobson. I'm the engineer on this crazy train."

"Yes, but my job is to keep the crazy train on the tracks."

Both Norman and the patient grabbed the rungs of the ladder and climbed into the past. Norman struck up a conversation along the way.

"I was thinking about your father's theory. What kind of killer are you?" Norman asked. "Do you need to kill? Do you want to kill? Or do you enjoy the kill? Which one is it?"

"Dr. Jacobson, if this is a multiple-choice question, you must add a fourth option—all the above. If you haven't realized by now, I'm not like other killers. Every day is different. Depending on the situation, I could fit into any of those categories."

The patient leaned forward and looked straight into Norman's eyes. "Dr. Jacobson, you know more about me than most people. I'm wondering what you're thinking. How would you categorize me?"

"As long as we're adding options, let's add another—none of the above. I don't think you fit into any of those categories. You don't enjoy killing at all. For you, it's a means to an end."

They continued to climb the ladder until they reached the mid-1980s. The patient stopped and turned to Norman. "In our last session, we talked about your first kill, and you mentioned it wouldn't be your last. Have you murdered others?" Norman asked.

"Funny, you should ask. We've arrived at the years where we can find the answers. Let's stop at 1985 to 1989," the patient said with a grin. Norman noticed the rungs in 1985 and 1987 were about to break.

"Let's go to these two years."

"Good choice Dr. Jacobson. I remember when I graduated from college, I crossed three more names off the list. Karen Henry (#4), Alex Patterson (#7), and Rick Cooley (#10). We should be able to find them here."

"What happened to each of them?"

"They all turned out to be easy targets. Karen was unconscious outside a bar, so I dragged her into the woods and beat her to death. Shot both Alex and Rick in the head at close range and then pummeled them with a baseball bat for kicks and giggles. It felt good to take out my frustrations on their lifeless bodies. I buried them in two different states, but the authorities never found them."

The patient stopped in other years and confessed to other murders. The number of victims was staggering. It was hard to keep count. Norman realized he was in over his head, and the physician-patient privilege was out the window. The public was now in danger.

"When will the killing stop?" Norman asked.

"When all have met their fate," the patient said.

"So, you're going to kill everyone on the list and then retire?"

The patient stopped climbing and pointed a finger at Norman.

"When I say, 'all have met their fate,' I didn't just mean the names on the list. If someone crosses my path and disrespects me or doesn't treat me with dignity, I'll hold them accountable for their actions. I'm the second in command—the judge, jury, and the executioner."

"Have you ever killed someone who didn't deserve to die?" Norman asked.

"Yes. I categorize them as collateral damage," the patient said.

"How often has that happened?"

"Not too often. One time, I had to kill a young woman because she was in the wrong place at the wrong time. I couldn't take any chances. She was a pretty girl who was engaged to be married. I took her life and her engagement ring."

"I can sense that you're not comfortable with collateral damage. Is that true?"

"Yes. I'd rather kill someone who deserves to die. Others are just obstacles and are in the way. Killing them is just part of the process. They're a necessary evil."

Norman had all the information he needed to draw a conclusion.

"In your own words, you proclaimed yourself judge, jury, and executioner," Norman said. "The judge decides what evidence is admissible to the court, the jury decides guilt or innocence, and the executioner carries out the sentence."

"Why do you separate the roles?

"That kind of power is dangerous if it falls into the wrong hands," Norman said. "Anyone can be an executioner, but only a select number of people can serve as judge and jury. If you were honest, you would admit that drives you. You don't just kill. You kill those who deserve to die."

"Your analysis is astute, Dr. Jacobson," the patient said. "But as Second in Command, I must serve justice."

"Based on my limited knowledge of the law, I know of four types of justice," Norman said. "Distributive, Procedural, Restorative, and Retributive. What type of justice are you serving?"

The patient smiled and said, "You forgot the fifth type—Vigilante justice."

They stopped talking for a few minutes. Norman sensed something was wrong.

"I've heard a lot over the years within these four walls," Norman said. "You're not the first. Other patients admitted to murder in the same chair you're in now."

"Yes, but they didn't have a story like mine." the patient said. "I've killed many people in my lifetime, and there's more to come. No one knows what I've done in the past or what I'll do in the future except for me…and now you."

The patient had a parched throat and asked for a drink. Norman got up and walked over to a small table and poured a glass of cold water. Within seconds, he felt something pressing against the back of his head. It was the barrel of a handgun.

"I guess you weren't thirsty, were you?" Norman said in a calm voice.

There was silence.

"I've never told the authorities about anything within the sanctity of my office. I adhere to the physician-patient privilege. There is nothing to worry about."

The silence continued.

It worried Norman. He needed to get his patient talking again.

The handgun pressed harder against the back of Norman's head. He closed his eyes as he prayed. Death was imminent, and there was one more opportunity to say something. Norman paused and said:

ONLY GOD CAN GRANT LIFE,

BUT ANY MAN CAN IMPOSE DEATH.

After a few more seconds, the pressure eased. Norman heard the patient retreat to the recliner. The two of them sat down, both drenched in sweat, but for distinct reasons. Norman wasn't out of the woods yet. The patient kept the handgun pointed towards him. There was still a good chance Norman wouldn't leave the office alive.

"I'm not sure if I made a mistake coming here." the patient said. "I've told you some of my deepest and darkest secrets. You can talk about physician-patient privilege all day long. But that's bullshit. There's no guarantee these conversations stay within these walls. I put my gun in the back of your head, intending to blow your brains out. You don't know how close I came to pulling the trigger. But I couldn't do it."

At that moment, both Norman and the patient came out of their hypnotic trances. They were like two bears emerging from a long hibernation. Both had no recollection of what they had experienced.

The patient got up, and before leaving the office, turned around to face Norman.

"I owe you a couple of grand. Next week I'll bring cash and pay my bill," the patient said. "I have to pawn a diamond engagement ring first. The take should be enough to pay off the balance.

The patient looked at Norman one last time, pointed his fingers at him like it was a gun, and said. "Remember that all conversations remain within these walls. Otherwise, there will be consequences." The patient pretended to pull the trigger.

"Bang."

Norman was at home three days later when Vivian walked in with the mail and a small package.

"Norm, can we talk about the cruise?" Vivian asked. "I want to go over the itinerary."

"Sure, honey," Norman responded. "Just give me fifteen minutes to go through my mail." Vivian walked out of the room.

Norman turned his attention to the package. Inside was a hardcover book. The title was Brainwashing: Objective Control of the Subjective Mind. The author was Dr. Mathews Ph.D.; the front cover had a dedication:

> I dedicate this book to the author, Dr. Carter Mathews, Ph.D. He had been working on this project for two years but never saw it to completion. He was a brilliant man and well-respected psychologist who devoted his life to studying the human mind. This book ensures his legacy lives on. But he wasn't just an author. He also was my father. Remain in spirit and rest in peace - Jack Mathews

---

The next day, Norman went into his office, sat with a cup of coffee, and booted his computer. As he waited, he went through his mail. The pile of letters were all sent to 'Dr. Norman Jacobson,' but one letter seemed odd because the return address bared the same name. When he opened the letter, inside was a folded 8-10 piece of paper. In the middle, printed in large capital letters, were the following words: "Retrieve the Video."

The most significant side effect of Jacobson's Ladder is a temporary loss of memory. By sending himself a note, he reminded himself to download the video from the session with his troubled patient.

The computer was taking a long time to boot up. Norman was eager to get to the share drive and download the video. That's when Jason Blackman walked in with some unwelcome news.

Jason was a one-man IT department. He was an expert in programming, networking, database creation, and general technical support. Norman paid Jason a healthy salary, but he was worth every penny.

"Norman," Jason said. "The server is down."

"What happened?" Norman asked.

"Problem with the network driver. The good news is I'll be able to fix it by the end of the day."

Norman looked straight at Jason. "Whenever I hear the words 'good news,' that means 'bad news' isn't far behind."

"You must have read my mind," Jason said. "That's why you're a psychologist."

The two shared a laugh, but Jason got serious in a matter of seconds.

"The bad news is we may have lost information from the past couple of days,"

Norman slumped in his chair. He knew he had lost the video of Jack. He ran his hands over his face and sighed in disgust.

"Jason, I may have lost something important. If you come across any video files with a date of February 19th, let me know."

"Will do," Jason responded.

"If you can work a miracle, I'll make it worth your while," Norman said. "I'll take you to a St. Louis Blues game."

"Always wanted to go to a major league baseball game live and in person. Thanks."

Norman smiled. Jason was a genius with computers, but as far as sports goes, not so much.

"Jason, I have good news and bad news. The good news is I have first-row seats."

"What's the bad news?" Jason asked.

"The seats are at the hockey arena and not the baseball stadium," Norman said with a smile.

At 5:30 p.m., Norman sat in the chair behind his desk. He had a faint recollection of climbing Jacobson's Ladder with his most challenging patient. Norman was on the verge of a significant breakthrough that would change the future of psychology. However, because of network issues, the video and any related evidence were lost forever.

Norman always envisioned he would end his career on a high note and ride off into the sunset. But now, that wouldn't be the case. Retirement was calling, and he was going to walk out of his office wondering what could have been. Norman turned out the light but left the door ajar a few inches. It was a symbolic gesture. He knew when the lights went out. The party was over. He cracked the door because he wanted a way to get back in, just in case the party started up again.

CHAPTER

16

Arcadia

Bar Harbor, Maine

THE ARCADIA BED AND BREAKFAST had been in the Brennan family for half a century. In 1962, Wilson Brennan and his wife bought a tract of land along Route 3 in Bar Harbor. It was on a desert island in-between Maine's Frenchman Bay and Arcadia National Park.

They built a spacious five-bedroom house with two appealing features. The east side had a front porch with half a dozen rocking chairs. Each morning, there was a glimpse of one of the earliest sunrises in the United States. On the west side was a well-shaded deck with outdoor couches. In the distance was a breathtaking view of a dense forest that extended to Cadillac Mountain and Arcadia National Park.

It seemed fitting to name the house 'Arcadia' after the park, but to the Brennan's, their 'Arcadia' had a deeper meaning. To them, it wasn't just a home but a place with a beautiful feeling. They didn't realize it, but Arcadia was also a synonym for 'Heaven,' which, all by itself, was the perfect descriptor.

After Wilson retired, the Brennans moved further inland to the rolling hills of Vermont. But they couldn't let Arcadia go. They kept the property in the Brennan family for future generations. Once Wilson and his wife passed, their grandson Wendell Brennan found himself in the same situation. He shared the beauty of Arcadia with the public and turned the house into a bed-and-breakfast.

Wendell traveled and left the management and operation of Arcadia with his wife, Kathleen. She looked after every aspect of the house and supplied home-cooked meals three times a day to the guests. Kathleen's distinctive touch made Arcadia a popular choice for those who wanted to escape the world and enjoy a relaxing vacation.

Breakfast was at 9:00 a.m. sharp each day in the main dining room. It was Kathleen's favorite part of the day because it allowed her to mingle with her guests.

On a Wednesday morning in October, both tables in the dining room were full. One table had five couples from various parts of the country. The other had a group of women who were lifelong college friends enjoying a long-overdue reunion.

Kathleen prepared a classic American breakfast buffet. Most guests preferred homemade pancakes and French toast, while others swore by the fresh scrambled eggs and crispy bacon. Anyone not falling into one of those two camps had a choice of cereals, pastries, and fruit.

"Good morning, everyone, you know the drill," Kathleen said. "I set the buffet up in the kitchen. Take as much as you want."

"Mrs. Brennan, the quality of your breakfasts is legendary," David Sutton remarked. "But the amount of food is more than we can handle. What do you do with all the leftovers?"

It wasn't the first time Kathleen fielded such a question. She had a stock answer.

"I'll let you in on a little secret. When you guys are out during the day, I take the leftovers into the woods to a group of forest dwellers. They offer us protection in exchange for breakfast."

"Protection from what?" Rita Bauer asked.

"There is a serial killer in these parts. They seem to prey on people coming through town. Don't worry; we've only lost three guests this year."

Everyone looked up from their breakfast plates at the same time with concerned looks on their faces. Kathleen waited a few seconds and then flashed a smile.

"You all can breathe now. I was only kidding. I send the extra food to a local shelter, where they put it to good use. Pardon me, but I get that question so often I wanted to have some fun with it."

Everyone laughed except for Natalie Becker at the end of the table. Natalie was with the college reunion crowd. She was sitting next to Lynn Walters, who was traveling by herself.

"What's wrong, Natalie? Wasn't that at least a little funny?" Lynn asked.

"To be truthful, it wasn't funny at all," Natalie said as she bolted from the table.

After the scene, there was silence.

"Kathleen," Barbara Harris said. "Natalie is from Shrewsbury, and she has friends who were part of the Shrewsbury Seven. She's sensitive to violence, especially talk about serial killers."

"What is the Shrewsbury Seven?" Kathleen asked.

"In the early 1980s, someone murdered two high school students, and five others went missing," Barbara said. "The police department and FBI investigated every lead, but everything turned out to be a dead end. A decade later, they closed all the open cases. They couldn't continue to fund the investigations after so many years of inactivity. But now, the Shrewsbury Seven is in the news again. There have been murders across the country with ties to Shrewsbury High School."

"Oh my, I'm so sorry. That was in bad taste. I didn't know. Let me go apologize."

The following day, there were two extra places open at the breakfast table. Everyone assumed both Natalie and Lynn overslept.

"Natalie is late for breakfast. I hope she is still not holding a grudge," Kathleen said.

"She shouldn't be," Barbara said. "I spoke to her last night after you apologized, and she was okay. I know when she travels, she likes to sleep late."

"Where's Lynn this morning?" Cathy Kramer asked. "I feel sorry she is all by herself. I wanted her to join us today."

"Lynn checked out around 7:00 a.m.," Kathleen said. "She had a family emergency and needed to leave."

After breakfast, the women got ready to go for a drive. They all met downstairs, except for Natalie. Barbara went to her room and knocked on the door. There was no answer, so she called for Kathleen to open the locked door. Natalie was missing. Her things were undisturbed, and her phone and handbag were on top of the dresser. It looked as if she got up and walked out of the house.

Kathleen called the police, and three officers came out to the house. After taking statements, they went out into the backyard and into the woods to investigate. It didn't take Officer Watson long to find Natalie. Someone strung her up in a tree with her hands tied and a bullet hole in her head. Someone pinned a piece of paper to her shirt. Someone wrote a note in a red marker.

IF YOU WANT TO SEE THE AUTUMN LEAVES,
YOU HAVE TO HANG IN THE TREES—JACK

A Honda Accord pulled into a Walmart parking lot off the interstate highway in Waterville, Maine. In the far corner was a Ford Taurus. The Accord parked next to the Taurus. The driver realized something was missing.

"Crap...of all things to forget," Lynn said. "Time to be welcomed to Walmart."

Lynn walked in and met 74-year-old Sam Armstrong.

"Welcome to Walmart, young lady," Sam announced.

"Hello, old man. Point me to your office supplies."

"Sure, hang a left, third aisle on your right. The Bic Ballpoints are on sale today."

Lynn went into the store and found two Sharpies, and headed to the cash register to check out. As Lynn left the store, she crossed paths with Sam once again.

"Honey, did you find the Bics?" Sam asked.

"Yes, but they didn't have my favorite color."

"What's your favorite color?" Sam asked.

"Red. The bolder and darker, the better."

Lynn returned to the cars and transferred all belongings to the Ford Taurus.

Lynn pulled out a piece of paper from a wallet. She took the Red Sharpie and drew a thick red line through "#4 - Natalie Becker."

The Ford Taurus merged onto the interstate, headed south. The next destination was Pittsburgh.

She had one more "friend" to visit.

CHAPTER

17

Number One

Jefferson Hills, Pennsylvania

THE 300 BOWL opened in 1970 with little fanfare. Back then, the bowling alley had a modest ten lanes and a small concession stand. It became a popular nightspot in the suburban Pittsburgh area. So, the owners expanded the property to accommodate the demand. Four decades later, the 300 Bowl grew into a modern-day entertainment complex with thirty bowling lanes.

On a Saturday afternoon in May, the Greater Pittsburgh area was set to crown the Over 40 Women's League champion. It was a thrilling tournament that came down to the Alley Kats and the Rockin' Bowlers. In the final frame, the Kats needed three strikes to win. They had one last hope.

Megan Griffin grabbed her bowling ball and stepped into the lane. She was an elite bowler in her early twenties. At one point, she tried to turn professional but fell short of qualifying. After five mediocre years, Megan gave up on her dream, got married, and then divorced. A few years later, she was miserable and returned to the one thing that made her happy. Megan started to bowl again.

Megan hung out at 300 Bowl on Sunday afternoons and targeted men with big egos and small bowling balls. She talked trash until it got under their skin. The men would always laugh and proclaim how they could beat her with one hand tied behind their back. That was Megan's cue to challenge them and see if she could get them to put their money where their mouth was. More often than not, Megan would walk away with two hundred dollars in her pocketbook. It was a nice complement to a steady paycheck.

~

Megan held the ball high and stared at the pins with laser focus. She got excited because she wasn't accustomed to winning anything. Megan stepped aside for a second to take a deep breath. At that moment, one of her teammates came up to her and offered encouragement.

"Meg, are you aware of what will happen if you strike out?" Paula Allen asked.

"I'm not an idiot," Megan said. "I know the situation. This ball is for the championship."

"Yeah, but a strike here, and you'll also have the best individual average, and you'll be number one in the entire league," Paula said.

Megan froze for a few seconds. When she heard the words "number one," she felt sick to her stomach. Those two simple words terrified her like nothing else.

Over the past decade, Megan received anonymous letters from all around the country. A white piece of paper was in each envelope with the following words written using a red Sharpie: "You're #1." Megan didn't understand what it meant, but the simple message made her feel insecure after a while. She contacted the police, but there was nothing they could do about it.

Megan shook it off and set up again in the lane. She stood in one spot and stared at the pins for what seemed like an eternity. She heard her teammates in the distance.

"Don't pull a Meatloaf. Two out of three ain't bad, but three out of three is better."

"Strike out the side, Meg. You can do it."

"One more, Megan, and we're champs."

The Kats were confident Megan would come through. Suddenly, an impromptu chant rang out. "We're #1. We're #1."

The chanting got louder by the second. Megan's heart was pounding, and she started to sweat. She was on the verge of a nervous breakdown. Megan wanted the chanting to stop, but she knew of only one way to do it.

With tears in her eyes, Megan took three strides and slung the ball down the lane. Typically, she'd start on the right side of the lane and have the side spin curve the ball before hitting the front pins. But by starting the ball down the middle, the same side spin produced disastrous results. The ball ended up in the left-hand gutter.

Everyone watched in stunned silence. Before anyone moved, Megan grabbed her things and bolted for the front door.

"What the hell just happened?" Paula asked. "She threw the ball into the gutter on purpose."

The Rockin' Bowlers backed into the Championship. They felt terrible and walked over to the Alley Kats to offer support. But some were more blunt than others.

"Sorry about the loss," Maria Richard said. "You guys had a great season. But to be honest, that bitch on your team had it coming to her."

Paula was shocked. She couldn't figure out where the hate was coming from.

"Look, I know you're new to the area, but you need to know something about Megan Griffin," Maria Richard said.

"What's that?" Paula asked.

"Megan Griffin is a mean person. She doesn't care about anyone but herself. She's quick to criticize and make fun of people to get a cheap laugh. Megan's only friends are on her bowling team. She leads a sad and lonely life and has no one to blame but herself."

"I didn't know. How do you know this?"

"I went to school with Megan," Maria responded. "Ask anyone who knew her, and each one of them has a story about her. Megan has tried to change these past twenty years. But you know what? You can change outside, but you are what you are on the inside."

When Megan got home, she made a beeline for the bedroom, got under the covers, and didn't emerge until Sunday afternoon. She was hoping when she woke up. It was all a dream. But she wouldn't be so lucky. Megan was in the middle of a deep depression, and it would take a while to fight her way out.

The phone rang. It seemed louder than usual because Megan's nerves were more fragile than ever.

"Hello," Megan said in a soft voice.

There was silence, but Megan heard someone breathing.

"Hello, who is this?" Megan asked with a hint of agitation.

Whoever it was, I ended the call.

Megan made herself an afternoon snack and spent the rest of the day watching television. She stayed awake until her eyelids closed and went to sleep around midnight.

At 3:00 a.m., the phone rang again. Chills ran down Megan's spine. She picked up the phone and again heard silence.

"Who the fuck is this?" Megan screamed.

Someone laughed on the other end.

"Hell-oo, Megan," a soft voice said.

"What the fuck do you want?" Megan screamed again.

There was more laughter, followed by a few seconds of silence before the voice answered.

"You're...Number...One..

CHAPTER

18

Breaking Point

Tampa, Florida

ON FRIDAY MORNING, Drake went to Political Donuts to pick up breakfast for the office. When he arrived, Drake walked in the front door, checking his cell phone, unaware of what was happening around him. When he raised his head to place his order, he sensed something was wrong. Not a single person was in sight.

When Drake looked closer, he noticed aprons tossed on the countertop, donuts were strewn on the floor, and the cash register halfway open. He pulled his service revolver and crept around the back of the donut shop to investigate.

Drake peered in a side window and saw Nikki and two other employees facing the wall in the corner of the back office. Billy Walsh, the manager, was opening a safe. Drake stumbled upon a robbery in progress, which wasn't how he wanted to start the weekend.

FBI protocol is first to secure the area and call for backup. They teach agents to diffuse or delay anything from happening until help arrives. However, if lives are at stake they need to respond. The situation at Political Donuts was dire, and Drake felt he needed to act.

After calling for backup, Drake made his way to the back door. He snuck in and reached the office. A middle-aged man was standing in front of Billy. The safe was at the far end of the room, and everyone's backs faced the door.

"FBI," Drake barked. "Put down your weapon and get on the ground."

The man stopped what he was doing and stared straight ahead, not wanting to make any sudden movements. Everyone was quiet and waited for the next move.

"I'm not getting down on the ground," the man said. "I've come too far to turn back now. If you want no one hurt, you'll let me walk out of here. We all get to live another day."

"Down on the ground," Drake barked again.

The man exposed his left arm, which brandished a hunting knife with a thick five-inch blade. His right arm remained hidden.

"Be smart and put the knife down," Drake said. "Keep your hands where I can see them and make no sudden movements."

"Don't push me, don't you dare push me," the man yelled. "You don't know who you're dealing with." The man swung around, grabbed Nikki with his right arm, and placed his blade at the base of her neck.

Drake had been in life or death situations before, but this was the first time involving someone he knew. In the background, were other voices amid slamming doors. Reinforcements had arrived. Drake backed the man into a corner. With Nikki's life in the balance, he gave the man one last chance.

"Final warning," Drake ordered. "Drop your weapon…now."

Drake looked the man in the eyes and realized he wasn't giving in. The blade was too close to Nikki's throat. Drake couldn't wait for the man to make the first move. Without thinking twice, he squeezed the trigger on his revolver, but the gun jammed.

The man panicked, slashing Nikki as she fell to the ground. He then bull-rushed Drake to get by him. Within seconds, shots rang out. One of the backup police officers confronted the man by the front door and shot the man in the chest, killing him instantly.

When Drake got to his feet, he went over to attend to Nikki. She fell backward and hit her head on the floor. A pool of blood gathered and was getting larger by the second. Drake took off his shirt and applied pressure to the wound. As he waited for the paramedics to arrive, Nikki's face was ashen, her lips trembled, and her eyes were full of fear. She prepared herself to die.

The paramedics arrived and took over within minutes. Nikki was off to the hospital, with Drake in tow. As he was driving, he thought of the cold, fearful look in Nikki's eyes as she cried for help. Drake was helpless. When they reached the emergency room, the staff took Nikki straight to an operating room for the fight of her life.

After the doctors addressed Nikki's wounds, they moved her to the intensive care unit. Drake paced the floor by the nurse's station for an hour until a doctor emerged from the operating room. He needed to find out how Nikki was doing.

"Excuse me, are you Dr. Graham?" Drake asked.

"Yes, I am."

"My name is Drake Merino. I'm with the FBI. I was at the scene and want to get an update on Nikki's condition."

"She remains in critical condition. I'm afraid she is in a coma." Dr. Graham responded. "Nikki lost a lot of blood, which has compromised multiple organs. But my bigger concern is the brain injuries resulting from her head hitting the ground. I'll be honest, Drake. I'm not sure she'd going to pull through. We'll do everything we can to save her. If you leave your contact information, we can provide updates as things change."

As Dr. Graham walked away, Drake stared straight ahead. He trudged through the hallways, passing by other patients with emotionless faces. Drake felt they were judging him for failing to save Nikki.

On the way home, Drake thought through everything that had transpired. Someone murdered his fiancé Taylor. Nightmares took control of his life. He was a recluse and a burden to his family, and he suffered a nervous breakdown that put his career in doubt. Now Nikki was dying, and he blamed himself.

Drake reached his breaking point. Everything was spiraling downward fast as depression and guilt overwhelmed him. Something needed to change. Drake couldn't continue down the same path. It was time for him to make a choice. Stay at home and hope his fortunes would change for the better or leave everything behind and start life over.

He chose to take the easy way out and run as far away as possible. Drake hoped to go far enough, so his problems couldn't follow in his footsteps. What Drake didn't realize is it didn't matter where he went. His troubles were still with him, only be a few steps behind.

Two weeks later, on a Saturday morning, Dominic stopped by Drake's house for another heart-to-heart talk with his brother. It was time to discuss Drake's future in the FBI. When Dominic pulled up to the house, he noticed Drake's car was missing. In the distance, he saw Kurt out on the lake. Dominic motioned for him. Kurt reeled in his fishing pole and high-tailed it back to the dock.

"Mornin' Kurt, have you seen Drake?"

"He left early this morning," Kurt said. "He told me he was going somewhere. I asked if he wanted to go fishing, but he declined. Now that I think of it, he seemed troubled by something."

Dominic stared back at Drake's house and said, "He mentioned nothing about going anywhere. I told him I'd be stopping by today. I'll call his cell phone."

He dialed Drake's number, but it went straight to voicemail. He tried three more times during the day, to no avail.

Something wasn't right.

By 9:00 p.m., Dominic became concerned and returned to Drake's house. He circled the premises. Kurt was still up and walked over to see what was happening.

"Kurt, Drake is missing. He's not answering his phone."

"I haven't seen him since early Saturday," Kurt said.

"Hate to do this, but I got to get into his house. Let's find a window to break."

"No need, Dominic. Drake gave me a spare key in case he locked himself out."

The two men unlocked the back door, walked inside, and turned on the lights. They were both shocked by what they saw. Everything was in pristine condition, and everything seemed to be in its place. The kitchen was spotless, and the living room looked good enough for company. A radio was on in the background, and a fresh scent was in the air. It wasn't like Drake to clean the house. He always thought, "Why bother if you never have visitors."

Dominic's eyes wandered to a note on the kitchen table.

To my brother Dominic:

The time has come for me to leave. I thought I could handle adversity. But that was until someone murdered Taylor. They say, 'Time heals all wounds.' Well, not this wound. It got worse with the nightmares and sleepwalking.

Everything crumbled around me. I kept telling myself things would get better, but they never did. But that didn't drive me to my decision. It was Nikki. I didn't save her when she needed me.

I can hear everyone say, "It's not your fault the gun jammed." Guess what, it didn't. That's just what I told the other officers at the scene. I froze and hesitated for a split second. Instead of going for the kill shot, the bastard slit Nikki's throat. Now she is in a coma fighting for her life. If she dies, I won't be able to live with myself. That's why I'm leaving.

As for Mom, do you remember what she used to always tell us? "Before you leave, make sure you clean your room." So that's what I did. I cleaned the entire house for the first time in a year. I bet you're impressed. No need to be because I'm never doing it again.

As for Dad, he taught us a lot and gave us everything we needed to carry on the Merino tradition. Dad raised us both to be big bad FBI special agents. But I cracked under pressure. For me, it wasn't meant to be.

As for you, my brother, thanks for being there for me. You saved my life more than once and always looked out for me. I wish I could repay you, but I can't. Maybe in another lifetime. Don't beat yourself up or blame yourself for my leaving. It's all on me. You did all you could do.

Where am I going? I'm not sure. Don't bother looking for me. I'm escaping so I can start over somewhere else. We'll see each other again, somewhere, someday. Wherever you go, I'll be with you in spirit. I promise you.

Love you, Brother

Drake

Tears came to Dominic's eyes as he finished reading the note. Kurt put his arm around Dominic's shoulder to comfort him.

"He'll be back, you'll see," Kurt said. "He's confused and needs time to clear his head."

After a brief pause, Dominic got emotional.

"The two of us are closer than brothers; we're one and the same. When one of us hurts, the other feels the pain. Now that he's gone, part of me is as well. I'll tell you what. This isn't the time to sit back and wait. I'm not sure where he is, but goddamn it, I'm gonna find him. If I don't, I'll never be whole again."

CHAPTER

19

Crossroads

Dallas, Texas

GLENN NORRIS was at Dallas/Fort Worth International Airport. After arriving from Los Angeles, he hit the restroom and walked over to a different gate. He waited for Vic Bradley, who was flying in from Boston. An hour later, Vic's plane landed, and the passengers disembarked except Vic. Glenn got impatient and pulled out his cell phone. As he dialed Vic's number, he spotted his friend walking from the jet bridge with a big smile on his face.

"The last one on is usually the last one off," Vic said.

"Why didn't you call me and let me know?" Glenn asked. "I was about to leave."

"I'll make it up to you and buy dinner," Vic said as they walked towards baggage claim. "It's been a while since we've worked together."

"It has been. Good to see you again, old friend."

"So, where are we going to discuss business?" Vic asked.

"I made reservations at Perry's. They have the best steaks in town."

At dinner, the waiter brought a bottle of Malbec for Glenn and Vic to enjoy while waiting for the feast to begin. They didn't waste time and took got down to business.

"Vic, I'm wearing too many hats right now," Glenn said. "I need to spend more time overseeing Project Diablo. That's why I want you to be my Director of Recruiting. Have you given it some more thought?"

"Yes," Vic responded. "This is a big commitment. So, I'd like to propose a compromise. I'll agree to sign a contract and work for one year. Then we can re-evaluate and see what makes sense for both of us. Will that work?"

"Yes. Thanks a lot, Vic." Glenn offered a warm handshake to solidify the agreement.

"So, how many teams are looking for recruits?" Vic asked.

"We have about 50 people across 15 major cities looking for volunteers," Glenn responded.

"How many volunteers are we targeting?" Vic asked.

"We don't want to exceed the population in neighboring towns, so we'll cap out at 1,000. Some volunteers will be part of Project Diablo, and others will be slated as extras to fill out the town. Your challenge is to travel across the country, monitor the recruiting process, and make sure we have the right mix of volunteers.

"Got it," Vic said. "Based on our email exchange, I'm aware of what you're looking for. These are people who want to escape their current situation for personal reasons. We'll tell all of them they're part of Project Diablo, even though we'll only monitor and evaluate a select group."

"We need to keep the volunteers in the dark about what we're doing. Some will have a more direct impact than others. Either way, they're helping the cause."

"So, what is tomorrow all about?" Vic asked.

"Tomorrow, we'll stage recruiting meetings with locals who expressed an interest in becoming volunteers. Our goal is to gain their commitment and get their signatures on a contract to be part of Project Diablo."

"I'm looking forward to seeing the master at work," Vic said.

"As the old saying goes," Glenn said, "I'm a jack of all trades and a master of none. But you, my friend, will help me by being a master of one."

~~

Cedar Hill, Texas

Tina arrived at The Coffee Press by 6:15 a.m. She was late and didn't look forward to walking by the line of anxious customers waiting to get their morning fix. These were the diehards who couldn't start a workday without their custom-made cup of caffeinated rocket fuel. An impatient crowd was ready and waiting with wisecracks as Tina unlocked the front door.

"Not sure if you know, but there are these things...what do they call them...oh, they're called alarm clocks," Josh said, dripping with sarcasm. "These devices make a loud sound at a specified time to awaken people from a deep sleep."

"Glad you're here. I was about to pass out from caffeine withdrawal," Rob chimed in. "I was getting desperate and almost walked over to Dunkin' Donuts. Because you came in late, do we get a free cup of coffee?" Rob asked, holding out his refillable cup.

Tina turned around with a smirk and said, "Is that all you got?"

Ray Nichols was one of the early birds waiting in line. He worked at Borneo, an international digital commerce company with a national call center near Garland, Texas. Ray dropped by The Coffee Press every morning, indulging in his favorite pastime—people watching.

He noticed everyone around him had a smile on their face and wondered if their manufactured expression of bliss had something to do with the coffee beans. It wasn't the beans because he drank the same coffee as they did and hadn't smiled in years.

Fifteen years prior, Ray left Boston College, where he failed in each of his four years. He never got a law degree but received a "graduation present" from the school, putting him into debt for $300,000. As graduation day approached, Ray was on the verge of a nervous breakdown. He kept his failures and debt hidden from everyone and didn't know how to explain it to family and friends. Ray needed divine intervention in the worst way.

A few days before graduation ceremonies, Ray dodged a bullet. He found out his grandfather had passed away, which provided a perfect excuse for him not to attend. But Ray didn't learn his lesson. He kept the ruse going for two more years until his finances ran out. At that point, Ray had to come clean in front of his parents. Ray felt better after he revealed the truth, but the burden of guilt remained. The weight on his shoulders just shifted from one to the other.

Ray returned to Cedar Hill, Texas, and lived at home with his mom and dad. With little work experience, he could only get menial jobs. Ray lived paycheck to paycheck and had no social life. Every day, he woke up and dealt with deep-seated feelings of embarrassment, inadequacy, and worthlessness. He tried to mask his pain with a myriad of prescription drugs, using whatever money he had to buy as many pills as possible from the black market.

Life couldn't have been worse for Ray. He was at his absolute rock bottom. Ray contemplated suicide, but he was too weak-minded to kill himself. So, he did the next best thing and ran away from his problems. Ray thought escaping his troubles gave him a chance to start life over. He had only one question.

Where should I go?

On Thursday morning, Ray awoke in a good mood. He sensed something positive was happening. He jumped up from his bed and drove to The Coffee Press, and sat in his usual seat. At some point, something drew his eyes to a bulletin board near the front entrance.

A sign on top read "Comings and Goings." The board aggregated job messages, advertisements, and information concerning upcoming local events.

Ray fixated on a small index card pinned to the board. What caught his eye from a distance was a single phrase, "Are You at a Crossroads?" Ray got up and read the card.

Are You at a Crossroads?

Looking for a change and want to start life over?

We're recruiting volunteers for a unique project with guaranteed employment. Compensation is above market value, and benefits include paid housing and healthcare. Employment agreements are for one year, with an option to extend.

This is a tremendous opportunity to start over again. For more information, meet at The Coffee Press Friday at 8:00 p.m.

For the first time in a long time, a smile appeared on Ray's face. His gut told him this was his opportunity.

On Friday night, Ray arrived early. He stood outside the entrance and waited for half an hour. As patrons walked in, he made eye contact with each person and wondered if they were also at a crossroads. As the meeting approached, Ray met four others who wanted to start their lives over, albeit for different reasons.

The Coffee Press closed shop while Ray and his four new friends stood outside by themselves. A few minutes later, a black Chevrolet Silverado pickup parked, and two men emerged. They walked over and introduced themselves.

"Hello, are you all here at a crossroads?"

Everyone nodded.

"Well then, let's introduce ourselves. My name is Glenn Norris, and this is Vic Bradley. And you are?"

"Hi, my name is Ken Greene."

"I'm Paula Carey."

"Ray Nichols."

"My name is Richard Lawson."

"Kate Bryant, nice to meet you."

"Great. First, my apologies. I know the message inside the shop on the billboard was vague," Glenn said. "The project we're here to discuss is being sponsored by one of the largest companies in the country. We can't give you many details. We can't even divulge the name of the company or the project."

Nervous excitement spread amongst the group.

"The project will study behaviors of people from various walks of life," Glenn said. "Volunteers will live and work within a test environment. We'll give you a full-time job, free housing, and health benefits. The only thing you must pay for is food and beverage and any other necessities."

"Can we bring anything with us, family or pets?" Kate asked.

"No," Glenn responded. "If you volunteer for the project, you must come by yourself and abide by one simple rule."

"What would that rule be?" Ken asked.

"Once you enter the town limits, you can't leave. No exceptions. You must stay for the duration of your agreement," Glenn said. "Likewise, nobody outside of town can communicate with you. No physical meetings, no mobile phone calls, and no internet. Once the year is complete, you'll have an option to leave or extend your stay."

"We're giving up a lot for our freedom. We'll be away from our families for an extended period. How is this worth our while? What is the compensation?" Ray asked.

"For the first year, each volunteer will receive a flat fee of up to $100,000. We base the amount on your qualifications," Glenn said. "Fees for future years are up for negotiation in the fourth quarter of each year. Don't forget. You'll also get free housing and healthcare."

Ray and the others were excited. Each of them had personal issues and wanted nothing more than to run away from their problems. Volunteering for the project enabled them to start life over with some money and a clean slate.

"You said that you'll monitor and evaluate us. What do you mean?" Richard asked.

"We'll use closed-circuit television, digital technology, and embedded team members to report activities as we see them. Within the town limits, we will record every movement and all activities," Glenn said. "Don't worry. After a couple of days, you'll forget anyone is watching you."

At that moment, Glenn handed out an application form and agreements to each person.

"Over the next week, please read the terms and conditions. We'll meet here next Friday night. We can answer questions and sign employment contracts. Once you have agreed on the terms and conditions, we will arrange travel to the town."

Someone from above answered Ray's prayers. He could run away and start his life over again. As everyone left, Ray hung around outside The Coffee Press. He looked inside and envisioned himself in his usual spot. Tomorrow he planned to arrive bright and early to do something he hadn't done in many years—drink his coffee with a smile.

CHAPTER

20

Orientation

Tümpisa, Wyoming

IN THE DISTANCE, Wyatt Thompson saw another plane cleared for landing. He walked out the front entrance of the Super 8 motel to get a closer look. Wyatt went over to a small hill, which provided a perfect view of the Riverton Regional Airport. His boss, Liam Jones, was already looking through a pair of binoculars.

"See anything, Mr. Jones?" Wyatt asked.

"Not sure," Liam responded. "That plane isn't the usual prop-jet."

"That makes 18 today, and it ain't noon yet," Wyatt said. "Where are all the passengers going?"

"Don't know," Liam replied, "but I can tell you they're not staying at the Super 8."

"Why? Are we too expensive? Maybe we should run a special," Wyatt said as he awaited a response.

Liam looked at his young employee and bit his tongue.

"Nothing to do with price, son," Liam said. "Folks aren't staying anywhere near here. Something strange is going on."

~

Riverton Regional Airport averaged 20 incoming flights each day in Wyoming, including public and private planes originating from Denver and Sheridan. But over the past few months, the flight traffic more than doubled. No one in town had an answer. It was a complete mystery.

The influx of people in Riverton was the talk of the town. At first, the possibility of increased traffic excited local businesses. But the covert visitors didn't go anywhere near downtown. Instead, they went straight from the airport to an undisclosed location. If not for the incoming planes, there was no way to know these visitors existed.

The people of Riverton held town meetings to get answers. But the local media wasn't cooperating. The Riverton Ranger newspaper buried articles and the evening newscast restricted airtime. Someone was paying the media to keep the story in the background.

The incoming flights were private planes carrying up to 30 passengers. They knew where they were coming from but were unaware of where they were going. After landing, the turboprops stopped short on the tarmac far from the terminal. Then, within minutes, a half-dozen SUVs swooped in like clockwork, picked up the volunteers, and sped off to an undisclosed location.

When the volunteers finally emerged from the vehicles, their eyes had to adjust to the bright sunlight. An older woman walked out from the front entrance of the building to greet them.

"Welcome," the woman beamed. "Welcome to Project Diablo. My name is Janet Barnes, and I'll be your host over the next three days. Don't worry. The guys will get your luggage."

Janet brought everyone inside the building to an oversized conference room with rectangular tables and chairs. Each place setting had a binder, pen, jar of hard candy, and an empty glass for ice water.

The fact they were volunteers in a life-changing project was the last thing on everyone's minds. The atmosphere in the room had a "seminar feeling." Everyone half expected a former hedge fund manager to come out and show everybody how to invest their hard-earned money. But since everyone settled into their seats, Janet put those thoughts to rest when she walked to the front of the room to address the group.

"Again, welcome to Project Diablo. My name is Janet, and I am a representative of the management team. The building you are in now is the project headquarters, but you'll find the locals in the town refer to it as the 'Mother Ship.' I'm not sure why."

Half of the volunteers in the room chuckled, while the other half was too tired to force even a smile.

"This is your home for general orientation, baseline health and wellness exams, and skills assessments," Janet said. "You'll also go through an interview process with the management team so that we can learn more about you. In front of you is a binder with more information and a detailed agenda."

The crowd seemed like a horde of zombies. Everyone in the room was listless, with eyes half-closed. Janet tried to wrap up as fast as possible.

"You've had a long day of travel, but before I let you go, two quick housekeeping items," Janet said. "First, we operate as a hotel here. We have a front desk, a small store with concessions, a relaxation area, and a workout facility. If you need anything, dial the operator from the phone in your room, and it will connect you to the front desk."

Janet saw the group was losing the battle and teetering on unconsciousness.

"Second, we'll meet in this room tomorrow at 9:00 a.m. sharp. We have a lot to cover, so please be here on time."

Janet picked up a binder and dropped it on the table on purpose to wake everyone up.

"Okay, let's go to the front desk and get you checked in," Janet said.

~

The following day, the volunteers showed up on time. Janet noticed everyone in the room had a familiar look on their face. The "Okay, you got me here, now what are you trying to sell me look." Janet's challenge was to make everyone feel as comfortable as soon as possible.

"Before we start, remember this is an interactive discussion," Janet said. "Any questions, raise your hand...oh, and state your name."

A palm shot up from the back of the room.

"Hi, I'm David Williams. To this point, we've received little to no information. Now we're here. Can you tell us more about Project Diablo?"

"Sure, I can give you an overview. But before I do, we need to discuss three basic rules. First, we can't divulge our location; second, we can't tell you the company sponsoring Project Diablo; and third, we can't share any information or data we collect. If we were to break any of those rules, it could jeopardize everything."

"Why is our personally identifiable information being withheld from us?" David asked.

"Our hope is the data we collect will lead to a breakthrough in modern medicine," Janet said. "Our goal is for everyone to live longer, more productive lives. This is medical history in the making. You'll be proud in your later years, knowing you took part."

Someone raised another hand to ask a question.

"My name is Teri Howard. What will you be studying?"

"Great question and an even better segue," Janet said.

A presentation appeared on a screen in the front of the room. "What we're studying is negative behaviors," Janet said. "Behavior is the way we act or conduct ourselves, especially in response to a situation or other stimulus. Our behaviors affect not only us but also the people we interact with daily."

Janet went ahead to the next slide to discuss the different behaviors, both positive and negative.

"We will focus on negative behaviors. They hide inside of us like a virus," Janet said. "The virus keeps spreading and doesn't stop until it takes over complete control of your thoughts and actions. That's why we monitor behaviors. We need to prevent them from spreading. If left unchecked, the behaviors could become habits and lead to addiction."

Janet felt continued as everyone in the room hung on her every word.

"Here's an example to show how destructive negative behavior can be," Janet said. "Think about a house in a neighborhood. The house has locks on every door and window. Does anyone know why?"

Brad Leigh raised his hand and answered, "To keep out strangers and other people who aren't welcome."

"Correct," Janet said, "Without locked doors and windows, at some point, someone will walk into the house, usually when we least expect it. Now, what happens once our unwelcome guest is inside our house?"

Barbara Johnson raised her voice and said, "They may take something or hurt someone."

"Good answer," Janet responded. "Once inside, we don't know what they'll do or how it will affect us. What else could happen?"

Blank looks filled the room.

"They might stay in the house and never leave," David said.

"If I had a prize, David, you'd be getting it," Janet said.

David flashed a huge smile as if he had won his elementary school spelling bee.

"When a stranger doesn't leave, that's the worst-case scenario," Janet said. "They take over control of the entire house. They end up making the owner live by their rules, or if they don't comply, leave the house for good."

"What does that have to do with negative behaviors?" Brad asked.

Janet set up a perfect analogy.

"In the house scenario, the home represents someone's mind. Strangers and unwelcome people represent various behaviors. If they stay short-term, it doesn't affect us much. But if they stay long-term and take over control, that's when they cross the line and become a bad habit."

Janet saw a lot of heads nod in the audience.

"One more thing about our house scenario," Janet said. "We want to keep our doors and windows locked at all times and only open them when we need to. If we secure our house, we can watch the behaviors come and go, which will ensure they don't take over."

Janet flipped to the next slide entitled "Project Diablo Mission Statement," which stated:

> Our mission is to understand negative behaviors, prevent them from developing into habits, and eradicate compulsion and addiction.

"Your contribution is critical to this project," Janet said. "Without volunteers, we wouldn't be able to develop treatments or discover solutions."

"Why go to all the trouble of building a town specific for Project Diablo?" Bill Henry asked from somewhere in the middle of the crowd. "You could put us all in a room, run a battery of tests, ask a bunch of questions, and get your information and data."

"True," Janet responded, "But that's the approach every company has taken since the beginning of time. Those old methods take a long time to go from research to development to production. This project is on a whole different level and needs an innovative approach. We work under the adage 'seeing is believing.' Instead of your telling us what is wrong with you from a closed room, we see it firsthand in a typical environment. That's why we need the town."

"How are you going to monitor us?" Grant Jacobs asked. "Are we getting ankle bracelets or chips implanted in the back of our neck?"

Nervous laughter filtered through the crowd as everyone awaited a response.

"Don't be silly," Janet replied, "I assure you we don't use ankle bracelets, and we don't implant chips in your neck."

Janet used Grant's words because, by doing so, she wasn't lying, only stretching the truth. They'd implant chips, just not in their neck.

"You're going to see closed-circuit television cameras everywhere," Janet said. "We equipped all public areas and residences with innovative technology so we can track vital signs and capture activities as they occur. But don't worry, after the first week, you won't notice them. We encourage you to be yourself and not change anything. Don't play to the camera. Just live your life as normal."

"Well, we reached the end. Any questions?" Janet asked.

"Yes," said someone in the front row. "Where in the town can I get a good cup of coffee?"

"Why yes, on Main Street. We have a coffee shop called Human Beans, which is popular with the locals. Everyone in town passes through at some point." Janet said, "By the way, what's your name?"

"Ray...Ray Nichols."

CHAPTER

21

Death Valley

Tümpisa, Wyoming

JAMESON BRADFORD never got up before 10:00 a.m. on a Saturday, but he made an exception on this day. Jameson was out of bed by 5:00 a.m. and in a helicopter an hour later. He was headed to Dubois, Wyoming, a small town in Fremont County along the Americas Continental Divide.

Cody was only 75 miles from Dubois as the crow flies, but the Shoshone Forest was in the way. The only other possibility was to drive by car, but the trip would've been over 200 miles and taken four hours. Jameson wasn't fond of road trips, so he called for the corporate helicopter, which he referred to as his "flying eggbeater."

After touching down in Dubois, Jameson jumped into a waiting black Chevy Suburban with tinted windows. Ten miles later, on North Horsecreek Road, they approached an area called Tümpisa. The locals named the town after an old Shoshone tribal word meaning "Death Valley." The Suburban pulled up to a brand new five-story 10,000 square-foot building. Two men waited to greet Jameson as he emerged from the vehicle.

"Hello, Mr. Bradford," Benjamin Franklin Pierce and John Francis McIntyre said in unison.

"Good morning, Glenn. Hi, Vic," Jameson said. "You can ditch the alias and go by your real names now."

Glenn Norris and Vic Bradley escorted Jameson to the cafeteria for a quick breakfast. Afterward, they went to the executive observation deck equipped with ten high-definition telescopes.

"So, is Phase 1 complete?" Jameson asked. "Can we bring in volunteers?"

Glenn and Vic looked at each other and smiled.

"We've already brought in 500 volunteers for a soft-opening. We're up and running," Glenn said.

"Look through the telescope," Vic said as he positioned it for Jameson. "Tell us what you think."

Jameson stepped onto the platform, took off his glasses, and looked through the high-definition lens. What he saw was impressive—a functioning town constructed in the middle of nowhere. By itself, the town covered ten square miles with a downtown area split by a wide two-lane street. Jameson saw small businesses and people milling around.

In the distance, Jameson noticed homes, apartments, parks, athletic fields, and strip malls. All buildings were no higher than three stories and were aged to give the environment character. The landscape was in various growth stages to appear as if the town was older than it looked. People were coming and going as if they were on their way to work, running errands, or visiting friends. In every respect, the town didn't seem different from any other town one in Wyoming.

"Wow, this is impressive. Let's go into the town."

"This is as close as we can get," Glenn said. "We don't want people to feel like it's a test environment. If we bring in visitors, everyone in the town will feel like they are part of an attraction. You'll notice we don't have a wall. We're using the latest technology with invisible boundaries."

"Interesting. How do the invisible boundaries work?" Jameson asked. "What if someone changes their mind and wants to leave?"

"No one is leaving this place," Vic said. "These people are getting paid a good amount of money, and they came here of their own volition. In many respects, they're leaving bad situations and coming here to start a new life. We have some volunteers here to live out their final days."

"Okay, then why do you need an invisible boundary?" Jameson asked.

"It's an insurance policy," Glenn said. "We built a half-mile buffer between the town limits and this building. If someone tries to leave by any means, they'll receive a strong magnetic pulse, stopping them in their tracks. We'll be able to pick them up and either return them or put them in a holding area."

"How does the magnetic pulse work?" Jameson asked. "Won't it affect everyone and not just the volunteers?"

"Dr. Sheldon Thomas, our resident dentist, takes care of that," Vic said. "He has a practice on the first floor. He handles technology for the invisible boundary, but he also fills cavities and cleans teeth in his spare time. Dr. Thomas is an excellent dentist. If you need a good cleaning, we can set something up before you leave today."

"What?" Jameson said with a puzzled look on his face. "A dentist in charge of security makes little sense. You're pulling my leg."

Glenn and Vic smiled and let the cat out of the bag.

"The volunteers visit Dr. Thomas for a routine dental exam during orientation," Glenn said. "While they're sitting in the chair, he implants a chip underneath their tongue with a serial number. The chip allows us to do a few things. Check vital signs, identify a location, and sync each person with the invisible boundary system."

"Why would someone let a dentist do that without questions?" Jameson asked.

"They don't," Vic said as he chuckled. "Somehow, Dr. Thomas always finds a cavity or two. He numbs them with Novocain and presto...they leave with a chip under their tongue and a filling in their mouth they never needed."

"Let me clarify Vic's last statement," Glenn said. "We have no problem finding cavities. So, you'll see higher than normal health and wellness expenses when you review the town's financial statements. Running a dental practice is expensive nowadays."

"Now I understand," Jameson said, " But I'll pass on the cleaning. Maybe next time."

Jameson stepped from the platform.

"Gentlemen, we're studying human behavior. Some of those behaviors are violent and abusive," Jameson said. "To understand how the mind works, we need to observe the volunteers within the test environment."

Jameson looked Glenn straight in the eyes.

"We need to get to capacity as soon as possible, which brings me to my next question," Jameson said. "What about your recruiting efforts? How's it going?"

"It's going well," Glenn said. "We're working with teams throughout the country to find volunteers from all walks of life. Our targets are individuals who are looking to disappear from society. Some will come here and hope to return home as a better person. Others will come here because they want to avoid a situation or set of circumstances. But a few will stay because they want to go out on their terms."

"Everyone has a back story, a reason for joining Project Diablo," Vic said. "We have people with mental disorders, overwhelming financial problems, insidious addictions, or terminal conditions. Each person has their cross to bear."

"That's a good start, but we're missing something," Jameson said. Glenn and Vic were avoiding the obvious and knew what was coming next.

"The concept for this project was to develop a drug to eradicate addiction. To do that, we need to understand a range of behaviors, from moderate to extreme. It sounds like you have a good sample of moderates so far. What about the extremes?"

"We've been looking and haven't—," Glenn said as Jameson cut him off.

"Apparently, not hard enough," Jameson said. "Do you even know what I mean by extreme?"

Glenn and Vic looked at each other for the answer and were speechless.

"To get the answer, all you need to do is ask yourself a question," Jameson said. "What is the most extreme act a man can carry out on another man?"

"Kill?" Vic asked.

"Precisely, Vic," Jameson responded. "To kill another man. But now, let's take it up a notch. What about a serial killer, someone that repeats his actions? What goes through a killer's mind before they take another person's life? If we can figure out what triggers a serial killer, then we can understand every other type of behavior."

"Are you sure, Jameson?" Glenn asked.

"Go out and find me someone who kills," Jameson said. "It has to be in their blood. Someone who shows no mercy and places no value on human life, the more depraved, the better. Go find me a goddamn killer and send him to the town. The whole project is riding on this. You've got one more job to do before Phase I is complete. Don't fuck it up, or there will be hell to pay."

Jameson stormed out as Glenn and Vic shook their heads.

"What do we do now?" Vic asked.

"Let me check my contacts in law enforcement," Glenn said. "There must be someone in custody that fits the narrative."

"What if they can't find anyone?" Vic asked.

"Then I guess you'll have to start killing people," Glenn joked.

Vic didn't think Glenn's little joke was so funny. But he felt that if he had to kill someone, Glenn would be in line to be his first victim.

CHAPTER

22

Coffee & Biscotti

Mediterranean Sea

ON THE DAY OF EMBARKATION, the Jacobsons boarded the QE2 and went to their cabin. Once inside, Vivian headed straight for the restroom. When she came out a few minutes later, she was ready to explore the ship but had one problem. Norman was sprawled out on the bed, and she was sleeping like a baby. Vivian knew he had not gotten enough sleep in the past month. Something was on his mind.

Vivian left Norman a note and went out to check out the ship by herself. Two hours later, she returned to the cabin, and Norman was still asleep. Vivian pinched his toes to wake him up.

"Are you going to sleep this whole trip?" Vivian asked.

Norman rubbed the sleep from his eyes. He was so tired he could barely utter a word.

"What...time...is it?" Norman asked.

"It's 4:30 p.m., and the party started without you. So, Rip van Winkle, when are you going to join in on the fun?" Vivian asked.

"I'll get up in a few minutes," Norman said, "I couldn't help myself when I saw the bed."

"Norm, if you're a good boy for the rest of the night, maybe I'll be saying the same thing later," Vivian said as she blushed. It wasn't like her to be so forward with Norman. But this was a new chapter in their lives, and she wanted to rekindle the feelings they had when they were newlyweds.

After dinner, a show, and drinks at the piano bar, they returned to their cabin. Inside, waiting for them, was a champagne bottle on ice, along with a note. Vivian read the note aloud.

"To make it through 50 years of anything is a major accomplishment. But 50 years of helping others is something to be proud of. Enjoy your retirement, Dr. Jacobson."

"That's nice. Who signed it?" Norman asked.

"Someone named Jack. Do you know who Jack is?" Vivian asked.

Norman suddenly got nauseous and sat on the bed.

"Are you feeling okay, honey?" Vivian asked with a concerned look on her face.

"I'm...I am okay. I must have had one too many vodkas at the bar," Norman said.

"Who is Jack?" Vivian asked again.

"A patient of mine. That's who I spent New Year's Eve with." Norman said.

"That's nice for Jack to send you off into retirement in style," Vivian said.

When Norman and Vivian first planned their dream trip, they didn't realize at the time that their dream would turn into a nightmare.

Norman sprung out of bed at 8:00 a.m. every morning, while Vivian stayed under the covers for another three hours. Before leaving, Norman kissed his wife and walked up to the observation deck to exercise. On this day, the Queen Elizabeth 2 was somewhere in the Mediterranean Sea. But it was so dark outside that the ship could have been in Miami, and he wouldn't have known the difference.

After jogging a few times around the deck, Norman grabbed a quick breakfast and found a quiet place on the boat to sit and write. He had a dual purpose in penning his seventh novel. Writing filled in the gaps while his wife relaxed in dreamland, but it also functioned as a form of therapy.

Norman couldn't stop thinking about Jack ever since he received the champagne bottle on the first night. He didn't understand why seeing Jack's name bothered him so much. With no one to talk to, the only option was for him to treat himself. He hoped documenting his thoughts on paper would ease his mind.

The go-to place for Norman on the boat was The Explorations Lounge towards the front of the ship. It was a vast room with floor-to-ceiling windows, cushioned chairs, and a small library and cafe with friendly baristas and delicious pastries. Norman would sit in the same chair by the windows and immerse himself in his book. He noticed other regulars around him. Some read books, others had quiet conversations, and a few took a mid-morning nap.

One morning, another gentleman about Norman's age sat next to him. Norman met the man earlier on the trip when they were with their wives at the piano bar. But this was the first time they saw each other in quite a while.

"Welcome to the front row," Norman said. "You received an upgrade."

"You've got it all wrong, my friend. This is a downgrade," Daniel said. "Because I have to sit next to you."

"Well, if you want to take ownership of that seat, you know the drill. You can't come, empty-handed."

Daniel shrugged his shoulders and asked, "Okay, what do you want?"

"I'll take a grande iced coffee with 2% milk and two packets of Splenda. Oh, and don't forget to get some of those chocolate biscotti."

Daniel visited the barista and returned with two iced coffees and a plate with half a dozen Italian biscuits.

"Haven't seen you in a while. Daniel, is everything okay?" Norman asked as he took his first sip of coffee.

"We had a minor emergency, and it forced us to leave the boat for a while to take care of something at home," Daniel said. "Nothing to worry about; everything is fine. We got back on in Rome. What about yourself? Are you enjoying the cruise?"

"Sure am. Especially, this right here," Norman said as he panned the room. "This is the perfect place for me to escape reality and write my next novel."

"What's the subject of the book?"

"The working title is *Killer Thoughts - Inside the Mind of an Active Serial Killer*. I figured there are thousands of books about killers. The only problem is every author tells the story after the fact leaving out all the suspense. What if you're reading a book and the serial killer was still at large? It could be someone in your neighborhood. What if you were the next victim? You could be in a future chapter and not know it. That's real suspense."

"Sounds like fascinating fiction. I would love to read it."

"But it's not straight fiction at all. I based part of the book on one of my patients."

Norman's cell phone interrupted the conversation. He looked at the number, and it was Jason Blackman.

"Excuse me, I don't normally answer long-distance calls, but this might be important," Norman said.

"No worries," Daniel said. "I'll sit here and enjoy my ice coffee and biscotti."

"Hello, this is Norman."

"Hi, it's Jason. How's retirement?"

"Can't complain," Norman responded. "We have the world at our fingertips. The weather is great. At night, we eat like kings and queens and then take in some entertainment. It's easy to get used to this kind of lifestyle. If I'd known how good this would be, I would have retired ten years earlier."

"I'll keep that in mind when I get close to retirement," Jason said. "But that's only if my wife lets me retire."

"I haven't heard from you in a while," Norman said. "Is everything okay?"

"Everything is great," Jason said. "I just wanted to ask if you still had St. Louis Blues tickets."

"I do," Norman responded. "Why do you ask?"

"When are you going to take me to a game?" Jason asked.

"Not for a while," Norman said. "I'm halfway around the world, and it's the middle of summer. The hockey season doesn't start until October."

"Oh, I was thinking baseball again," Jason said. "Well, if I send the files to you now, will I still get to go to a hockey game later this year?"

"Send what?" Norman asked.

"The video you were looking for," Jason responded. "I was able to recover the information that was lost when the server went down. I have the data files, but I can't open them without a password."

"You got the video?" Norman asked. "Is the title 'Jack Session - February 19th'?"

"Yes, the video is an hour-long," Jason responded. "Do you want me to hold it until you get back?"

"No. Send the files to me, but encrypt them first. I need to review it as soon as possible," Norman said.

"What about hockey tickets?" Jason asked. "Are you good for it?"

"I will miss the beginning of the season," Norman said with a smile. "You can have full access to my season tickets until I return home. I'll make the arrangements."

"Thanks Norman," Jason said as he ended the call. "I'll send the file now."

Daniel tried to ignore the conversation but couldn't. Norman was an average-sized man with a booming voice. Daniel pieced the facts together. First, Norman was a psychologist; second, he authored a book about an active serial killer; and third, he based the story on a troubled patient. It all sounded familiar.

"Daniel, I have to run," Norman said. "I have to watch a video and write a synopsis. Meet you here tomorrow at the same time?"

"I'll be here," Daniel responded. "But tomorrow, it's your turn to bring the ice coffee and biscotti."

CHAPTER

23

Broken Privilege

Mediterranean Sea

THE FOLLOWING DAY, Norman got out of bed at 6:00 a.m., took a quick shower, and got dressed. He leaned over to kiss Vivian on the cheek, just hard enough to wake her up.

"What time...is it?" Vivian asked as she stretched her arms above her head.

"Almost 6:30 a.m.," Norman replied as he slipped into a pair of shorts.

"Where are you going this early?" Vivian asked. "Don't you realize you're retired? There's no good reason to get up before sunrise."

"I couldn't sleep," Norman said. "Got a lot on my mind. I have to find a quiet place to write for a couple of hours and then hang out with Daniel for a little while. I'll be back in time for lunch."

Norman woke up early because he wanted to watch the Jack video a second time. He sat through it the night before, but did so in a perpetual state of shock. Norman needed to see the recording again to understand Jack's dark side. Norman spent an hour with Jack on Jacobson's ladder to reveal the patient's repressed memories. Instead, it uncovered a dark secret. Jack was not just a troubled soul but a prolific serial killer who orchestrated a murder spree spanning two decades.

There had been situations in the past where Norman struggled with the "physician-patient privilege." He was proud to keep that promise with all his patients over his career. But this was a situation where his obligation to the public outweighed loyalty to his patient. Norman needed to do something.

Norman made it to the Explorations Lounge at 7:15 a.m. and reserved two chairs by the windows. He was proactive and had Daniel's ice coffee and biscotti ready and waiting. Daniel showed up with a huge smile on his face.

"Now that is what I call service," Daniel said.

"That's what happens when you retire," Norman said. "You have time to do the little things in life."

The two men relaxed for half an hour and talked about various topics. Daniel was looking for the right time to ask a specific question.

"I thought about your book," Daniel said. "What's the name of your serial killer?"

"For now, I'm using Jack," Norman said. "But I will most likely change the name before I publish the book."

Daniel had a hunch that would be Norman's answer. Norman didn't know, but Daniel was on to something.

"I found something interesting that might give you some ideas for your serial killer. Let me show you," Daniel said.

Daniel opened a laptop and navigated to KDKA-TV's website, a CBS affiliate in Pittsburgh. He searched the archives, found a video, and clicked on play. Trace Gordon, a local Pittsburgh news anchor, appeared on the screen. He was reporting on a story from the night before.

Trace: We have breaking news overnight of a murder that occurred outside of Pittsburgh. Shawn Johnson is here with the latest.

Trace turned around to face a giant screen behind him. The camera caught Shawn Johnson playing with his earpiece, but he regained control in time.

Trace: Shawn, the police, and the FBI aren't letting out much information, are they?

Shawn: That's right, Trace. Local law enforcement and the FBI on the scene aren't saying much at this hour. Word is spreading. A serial killer may be on the loose. Here are the facts as of this moment. A middle-aged woman was slaughtered here in a small town outside Pittsburgh last night. We know her identity. She is Megan Griffin, 42 years old of Jefferson Hills. A lot of communities are nervous around here this evening.

Trace: Shawn, were the police able to tie this murder to any others we've heard about in recent months?

Shawn: Investigators aren't saying anything at this point. The investigation is ongoing. But my sources close to the crime scene say a link is possible.

Trace: How can they be so sure?

Shawn: My sources observed the crime scene and said it was far too gruesome for television. But something was left behind, which seems to be the killer's "calling card."

Trace: Are you at liberty to say?

Shawn: All I can tell you is they told me someone wrote a message written on the wall.

I NEVER FORGOT WHAT YOU HAD DONE.

REVENGE IS SWEET; YOU'RE NUMBER ONE—JACK

Norman added everything together.

- Jack grew up with the Shrewsbury Seven (7).
- Jack admitted to killing classmates in high school (4).
- Jack was tied to murders in Bar Harbor and Pittsburgh (2).

The total was 13 victims, who matched the number of targets on Jack's list. Norman's entire body shook, and his face turned pale.

"Norman, are you okay?" Daniel asked.

"I...I should have known. I...I should have broken privilege a long time ago and reported Jack to the authorities."

Daniel knew what he was doing. He shared the video with Norman because he strongly suspected Norman's killer was the same Jack that his sons were looking for.

"Norman, I need to be transparent with you," Daniel said. "I worked for the FBI for many years and retired not too long ago. I still have contacts and can put you in touch with the investigation team handling the case. You have a wealth of information. Help us find Jack."

"How can I do that when I'm in the middle of nowhere?"

"Don't worry. I can set up a secure call on an encrypted phone line. This ship is the safest place for you to be. I'll arrange everything."

Daniel reached into his pocket, pulled out one of his old business cards, and handed it to Norman.

Sonny Merino, Director U.S. Department of Justice,

Federal Bureau of Investigation

FBI Criminal Investigative Division, Washington, D.C.

Norman seemed puzzled and asked, "Who is Sonny Merino? I thought your name was Daniel?"

"Daniel is my given name. That's how family and friends refer to me. When I started at the FBI, we had three Daniels in the same office, and it got confusing. They gave us nicknames for the first week. I got stuck with Sonny. If you asked anyone at the FBI who Daniel Merino was, they would hesitate before answering. Everyone knows me as Sonny Merino."

Even though Sonny was retired, his sons still shared case information with him to get his thoughts and opinions. He was aware Jack was responsible for Taylor's murder, and he realized this was an opportunity to end Jack's wrath once and for all. Sonny excused himself to look for a safe place to make a call. He secured a small conference room on the boat and dialed Dominic's cell phone. Sonny stayed silent and let the two men talk.

"Hello, Dominic Merino." There was an awkward moment of silence. "Hello," Dominic said again.

"Hello...I need to speak to someone."

"I'm all ears," Dominic responded.

"I know...a killer."

Dominic received thousands of similar calls. His intuition told him this was another wasted call, but he played along anyway for kicks and giggles.

"Don't we all," Dominic said. "What's the name of your killer?"

"Jack," Norman responded. "Jack Mathews."

Dominic dropped his coffee cup on the table and spilled liquid caffeine all over his desk.

"To whom am I speaking?" Dominic asked.

"I'd rather not say," Norman responded. "For the time being, you can call me 'Doctor' because I am one."

"Before I ask you questions, I want to make you aware that I'm recording this conversation. We'll keep your name anonymous and only publicize it with your express approval."

"I understand," Norman replied.

"I'm a well-known psychologist, and one of my patients was Jack Mathews," Norman said. "Before my retirement, Jack confessed to several murders under hypnosis. I've got a video as evidence. I watched it yesterday for the first time."

Dominic's mind was about to explode. He was furiously writing notes as he listened to what Norman said. All the while, he was thinking about three questions ahead.

"Has Jack been in touch with you?" Dominic asked.

"Jack monitored my whereabouts and kept reaching out to me until last month," Norman said. "I've not heard anything since. I'm breaking physician-patient privilege here, but I have no choice. If Jack finds out, my life is in grave danger."

Norman disclosed everything about Jack. He mentioned specific details of murder scenes, a troubled upbringing, and plans. Dominic knew the doctor was telling the truth because Norman knew about classified information found at the crime scene. It was the best lead Dominic had received since Alden Moore's murder.

"What's next?" Norman asked. "When Jack finds out, he'll come looking for me."

"There's nothing to worry about," Dominic said. "You're safe on the ship, and when you return, we'll provide 24/7 protection."

"Very much appreciated, but I can't rest until Jack is in custody."

"Jack won't be taken alive. We have a shoot-on-sight order."

"That's a huge mistake," Norman said. "If you keep Jack alive, medical research can gain an understanding of the criminal mind. They could use the information to prevent monsters like this in the future."

"Public safety comes first," Dominic said. "I have to follow orders."

"Agent Merino, at some point, you'll find Jack and have to bridge the gap between the sane and the insane. If you don't understand how Jack's mind works, then you'll be at a disadvantage. No one knows Jack better than me. I've been in the darkest areas of Jack's mind, places no other psychologist has been. Let me help you put an end to all of this."

Dominic wasn't honest with Norman. The order to shoot on sight didn't come from the FBI; the order came from Dominic himself. As far as he was concerned, the only option for Jack was a body bag.

"Agent Merino, have you ever heard of the old saying 'revenge is a dish best served cold?'" Norman asked.

"Yes, I have," Dominic responded.

"Most people have," Norman said, "but few know what the phrase means. We live in a society of instant gratification. Whether it's buying something tangible or making something happen, our nature is not to wait any longer than we have to. This is most dangerous when dealing with anger. When someone hurts us, we want to respond in a fit of rage. We think it will make us feel better, but that feeling goes away rather quickly. Vengeance is more satisfying when exacted after the harm that instigated it."

"Doctor, I understand your point," Dominic said. "But this situation is different. We are dealing with a ruthless serial killer who has taken many innocent lives. Jack deserves to die."

"Agent Merino, death is not always the answer," Norman said. "Sometimes, a delayed death is warranted. Putting a bullet into Jack's head satisfies only you. But what does that do for the family and friends of Jack's victims? How do they gain closure? That's why, before you make any rash decisions, we need to look at the big picture. Before you pull a trigger, think of the victims."

Dominic was having second thoughts.

"You may be right. The death penalty may be too good for Jack. Perhaps something good can come out of this."

"Glad you can see my point of view," Norman said.

"Doctor, I think you can be of value to our investigation," Dominic said. "I'd like to consult with you regularly. You understand Jack better than anyone else. Maybe you can help us put an end to all this. I'll be in touch."

Dominic ended the call. For the first time in a long time, Dominic felt he had made some progress on the investigation. He agreed with everything Norman said, with one exception. Dominic wasn't sure what would happen when he came face-to-face with Jack. Would revenge be served warm or cold? There's no way to know until the moment arrives, because the answer depends on who's serving the dish.

CHAPTER

24

Something Big

San Francisco, California

WHEN THE PHONE RINGS in the middle of the night, it's never good news, especially on a Sunday morning. Travis rolled over and picked up his phone. The bright light emanating from the screen made it impossible to see the number of the incoming call. He sat up in bed and answered, not knowing who it was.

"Travis, this is Owens."

"What do you want?" Travis asked.

"We responded to a reported disturbance in the Mission Bay District. We picked up someone of interest," Owens said in a soft voice so that no one could hear the conversation. "All I can tell you over the phone is it's something big."

"Are you aware it's 3:00 a.m. on a Sunday?"

"I know the time. Sorry to disturb your beauty sleep. There's only one thing I would wake your ugly ass up for."

"All right, I'm awake now and on my way," Travis said as he rubbed his eyes and let out a big yawn. "Where are you?"

"I'm at the Bay View Boat Club off the San Francisco Bay Trail, Pier 54."

"See you in half an hour," Travis said, as he let out a final yawn.

Travis kissed his wife Diana, who was in a deep sleep. He left a note and drove to the Mission Bay District. He flipped on the radio and listened to news reports about police activity near Pier 54. The media speculated on a murder scene with multiple victims. He would find out for himself within minutes.

When Travis arrived, law enforcement had roped off a large area which kept the media and other onlookers back a hundred yards. He counted a dozen police cars and several ambulances. Travis flashed his FBI badge to get through the blockade and parked right outside the Boat Club. Owens came out to greet his boss.

"You made it here faster than I thought," Owens said.

"Not much traffic this time in the morning," Travis responded. "What's up?"

Owens pulled Travis aside to give him an update.

"The police got a call complaining about suspicious activity here at the boat club," Owens said. "They responded at once and found two people murdered. Both suffered gunshot wounds to the forehead, and the killer posed the bodies on bar stools."

"Okay, a double homicide by a shock jock. Not your everyday occurrence, but you can handle it, Owens. Why the need to get my ugly ass out of bed?" Travis said in a sarcastic tone.

"That's not all," Owens said. "I got a call from Bill Patterson, Chief of Police. He asked me to meet him here as soon as I could. When I arrived, both of us inspected the murder scene. We both felt the killer was still in the vicinity. Our teams secured the entire pier, so we could search building by building to see what we could find."

Bill Patterson walked up to join the conversation.

"Mornin,' Travis," Bill said. "Don't be mad at ole Owens here. He's only doing his job. I told him to call you."

"Just getting Travis up to speed," Owens said. "I got to the part where we conducted our search."

"Thanks Owens, I'll take it from here," Bill said as he led the two men inside the boat club.

At the bar were a man and a woman on barstools. Their torsos leaned forward and draped over the counter as if passed out drunk. Next to each was a tall shot glass filled with blood. On the menu board, instead of the happy hour special, was a bloody message.

IT'S CLOSING TIME, FAMILY, AND FRIENDS.
GOOD THINGS MUST COME TO AN END-JACK

"The killer tried to sign the bottom of the note, but it was illegible," Bill said. "He must have run out minutes before we arrived."

Travis's jaw dropped. Based on what he saw at the murder scene, he had an idea who the killer was but bit his tongue for the moment.

"We broke up into teams and searched." Bill said, "We found the suspect in an abandoned building further on the pier. Owens said to call you first because this might have national implications."

"Let's have a look, shall we?" Travis said.

~

The three men walked along the pier to an abandoned building. Travis looked up and saw a light emanating from a room on the second floor. A SWAT team surrounded the building. At the top of the staircase, armed police officers were guarding the suspect.

"Can I see the suspect by myself?" Travis asked.

"Sure," Bill said as he nodded to the officers to let him through. After five minutes with the suspect, Travis returned but didn't seem like himself.

"Are you okay, Travis?" Bill asked.

"I'm fine, but I was a little surprised at what I saw," Travis said as his voice quivered. "Owens was right. This is a national FBI matter.

We need to find someplace for a private call with Headquarters in Washington."

Travis and Owens found a secure room and made sure no one followed them.

"Do you realize who that is?" Travis asked.

"I know who it is," Owens said. "Why do you think I got your ugly ass out of bed?"

"We have to act quickly," Travis said. "I'll talk to Bill and tell him the FBI is taking over the investigation, and we will assume ownership of the suspect. Call the response team and get them here to provide transport. Then we'll discuss the next steps."

"Got it, I'm on my way," Owens said as he darted towards the door.

"Owens, one more thing. You were right. This was something big," Travis said as he grinned. Owens ran out the door.

Travis found out Glenn worked as a consultant for Jameson Bradford. Travis met Jameson in Washington, D. C. when he worked at FBI headquarters. Over the years, they crossed paths at various government functions along the beltway. Travis had a high-profile position and knew all the right people in law enforcement. Jameson was a successful and influential businessman with an agenda. That's the perfect recipe for forming powerful friendships. When one person has valuable information, and the other has deep pockets filled with money, it's a match made in heaven.

Travis already had in-depth knowledge about Project Diablo. He was aware Jameson was desperate to find a serial killer, and that Glenn was under significant pressure to find one. Travis thought if he could help his two friends with their problems, it would be a win-win for everybody. They would get their serial killer, and then Travis could retire. It was like playing poker and knowing everybody's hole cards. All he needed to do was wait for the right situation to get the biggest return. Now was time to go all-in and push his chips to the center of the table.

Travis pulled out his phone to send a text message to Glenn.

Travis: I have something u might be interested in.

Glenn: What would that be?

Travis: Got u a Killer

Glenn: Okay, See you in two days.

Travis: Can't wait...Tomorrow

Glenn: When did u make the rules?

Travis: We hooked a big fish. It might get away. Timing is critical.

Glenn: How big is the fish?

Travis: Bigger than our goddamn boat.

Glenn: Okay, we'll be there tomorrow. This better be big or else.

Travis: Bring a big briefcase. We can't do business without a big briefcase.

Glenn: Understood.

Travis walked outside, where Bill was waiting for him.

"I saw Owens leaving to get a response team," Bill said. "What's going on?"

"The FBI is taking over ownership of this investigation. We'll be sending a response team to take the suspect into custody."

"You can't do that. The FBI needs to work with local law enforcement. You're bending the rules," Bill said.

"This is a federal matter, and we must assume ownership," Travis said. "This is a unique case, and rules need to be bent."

"I'm going to—" Bill said. "Do absolutely nothing," Travis said, completing the sentence. "If you try to contact anybody, that will be something you'll regret for the rest of your life."

"Is that a threat?" Bill asked.

"It's only a threat if you perceive it as one," Travis replied. "I'm not trying to be difficult. It's just that this case is too important and needs the full attention of the FBI."

Bill knew Travis tied his hands and had no choice but to submit to Travis's request.

"One other thing, Bill," Travis said. "Make sure no one divulges any information to the media or the public until further notice."

Bill wasn't happy with the situation but had to play by the rules. Once the FBI assumes control of an investigation, there's little local law enforcement can do. Back at the San Francisco field office, they put the suspect into a small cell. Travis asked Owens to his office to discuss the next steps.

"We'll have a visitor here tomorrow to negotiate," Travis said. "I told them to bring a big briefcase."

"How much are you going to ask for?" Owens asked.

"I'm not sure," Travis responded. "But it will be something big."

CHAPTER

25

Dynamic Duo

San Francisco, California

EVERY MONDAY AT 10:00 A.M., Dominic Merino held a conference call with all FBI field offices to provide an update on the national investigation. But it was also an opportunity to share leads and information amongst the offices. Dominic wrapped up each call with a reminder.

"Jack is moving from east to west, focusing on the suburbs of major cities. I'm asking all the FBI field offices west of the Mississippi River to be on alert. Make sure your agents keep their eyes open and ears to the ground. If they see or hear anything, have them bring it to your attention and call us at once. Stay safe."

In the FBI's San Francisco field office, Travis Andrews ended the call. He looked at Glenn Norris, who was sitting across the conference room table. They both had smiles on their faces.

"Travis, you didn't speak up," Glenn said in a sarcastic tone. "Why didn't you tell them what you know? Why not do the right thing?"

"I haven't done the right thing for most of my life, so why start now?" Travis responded.

Laughter filled the room as the men got up to shake hands.

"My parents brought me up in a strict household. They enforced strong values and beliefs," Travis said.

"Appearances can sometimes be deceiving,". Glenn said with a smirk.

"You're right. But you know what? No matter how strong you think your values and beliefs are, we all have something in common."

"And what would that be?"

"Our values and beliefs have a price. The only difference is some people have a higher price than others." Travis said with a smirk. "Let's go get lunch."

~~~

Travis Andrews was an FBI deputy special agent in charge of the San Francisco field office. He was a 30-year veteran who worked most of his career in Washington, D.C., before transferring to the West coast. Few were aware Travis had two distinct personalities. Travis was a well-known and well-respected leader, but he was also a selfish opportunist. He preyed on people and situations for his benefit.

Over his career, Travis learned from the best how to bend the rules. He started small but worked his way up to confiscating drugs and weapons seized from crime scenes. If Travis were honest, he'd tell you that working for the FBI was his side job. At his core, Travis was a deal maker. His strong suit was accumulating assets and turning them into money. But now Travis was taking it to another level. He was on the verge of making the biggest deal in his life.

The two men went to Vincent's Italian Bistro, where Travis had a regular table in a back room. It was his go-to spot to discuss business and close deals. He was friends with the owner and forked over a healthy sum of money under the table to guarantee privacy. If someone wanted to listen in on a conversation, they'd need to enlist the local FBI office. But as long as Travis was in charge, there was no cause for concern.

"Vinnie, got the room ready?" Travis asked.

"Sure, Mr. Andrews, I'll grab some menus."
~~~

Travis walked Glenn to the back room. They sat and ordered a bottle of Chianti Classico. They got a head start on business while Vinnie was in the kitchen making magic.

"Based on our prior discussions, your top priority is to find a killer," Travis said. "I found you one. But this, my friend, is no ordinary run-of-the-mill killer. Oh, no, this is the one you want more than any other. But before I turn the killer over to you, we need to work out the finances."

"What's your price?" Glenn asked.

"Let me first ask you a question. What are you prepared to pay for an everyday serial killer? Someone who fits the narrative but isn't well-known?"

"I'm allowed to spend up to $5 million," Glenn said.

"That's a fair price, but if you want to shop in one of the high-end stores, you'll need to call the bank and get an increase in your credit line," Travis said.

"I didn't realize you had a price list. Aren't all killers the same? Why a premium?" Glenn asked.

"Three reasons. First, killers are like fast-food restaurants. They're in every town and are prey on the public," Travis said. "Serial killers are unique. They are more like a one-of-a-kind underground five-star bistro only serving a limited clientele. As you can see, one is more prevalent and cheaper while the other is hard to find and expensive."

"Fair point," Glenn said. "What's the second reason?"

"We found the killer at the crime scene and kept the story out of the public eye," Travis said. "We had to discredit witnesses and rumors. We had to convince the media it was a non-story. It wasn't easy."

Travis took a long sip of wine.

"The third reason?" Glenn asked.

"Oh, I almost forgot. The killer is in our office, locked downstairs in a secluded room. The killer in question goes by the name of Jack."

Travis smiled as he revealed his royal flush and raked in all the chips. Travis was backing Glenn into a corner, and there was nothing he could do about it.

"There is no market for this commodity. It's more than unique. I guess you could say one-of-a-kind," Travis said.

Vinnie stopped by the table and asked, "Sorry to interrupt, Mr. Andrews, but would you like another bottle of wine?"

Travis smiled and said, "Sure, Vinnie, but let's up the ante here. What's your most expensive bottle of red wine?"

Vinnie's eyes opened as wide as possible.

"I have a Giuseppe Quintarelli Amarone Classico Riserva from Veneto, Italy. Goes for $1900 a bottle."

"That is a bit pricey," Travis said. "Why such a hefty price tag?"

"It's the only bottle you'll find in the United States," Vinnie said. "It's all about supply and demand."

Travis looked Glenn straight in the eyes and flashed a big smile.

"Makes perfect sense to me," Travis said. "Bring us the bottle and two glasses."

Glenn slumped in his chair, looking like a prizefighter who had taken one too many punches to the head.

"Well played, Travis," Glenn said. "You have me in an awkward position. Give me the bad news. I'm a big boy and can handle it."

"The price for you is $10 million," Travis said as he leaned back in his chair, watching Glenn's jaw drop. "Remember, everyone has their price."

Glenn was speechless because it was much more than he thought. So, they went to lunch to continue the negotiation. However, Glenn only got Travis to come down to $8 million.

"I need to talk with Jameson before we move forward," Glenn said.

"Talk to the Almighty man himself then," Travis said. "Get back to me this evening, or the deal is off the table."

"Call you by 9:00 p.m.," Glenn said.

~

After a long lunch, Glenn left the restaurant and headed to the hotel. He found a quiet spot in a remote part of the lobby and called Jameson.

"I got your killer," Glenn said.

"Fantastic," Jameson said with glee.

"But there's a problem," Glenn said. "A sort of good and bad problem."

There was an uncomfortable silence on the other end of the line. Glenn felt Jameson's blood boiling.

"I out-kicked my coverage on this one," Glenn said. "I found the perfect killer. But it will come at a significant cost."

"Did you already commit?" Jameson asked.

"No, not yet," Glenn said. "The price tag for the killer is $8 million."

"A little pricey," Jameson said with a hint of disappointment. "We can target someone else. Let's pass for now."

"Jameson, when you hear the name, you might want to reconsider," Glenn said.

"Why is that?" Jameson asked.

"Because your killer is Jack."

Jameson let out a hearty laugh.

"No way you got your hands on one of the most notorious serial killers of the century," Jameson said. "Where did you bump into, Jack? In a pizza shop making calzones?"

"Jameson, I'm as serious as a heart attack," Glenn said. "There was a report of multiple homicides on the pier, and the police arrived in time to apprehend the killer. Travis took Jack into custody from the San Francisco Police Department."

"Really?" Jameson said like a little boy getting his first puppy. "We can get Jack?"

"Yes," Glenn said.

There was another period of silence, but this time, it wasn't uncomfortable at all. Glenn knew Jameson was pleased.

"This is more than we expected," Glenn said. "The price is unreasonable, and this is a dangerous situation. I'll tell Travis we're passing on this. I wanted to at least bring it to your attention."

"Don't you dare," Jameson said. "You're right. Jack is the perfect killer. We'll learn more from Jack in a year than we would from any other killer in a decade. This will fast-forward Project Diablo by years. Go back to Travis and try to negotiate him down if you can. We must get Jack."

"Is all this worth $8 million?" Glenn asked.

"Jack is worth every penny," Jameson said. "$8 million is mere pocket change nowadays. How much money did you bring with you?"

"Three briefcases filled with Benjamins," Glenn said. "I would say somewhere around $2.5 million."

"Perfect. Give it to Travis as a down payment and tell him the rest will come when Jack is in our possession."

"Are we still going to use the same game plan for Jack that we would use for any other serial killer?" Glenn asked.

"No," Jameson responded. "We can't force Jack into the town. We need to be careful. This will make or break Project Diablo. This investment has to pay off. I hate to lose money, even pocket change."

"How are we going to get Jack into the town?"

"Somehow, Jack has to enter the town like everyone else, as a volunteer," Jameson said. "It's the only way."

"What about orientation?"

"Skip normal orientation procedures," Jameson said. "We can worry about that later. Just get Jack here as soon as you can. My money and resources are at your disposal."

"Okay, let me call Travis and get the ball rolling," Glenn said.

As Glenn ended the call, he realized this would not be easy. How was he going to get Jack out of San Francisco with no one noticing?

Glenn had an idea. He called his trusty sidekick Vic Bradley. Since Glenn's promotion to SVP of Project Operations, the two friends hadn't worked together very much.

The phone rang for quite a while until Vic picked up the phone. Glenn and Vic knew each other's voices as if they were brothers.

"Time to get the Dynamic Duo together again," Glenn said without announcing who he was.

"Do you mean Benjamin Franklin Pierce and John Francis McIntyre?" Vic asked.

"No idiot, Batman and Robin. They were the Dynamic Duo," Glenn said. "Look, I need you out here fast. There's something we need to take care of for Project Diablo."

"Holy road trip, Batman. I'll be there tomorrow morning."

Glenn was a little uneasy about the prospects of dealing with Jack, but he felt better knowing his trusty sidekick Robin was on the way.

CHAPTER

26

First Cut

San Francisco, California

THE NEXT DAY, after lunch, Glenn went to a local park near the FBI office. He walked around for a while until he spotted Travis sitting on a bench. Glenn sat next to him with an oversized briefcase and stared straight ahead. He typed a message on his phone and handed it to Travis.

The briefcase is yours. Inside is a down payment. Once Jack is in our possession, you'll receive a second payment. We will pay the balance once we're on the plane to Wyoming.

Once Travis read the message, Glenn removed it from his phone. The men shook hands and parted ways. That's how you close a deal to purchase the services of a serial killer.

Travis drove home and went into his office to open the briefcase. Inside was $2.5 million. He stared at the newly minted $100 bills for five minutes to savor the moment. It was more money than he had ever seen in his lifetime. He took all the money and placed it into a hidden safe.

In criminal organizations, members share a taste of their earnings with the boss who accepts the tribute, and in return, he offers protection. Travis ran into his FBI field office the same way. The only difference was Travis took his cut first before anyone else. But sometimes, he couldn't help himself and took it all. This was one of those times.

Travis walked into the kitchen and saw his wife, Diana, and two girls, Emma and Haley. After hugs and kisses, Diana looked at Travis.

"You know the drill," Diana said, "Feed the dogs, and then I'll feed you."

After Travis fed the monsters, he walked back into the kitchen.

"Hope you're hungry. Got to get rid of these leftovers," Diana said.

"Dee, I'm not all that hungry. Went to a big lunch with an out-of-town agent, which didn't end until mid-afternoon," Travis said. "But I skipped dessert, so if you're hiding anything, let me know. I always have room for dessert."

"That's why Daddy has a big belly," the girls said in unison. Travis smiled because his little girls were correct in their assumptions.

"I have a freshly baked apple pie. Help yourself," Diana said.

Travis grabbed a glass plate and knife and cut himself a double slice, which was a quarter of the entire pie. When he transferred it to the plate, he let out a big laugh.

"What's so funny?" Diana asked.

"Nothing, Dee," Travis said, chuckling to himself as he walked away.

Travis laughed because he learned something valuable.

Whether it's a briefcase full of money or a freshly baked apple pie, it's always best to make sure you get the first cut.

After dessert, Travis thought about going back for more. But he showed some willpower. Travis knew he could wait because there would be more money and apple pie soon.

Dr. Steven Murphy was on his way to lunch, walking in the hallway on the fourth floor of UCSF Medical Center. But he never made it to his intended destination because another doctor blindsided him.

"Steve, we need to talk," Dr. Jason Payne said. "I can't wait."

"Dammit. I almost made it out the door," Steven muttered to himself.

Jason pointed towards one of the larger hospital rooms, and they both stepped inside.

"Steve, I heard troubling news from my lawyer. The City of San Francisco is going to announce a class-action medical malpractice suit against both of us. Is it true?"

"I'm not sure," Steven said. "I've heard rumors."

"What are we going to do?" Jason asked. "If anyone finds out what happened and what we did, it's all over for both of us."

The two doctors sat down. Jason's head was in his hands as negative thoughts raced through his head.

"Jason, it was only a matter of time before the insurance companies caught on to our little scheme," Steven said. "The stakes got higher when people died for unknown reasons. But don't worry."

Jason looked up with red eyes and asked, "What do you mean, don't worry? It's all over, and we're going away for a lifetime."

"You're right. We're going away, but not where you think," Steven said.

A confused Jason cocked his head like a six-week-old puppy dog.

"You don't start an operation like ours without having a backup plan," Steven said. "I've thought long and hard about this. We can disappear before the shit hits the fan."

"How are we going to do that?" Jason asked.

"We can volunteer for Project Diablo."

"What's that?" Jason asked.

"It's a secret project conducted by one of the largest companies in the world," Steven said. "They need volunteers to live and work in a prefabricated community. There's good pay, a job, housing, and other benefits."

"What else is there?" Jason asked.

"Anonymity," Steven said. "They hide the town from public view. It's not even on a map. No one knows where it is. It's like falling off the face of the earth."

"What's the catch?"

"Once you enter the town, you can't leave until your contract expires. After one year, there's an option to extend. If you choose, you can remain until your dying day."

"What experiments are you performing?"

"They can't tell us outright because it would jeopardize the project. All they can say is it's a myriad of things. The sponsor looks at each person as a unique case and a separate study."

"How long are we going to stay?"

"At least until we fall off the radar," Steven said. "We can reassess the situation after the first year and then go someplace else. But we should prepare to stay for a long time. Perhaps until the end."

Steven could see the gears turning in Jason's head.

"If we both disappear, it will be harder for them to investigate the case. I don't want to spend a day in prison," Jason said. "I've got nothing holding me here. This is an opportunity to escape for a while, if not forever."

"A bus is leaving from this hospital on Friday evening. I'll put you in touch with a gentleman by the name of Rob Gardner. He is the Director of Volunteer Recruiting for the town. Rob will ask questions, give you a contract, and reserve a spot for you on the bus."

"Thanks, Steve. I feel better already," Jason said. "I hate to run away from a problem, but sometimes there is no other choice."

Behind the two doctors was a bed. They forgot there was a lone patient in intensive care. The person moved. Jason walked over and grabbed the patient's hand.

"Looks like we're waking up," Jason said. "About time you opened your eyes."

He turned to Steve with an unmistakable wink.

Steven responded with a thumbs-up as he walked out of the room.

~

The following day, Jason got off the elevator with a spring in his step. He stopped by the nurses' station and chatted with Valerie. But she wanted to play with her hair rather than carry on a conversation.

"Hey, good-looking. How's the patient today?" Jason asked.

"Kind of cranky. Asking a lot of questions," Valerie responded, without even looking up at Jason.

"Only a few more days, and this will all be over," Jason said. "Then you can play with your hair all day long."

"Always a comedian," Valerie responded. "Stick to your day job."

Jason took a deep breath and walked into the patient's room. The patient was sitting up and watching television.

"Are you my doctor?" the patient asked.

"Yes. My name is Dr. Payne."

The patient tried to laugh, but the meds weren't kicking in. That meant only one thing. The patient was in a lot of…pain.

"I get the same reaction every time," Jason said. "It's getting old, so on Monday, I plan to change my name to Smith or Jones or something like that."

"How are you doing today?" Jason asked.

"I couldn't tell you the day or time, where I am, or what happened. Other than those minor items, I'm doing fine. Can you fill in the blanks because inquiring minds want to know?"

"What's the last thing you remember?" Jason asked.

"I was in a holding cell at the FBI office in San Francisco, being held against my will. I hadn't eaten for a while, and after my first meal, I blacked out and woke up in this bed with stitches in three places. What the hell happened?"

"You suffered an acute case of appendicitis, and we brought you here to this hospital for emergency surgery," Jason said. "There were complications, and the wound didn't heal properly. You lapsed in and out of consciousness for two days. You may recall things you saw or heard, but you couldn't speak until yesterday."

"What happens now? How long do I stay here?"

"They didn't say," Jason responded. "You were a special case, and they hid your identity. They told me to refer to you as 'the patient' for the time being."

"Doctor, there's no way I'm going back, and you will see to it."

Jason was speechless.

"Tell me all about Project Diablo. I am extremely interested in what you were talking about yesterday. Just like you said, I recalled every word; but couldn't join in on the conversation."

"What do you want from me?" Jason asked.

"I want you to put me in touch with Rob Gardner and make sure I've got a seat on the bus on Friday."

"I...I can't do that," Jason said.

"You can, and you will, Dr. Payne. If you don't, I'm going to the authorities, and before you know it, we'll be in adjoining cells down at FBI headquarters. Trust me. You don't want me as a next-door neighbor. I'm not a nice person."

"I'll see what I can do," Jason said as he backed out of the room. "I can't make promises, but—"

"Make it happen, or your life will go to hell, and you won't be coming back."

CHAPTER

27

Bad Actors

Tümpisa, Wyoming

THE CAVALCADE OF TURBOPROPS at Riverton Regional Airport began at 7:00 a.m. each day. It continued nonstop until incoming traffic slowed to a crawl around 9:00 p.m. After the last flight touched down, most non-essential personnel went home. The airport dimmed its terminal lights and took a collective nap.

Logan Smith and Sarah Miller would tell you they were the head of airport security detail between 10:00 p.m. and 6:00 a.m. But the truth was they were babysitters for a 1,200-acre airport. On most nights, they walked and talked because there was usually nothing to find or investigate.

One morning around 3:00 a.m., Logan and Sarah were behind the airport in front of a hangar. They were both fighting to stay awake, so they kept walking and talking.

"I'm not sure how much longer I can do this," Logan said. "This is an easy job, and it provides a steady paycheck, but working these hours is draining."

"I hear you," Sarah said, "the hours suck, but I say milk it for as long as you can. You'll never have another job as easy as this."

A large van accompanied by three SUVs appeared on the tarmac on one runway. They were hard to notice because there wasn't enough light.

"What the hell is that?" Sarah asked.

"Don't know," Logan said. "Only saw one airplane come in this time of the morning once, and it was for an emergency landing. Let's call the police station."

As Sarah plugged numbers into her phone, the two of them walked towards the vehicles. She reached Cooper Johnson from the station to ask for backup.

"Cooper, we have a situation here at the airport," Sarah said between breaths. "Unauthorized vehicles are on the tarmac."

"Sarah, orders are to stand down," Cooper said. "We received notice of a flight coming in. No need for you to be concerned. Do not engage, repeat, do not engage." Sarah stopped walking and relayed the message to Logan.

"Kind of strange no one told us," Logan said. "You'd think the first call would be to security."

"Logan, look over there," Sarah said, pointing to the east side of the airport.

A light appeared in the distance, getting larger by the second. It wasn't the typical 30-person turboprop, but a much broader plane twice the size. After landing, it taxied towards the waiting vehicles. After powering down, 15 minutes passed before anyone deplaned.

Even though the plane could've held 50 people, only a dozen walked off. One was on a stretcher and put into the back of the van. It was hard to tell from such a distance, but it was a medical emergency of some sort. The lone van and three SUVs took off in the darkness, and the airport once again hugged a pillow and went back to sleep.

"I don't understand what it could be all about. Think they're going to Riverton General?" Sarah asked.

Logan looked at Sarah and bit his tongue.

"There aren't any outstanding medical facilities in the entire state of Wyoming, let alone a small town like Riverton. It has nothing to do with that," Logan said. "These folks aren't going to any hospital anywhere near here. Something strange is going on."

After a long ride, the vehicles arrived at Project Diablo Headquarters. They drove straight to a private entrance and into a secured garage. Three men took the stretcher to the on-site medical facility. Right behind were Steven Murphy, Jason Payne, and Rob Gardner.

The men brought the patient to a private room. Armed security guards kept watch outside and in the hallway. The group of men sat down to relax in a lounge area. It had been a hectic 24-hour stretch for everyone involved. Glenn walked in with a big smile on his face.

"Nothing makes me happier than when everything goes according to plan," Glenn said. "Now we have Jack."

Glenn orchestrated the whole ordeal. It turned out to be one big ruse. Jameson's orders were for Glenn to get Jack to enter the town as a volunteer. In Jameson's own words, he said, "My money and resources are at your disposal. Just get it done."

Glenn paid off executives at the UCSF Medical Center, flew in resources from Pharmatech, and hired local actors to play bit parts to make it all work. That was on top of the payments Glenn made to Travis Andrews.

The first step in the deception was to lace Jack's meal at FBI headquarters with a corrosive agent. The abdominal pain was so severe. Jack passed out within half an hour. Glenn then sedated Jack for the ride to UCSF Medical Center.

Glenn commandeered the entire fourth floor for a week. There were only two UCSF executives who knew what was going on. They kept their mouths shut for a healthy sum of money. As for the rest of the hospital, the UCSF executives told everyone that the hospital closed the floor for a movie production.

With the stage set, Glenn turned Jack over to Drs. Murphy and Payne. But they took Jack as a patient under false pretenses. Because the doctors had no affiliation with UCSF. Instead, the two doctors were part of a medical team employed full-time by Pharmatech. Dr. Murphy, played by Dr. Randolph Mills, performed the emergency appendectomy. Dr. Payne, played by Dr. Clint Ferguson, implanted a tracking mechanism in the abdomen.

After surgery, Jack stayed in intensive care and was brought in and out of consciousness. Jack could hear what was going on but couldn't move a muscle. They timed it, so Jack would listen to the doctor's private conversation about their plans to disappear. The opportunity to escape was too hard for Jack to resist.

"If there were an Academy Award for best actor in a short film about a serial killer, it would be hard to choose between Randy and Clint," Glenn said.

"What about my performance playing the part of Rob Gardner?" Vic asked. "I was acting as the Director of Volunteer Recruiting for the town."

Glenn looked at Vic and said, "I hate to break it to you, but you are the Director of Volunteer Recruiting for the town. You were playing yourself. The only difference was your name."

"I guess you're right," Vic said as he feigned disappointment. "Can I at least get a Daytime Emmy award?"

Meanwhile, Jack was still in recovery. The doctors sedated Jack for the flight to Wyoming. It would take a while for Jack to recover and be normal again. Or as normal as one can be if you're a serial killer.

CHAPTER

28

Three Wise Monkeys

Tümpisa, Wyoming

ON THE LAST DAY OF ORIENTATION, the Project Diablo Management Team subjected the volunteers to numerous physical and mental tests, including a health and wellness exam. They endured a full day of questioning, testing, flexing, pinching, pricking, prodding, pushing, and pulling. But before heading to the town, the volunteers had one last item on their agenda. They paid a visit to Dr. Thomas, the resident dentist, for a thorough examination. After an hour in his chair, the volunteers left with more than just clean teeth and healthy gums. Unbeknownst to them, they also left with a parting gift.

While the patients were numb, Dr. Thomas implanted a tiny computer chip below their tongue. The chip captured each volunteer's vital signs, accumulated information on biochemicals and neurotransmitters, and tested blood and body fluids. Researchers used the real-time data to look for trends and see if there were linkages to observed behaviors.

The dental exams took place on the second floor next to SODA, the Subject Observation and Data Analysis department. SODA was home to a functioning medical research center, a state-of-the-art information technology department, and a high-tech video and audio command desk. Behind closed doors were a team of doctors, analysts, and technical personnel who collected, analyzed, and reported volunteer data.

SODA was also where Jameson liked to hold his executive update meetings every Wednesday evening. Jameson led the weekly discussions from his regular spot at one end of a long rectangular table. Around the table was the Project Diablo executive management team.

- Glenn Norris - SVP of Project Diablo Operations
- Vic Bradley - Director of Volunteer Recruiting
- Patty Allen - Director of Procurement & Supplier Services
- Tim Foley - Director of Infrastructure &Facilities
- Dr. Deborah Thornton - Director of Medical Practices,
- Jerry Foster - Director of Volunteer Data Collection
- Harrison Bradford - Project Diablo CFO & Controller

Jameson called for a special executive meeting to discuss Phase III of Project Diablo. Seated opposite Jameson at the other end of the table was Harrison, who was attending his first weekly meeting.

Projected on the wall was a live feed from a surveillance camera located somewhere in the town. The live picture showed someone in a bed, sprawled out under the covers, in a deep sleep. Everyone in the conference room was on edge as they waited for the subject to awaken. In some respects, what they were watching seemed like a Frankenstein movie. You could almost hear Dr. Henry Frankenstein say, "It's just resting. Waiting for a new life to come."

Jameson rose from his chair and walked to the front of the room with a smile on his face. Harrison felt like he was waiting for his father to send him to the concession stand with a five-dollar bill to get a big box of popcorn. At least he hoped that was the case, because Harrison hated to watch a good movie on an empty stomach.

"Welcome, everybody," Jameson said. "This is a special night. Before turning this meeting over to Dr. Thornton, I wanted to say a few words about Project Diablo."

Glenn and Harrison suspected Jameson was going to provide insight into his grand plan.

"As you know, the scope and scale of this project are far beyond what any company has ever attempted. What we've created here is the most realistic test environment in the world. Research and development are providing us with information we never thought possible. When we started, our goal was to develop a drug to change human behavior. That's still our primary goal, but I want us to think bigger and broader. We need to determine if the information has other uses. Why shoot for the moon when you can be amongst the stars?"

Jameson asked Glenn to join him at the front of the room.

"Three years ago, we started Project Diablo," Glenn said. "After a lot of hard work, here we are, sitting around this table with plenty of pride. We've studied a considerable number of individuals from all walks of life. We already got a wealth of information, and now we move forward. Starting this evening, we're entering the third phase of Project Diablo."

Glenn took a long drink of water and continued. "In the first phase, we constructed the town and found volunteers, developed the town's infrastructure, and set up operating procedures. Then, in the second phase, we focused on analyzing and testing volunteers. Finally, in the third phase, we will test prototype drugs and monitor the results."

"How are we going to administer the drugs to volunteers in the town?" Vic asked.

"Infuse the water system," Deborah replied. "We'll alter the water in every house, business, and public facility. Even the bottled water shipped into the town. That's how we can make sure everyone takes part."

"Each person drinks different amounts of water. How does that affect the results?" Tim asked.

"That's a good thing," Deborah said. "The data will tell us how someone reacts if we over or under administer the drug. We'll track everyone's consumption based on surveys and closed-circuit television."

"When will we administer the drugs?" Harrison asked.

"We've already started," Deborah said. "Two months ago, we infused the water system with our first drug called Inclinerol, which didn't perform well. This month we're trying Demeanorin, which is stronger. Research and Development is optimistic we will have better results."

Jameson interrupted and took back control of the meeting.

"As Dr. Thornton just told you, we've begun detailed testing. The original timeline for this phase was five years. That has now changed. We're bringing in new volunteers with more extreme negative behaviors, which will challenge our team to develop the best drug possible."

Jameson stood up with a grin from ear to ear. He looked like a little kid unwrapping a present who already knew what was inside. He was bursting at the seams and couldn't wait to tell us something.

"At Pharmatech, we take things to the next level. We push the envelope. That's why we're the most profitable company in the world. That's how we developed Restorex, and that's how we'll develop this drug."

Jameson walked around the conference room table to make sure everyone in the room paid attention.

"All of you have a question on your mind, so I'll provide an answer. What is the next level for Project Diablo? Well, I'm about to show you. We have one volunteer who will provide the ultimate challenge for our Research and Development team. If one of our prototype drugs works on this volunteer, it will work on anyone. If successful, this one volunteer will single-handedly cut the Project Diablo timeline in half."

Jameson continued to walk around the table. He paused for a few seconds between sentences to make sure his message was clear.

"Prepare yourself for what you're going to witness. This phase will yield valuable information but at a significant cost. I'm not talking about monetary cost. I'm talking about the cost of our values, beliefs, and our overall sense of morality. The old saying is, 'In life, sometimes we take great risks to get even greater rewards.' This is one of those times."

"Now, let's say hello to our newest volunteer…Jack."

Everyone was in complete silence.

The body under the bedcovers moved. Limbs stretched as arms and legs poked out between the sheets. A head emerged and swung around, pointed straight at the camera lens. Jameson lowered the volume and addressed the group.

"During this phase of Project Diablo, you'll see and hear horrible acts. People will suffer, and some will die. Your conscience will compel you to do something. But you must resist."

Everyone held their breath.

"Remember the old tale about the three wise monkeys. See no evil, hear no evil, and speak no evil. Can you control your consciousness and your emotions? If your answer is yes, then welcome to the team that will change the world, but if your answer is no, then the time has come for you to walk out the door."

Jameson sat and leaned back in his chair, clasped his hands, and put them behind his head. He waited for a response from each person in the room. Glen and Harrison looked at each other with the same thought on their mind.

There was only one correct answer, "Yes."

If anyone thought otherwise and walked out the door,

They wouldn't be walking for very long.

CHAPTER

29

Killer Drugs

Tümpisa, Wyoming

JAMESON AND HARRISON arrived at Project Diablo Headquarters for their weekly executive update meeting. The schedule started with a general update, included a review of ongoing clinical trials, and ended with a discussion regarding expectations as they entered phase three.

"Today, Jerry Foster and Dr. Thornton will update us on Demeanorin," Jameson said. "Deborah, I've heard positive reviews through the grapevine. So, please don't disappoint me now."

"No need to worry, Jameson. It's all good news." Deborah said as she stood in front of the group.

"We've evaluated Demeanorin for two months, and the drug has performed much better than our last trial for Inclinerol. In the town, we have 126 volunteers with chips implanted underneath their tongues. The chips enable us to collect information on-demand as often as we need it. Without going into too much detail, we can tell you Demeanorin has a minimal effect on heart rate, body temperature, respiration rate, and blood pressure."

"What about changes in behavior?" Tim asked. "That's the primary reason for our testing. Have we seen any improvement?"

"Yes," Jerry said. "We measure behavior by calculating a wellness score that combines 25 different factors, including facial expressions, verbal triggers, social interactions, sleep patterns, cognitive performance, changes in appetite, and adjustments to daily routines."

"Do you have the wellness scores?" Vic asked.

"Here they are," Jerry said as he projected a slide on the wall. "The scale is one to five. One represents a complete change of behavior, while five represents no change at all."

Focus Group	# Of People	% Of Town	Wellness Score
Supporters	850	87.1%	3.3
Subjects	100	10.2%	2.8
VIPs	25	2.6%	2.5
Jack	1	0.1%	1.3
Total	**976**	**100.0%**	**3.2**

"Something to note about this chart," Jerry said. Outside of the supporters on the top line, we chip and monitor everyone else. The only difference is frequency. We check subjects weekly and track VIPs daily. Jack, as you know, is a unique case. A separate team watches Jack around the clock.

"Looks like Jack's behavior improved," Harrison said. "Can you provide more details?"

"Sure," Jerry said. "We monitor Jack more than anyone else. When Jack first arrived in the town, it was a tricky situation. Jack came here with multiple compulsions and, if pushed, was prone to commit extreme violence. So, we weren't surprised when we learned Jack was a loner with few friends."

"Inclinerol did not affect Jack, but Demeanorin did," Deborah said. "Suddenly, we saw Jack venturing out in public and interacting with others. Jack didn't turn into a social butterfly overnight but seemed closer to normal. It was quite the turnaround."

Jameson felt compelled to add context.

"You're right," Jameson said. "It's a remarkable turnaround. But let's not sell this short. This is a breakthrough. Jack gets more attention for a good reason, and I'm about to tell you why."

Jameson dropped a bombshell in the middle of the table.

"Jack is a serial killer," Jameson said. Gasps filled the room.

"How could you let a serial killer loose in a town with innocent people?" Tim asked.

"Remember what I told you in December," Jameson said. "I said you'll see and hear horrible acts. People will suffer, and some will die. Your conscience will compel you to do something. But you must resist."

"When you said, 'people will die,' you didn't mention murder," Patty cried.

"Remember what else I told you," Jameson said. "In life, sometimes great risks are taken for even greater rewards."

"Has Jack harmed anyone?" Deborah asked.

"No," Jameson said. "But as you can see, based on the results, Jack has changed for the better. The hope is Jack continues to progress, and this becomes a non-issue."

"We can't say for sure that Demeanorin or any drug will be successful long term," Tim said. "Anything could trigger Jack to kill again. How are you going to feel Jameson with blood on your hands?"

Jameson reclined in his chair and flashed a big smile.

"See no evil, hear no evil, and speak no evil."

Jameson got up, walked over to the conference room door, opened it, and said, "Tim, if you don't want to be part of the team that will change the world, here is your chance to leave."

Tim didn't move.

Jameson shut the door and sat down once again.

"I knew you wouldn't budge," Jameson said. "Just do your job. If you don't, you can leave and suffer the consequences."

After the meeting, the Bradfords returned to the flying egg-beater for the hour flight home. After a long day, Jameson couldn't keep his eyes open and took a nap. That left Harrison alone with his thoughts for the entire trip. As they approached Cody, Harrison gazed out the window at Mount Washburn. The view was as spectacular as ever, but the mountain didn't seem the same from the air.

Harrison remembered when Jameson told him the mountain represented Pharmatech, and everything else below was within its domain. But his father conveniently left out one crucial fact.

Pharmatech may indeed be the mountain, but Jameson was climbing fast, trying to get to the top.

CHAPTER

30

Hail Mary

Tümpisa, Wyoming

THE FOLLOWING DAY, Glenn recalled Jameson's actions at the meeting. Something seemed odd. He felt Jameson acted more like a mad scientist rather than a CEO of a pharmaceutical company. Glenn wasn't sure if anyone else noticed. He had to find out, so he took a chance and contacted Harrison Bradford.

"Harrison, this is Glenn Norris. Do you have a few minutes?"

The call startled Harrison. Ever since he met Benjamin Franklin Pierce and John Francis McIntyre (a.k.a. Glenn Norris and Vic Bradley), any conversations with them were off-limits. Harrison sensed something was wrong.

"Sure, what's going on, Glenn?"

"After yesterday's meeting, I'm concerned about Jameson," Glenn said. "I'm not sure what you may have seen or thought. But from what I could tell, his priorities have changed. Project Diablo is not about understanding and changing human behavior for the greater good. Project Diablo has turned into something more ominous."

"Didn't he tell you at the beginning what his intentions were?" Harrison asked.

"Jameson told me he wanted to study the mind of a serial killer to understand what triggered someone to kill," Glenn said. "He said it would be the ultimate challenge. I never thought he would sit by and put people at risk of being killed in the name of science. I think we're just pawns in his sick game. At some point, he'll sacrifice all of us to get what he wants."

"And what do you think that is?" Harrison asked.

"Jameson wants to be the most powerful person in the world," Glenn responded.

Harrison wasn't the least bit surprised. He thought the same thing every time he looked at Mount Washburn.

"When you're as rich as Jameson, you become desensitized," Glenn said. "You can go anywhere and do anything you want. Money and relationships don't mean as much anymore. The only thing you want to attain is the unattainable. In Jameson's case, he is searching for the one thing he doesn't have—absolute power and control."

"I agree with you completely, but there's nothing we can do," Harrison said. "We can't change him. The horse is already out of the barn."

"True," Glenn said. "But an opportunity may arise. If we can get enough pawns together, we can overthrow the king."

"We just need to get all the pawns on the same chessboard," Harrison said. "So, let's work together and see what we can do."

"Sounds like a good idea," Glenn replied.

"All this time, I thought you were in lockstep with Jameson," Harrison said. "Why the change of heart?"

"I'll admit I may not be perfect. But I can't stand by and see innocent people die. I'm not Jameson's puppet, someone without thoughts and feelings."

Harrison let out a big laugh.

"What's so funny?" Glenn asked.

"When we first met, I thought you and Vic were androids because neither of you spoke a word," Harrison said.

Now Glenn let out a big laugh.

Glenn and Harrison realized they had something in common. They were both concerned about Jameson. But now they learned they could confide in each other and work together to stop him. The only problem was the king's horse was out of the barn. If they wanted to topple the king, the other pawns would have to join the cause.

What they didn't realize was the other pawns were on their way.

Cody, Wyoming

A few days later, something clicked. A thousand light bulbs went off in Harrison's head. He figured out how to conquer the mountain.

In the middle of the month, Pharmatech designates one week as "Vendor Pay Week." That's when Harrison's accounting team prepares vendor payments for invoices that need to be paid. Once Harrison signs the payment requests, he sends them to the bank for processing and disbursement.

Before his team arrived for the day, Harrison emailed his managers and asked them to send him all open payment requests. By noon, Harrison had them all in a single folder on his desk. He called Glenn to tell him the good news.

"Glenn," Harrison said. "I've got good news. I figured out how to capture the king and shut down Project Diablo."

Harrison picked up the folder on his desk.

"I have a folder in front of me. Care to guess what's in it?" Harrison asked.

Glenn didn't understand and replied, "I have no idea."

"Inside this folder are all the vendor invoices to be paid this month. All I need to do is pull one invoice out of the batch, and the rest takes care of itself."

Glenn was now more confused than ever. He wondered if another Bradford was going insane.

"Harrison, you've got to help me on this one. I've got no idea where you're headed."

"Okay, here's the deal. In this folder are invoices for all of our vendors. One of those is Wind River Power. They control the town's electrical grid. Almost 70% of Wind River's revenue comes from the town. Without Pharmatech as a customer, they wouldn't exist. So, when I remove the Wind River invoice from the batch, guess what? It doesn't get paid. Then in 45 days, the calls and emails will come in fast and furious."

"I'm not an accountant, but I see where you're going now," Glenn chimed in.

"I'm not sure how long it will take, but at some point, Wind River will reach their breaking point," Harrison said. "They'll threaten us, and I'll play hardball. You can guess what happens next."

"Wind River will shut off the power to the town," Glen answered. "Everyone will have to leave."

"Project Diablo Security won't be able to stop them," Harrison said. "Chaos will ensue, and there will be a mass exodus."

"What about Jameson? What happens when he finds out?"

Harrison paused for a few seconds to gather his thoughts.

"Glenn, did you ever wonder why I wasn't part of Project Diablo from the beginning?

"No. Why?"

"Before I was born, my mom pressured Jameson into having a child," Harrison said. "She passed away during childbirth, and ever since, he blamed me for her death. I'm his biological son, but he treats me like an adopted child. We never had a regular father-son relationship. I suspect that's why he never trusted me."

"But he trusts you with billions of dollars," Glenn said. "Otherwise, you wouldn't be his CFO and Controller."

"Putting me in this position wasn't a matter of trust. All Jameson needed was someone with experience whom he could control and hold accountable. Do you know what he used to always tell me?"

"What?" Glenn asked.

"He said, 'Harry, you're the financial quarterback of this company. Keep getting first downs, ten yards at a time. There's no need to go for the Hail Mary. We don't take unnecessary chances. Play smart and execute the game plan. Oh, and don't throw an interception or fumble the ball. If you do, you'll have to deal with me.'"

Glenn then asked the obvious question.

"Harrison, it doesn't sound like a happy situation. You seem miserable. Why do you continue to work for Jameson?"

"I won't lie. This job was a great opportunity. Initially, I thought I would leave at some point. But then I learned something."

"What?" Glenn asked.

"The same thing you figured out," Harrison said. "Jameson wants to be all-powerful. For the longest time, I thought I was the only one who saw it. Then, when you mentioned it the other day, it confirmed everything."

Harrison heard a gasp on the other end of the phone.

"I'm still at Pharmatech for one reason," Harrison said. "I felt it was my responsibility to put an end to Jameson and his ego. I just didn't figure out how to do it until now. Someone must stop him. Who better to do that than his only son?"

Harrison paused for a second and smiled.

"Screw the first downs," Harrison said. "I'm throwing the Hail Mary to the end zone."

CHAPTER

31

Armor All

Cody, Wyoming

BRANDON TURNER wasn't afraid to speak his mind. He always thought if you don't ask, you don't get. That's why whenever something didn't look right, he always asked questions.

Harrison hired Brandon straight out of college from his alma mater, the University of California at San Francisco. What made Brandon unique was his unceasing ability to seek the truth. He was Harrison's black knight who guarded the golden bridge and let no one pass without approval.

He never envisioned a day when he would ask Brandon to forego everything he believed. But the day arrived, and the time was now. Harrison took Brandon to a working lunch at Y. O. Ming's, a local Asian restaurant only a ten-minute drive from Pharmatech. As they waited for the fortune cookies, Harrison broached the subject. He was about to ask Brandon to bend the rules.

"Brandon, I asked you to lunch today because I need a favor," Harrison said

Brandon worshiped Harrison. He patterned his work habits around his boss and mentor. If Harrison did or said something, Brandon took it as gospel.

"Sure thing, Harrison. Consider it done," Brandon said.

"But I haven't even asked for the favor yet," Harrison said.

"I know," Brandon replied, "I just wanted to let you know nothing is too much to ask for, that's all."

If you looked up the word 'gullible' in the dictionary, you would find a high-resolution picture of Brandon Turner along with his email address and phone number. Inside the office, Brandon was serious as a heart attack. But outside the office, Brandon was the brunt of most jokes. It took little to reel him in and pull the wool over his eyes. Harrison couldn't resist having some fun at Brandon's expense.

"I appreciate that," Harrison said. "Here's the favor. I want you to take my car and get it washed every Friday morning. Make sure you're done by noon. Oh, and don't forget the Armor All. I love shiny tires."

Brandon took out his calendar, checked dates, and asked, "When would you like me to start?" Harrison broke into a huge grin, and Brandon realized someone had tricked him once again.

"Let that be a lesson, Brandon. Never agree to do something before you know what that something is."

"I...I knew you were kidding me. I...I was playing along with your little joke."

Harrison didn't believe him.

"In all seriousness, we need to discuss something of importance."

"What is it?"

"First, let me ask you a question. When you see the word 'ethics,' what comes to mind?"

"Ethics are the morals and principles which govern our behavior. It defines who we are and what we stand for. Without ethics, we have no basis for our beliefs and values."

Brandon's in-depth definition impressed Harrison.

"We know each other pretty well," Harrison said, "and we're cut from the same cloth. Both of us respect our ethics and live by the same code of conduct. We would never break the rules because that would go against everything we believe in. But sometimes, Brandon, we need to bend the rules for the greater good."

"What do you mean by the greater good?"

Harrison paused for a few seconds to gather his thoughts.

"I've come across information which shows one of our projects poses a threat to society. We need to shut it down."

"What's the threat?" Brandon asked.

"I can't divulge too many details," Harrison said in a soft voice. "All I can tell you is it's a research project which takes place in a prefabricated town. Time is of the essence. We need to act now. That's why I've ceased paying Wind River Power."

"What does not paying Wind River have to do with shutting down the project?" Brandon asked as he cocked his head at an angle like a confused puppy.

"I don't have a lot of options. But the one arrow in my quiver is the power of the pen. Nothing gets a vendor's attention faster than when invoices go unpaid, and the money stops flowing in. The vendor will reach a breaking point. Now, if you're Wind River and your biggest customer makes up 70% of revenues, the breaking point comes much sooner."

"Why are you telling me this?" Brandon asked. "What do you want from me?"

"I need you to do something which goes against your ethics," Harrison said. "Brandon, I'm asking you to bend the rules. If Wind River calls, try your best to avoid them or make up an excuse not to talk to them. If they pressure you to talk, let them know they have to contact me."

"Don't worry. I can bend the rules. What happens once Wind River reaches their breaking point?"

"Wind River will cut off the power to the town," Harrison said. "The town won't be able to continue operating. Everyone will leave. It will be a mass exodus. No one will stop them."

"It's a brilliant plan. What will you tell Jameson?"

"Not sure," Harrison said. "Right now, I'm just focusing on shutting down Project Diablo."

"Jameson will be pretty upset," Brandon said. "You better wash his flying egg-beater. Oh, and don't forget the Armor All. I hear Jameson loves shiny tires."

CHAPTER

32

Cops & Robbers

Tümpisa, Wyoming

EVERY MORNING BOBBY WOKE and was out the door to work by 8:00 a.m. He spent an hour going through his daily routine before heading to the office. Bobby used the extra time to run errands, spend time with the town locals, and give thanks to someone above.

When Bobby left his apartment and began his daily walk along Main Street, his first stop was Crowder's Convenience Store.

"Good morning, Mr. Crowder," Bobby said with a big smile. "Beautiful day, isn't it?"

"Sure is," Michael Crowder replied.

"Do you have today's paper this morning?" Bobby asked.

"Not yet," Michael said. "The mothership is late with their deliveries today. It should be here soon. The delivery time changes every day. Sometimes I wonder if we're living on another planet, and everything comes in by spaceship."

Bobby laughed as he waved goodbye and continued along the street. On the right, he saw Carol Hutchinson, who owned the Main Street Deli. It was the best place to get lunch in the town.

"Morning, Carol," Bobby said. "You got my roast beef sandwich waiting for me?"

"Sure do," Carol responded, "but I don't have any chips. Waiting for a delivery from the mothership. If this keeps happening, I'm gonna start growing my own potatoes."

Bobby chuckled and said, "I'm not sure of much in this world, but the one thing I know is you can't grow squat around here."

After Bobby nodded and waved goodbye, he crossed the street again and walked into Stains &Wrinkles, the local dry cleaners.

"Morning, Simon," Bobby said. "You got my shirts today?"

"Not yet, Bobby," Simon said, "the mothership is late again today."

Simon shook his head as Bobby let out a huge laugh.

"Not the first time I heard that today," Bobby said. "I'll come back on my way home."

The last stop on the street was Human Beans, the local coffee house. Everybody in town stopped in at some point to grab a cup of joe, read a book, or just socialize. Bobby strolled in and said hello to the regulars, and headed towards the bar to put in his order.

"Morning, Jordyn," Bobby said. "What's brewing today?"

"Hi, Bobby," Jordyn said. "We have two choices today. Yellowstone Medium Roast or Rocky Mountain Dark Roast."

"Give me a Rocky Mountain with room. I'll take care of the rest," Bobby said.

The walk on Main Street was the part of the day Bobby looked forward to more than anything else. He enjoyed socializing with the business owners and speaking with the townies.

Bobby arrived nine months prior as a volunteer, but in that brief time, he reconnected with a feeling he hadn't had in a very long time. The town felt like home.

After leaving Human Beans, Bobby needed to take care of one last thing before going to the office. Every day, he walked over to a nearby park and found a random bench. Bobby sat for a moment and reflected on where he came from. He looked at the sky, closed his eyes, and whispered, "Thank You."

Bobby wasn't a religious person. But he knew someone above was looking out for him. That someone was most likely named Karen. It had to be her. There was no other way to explain how Bobby could have turned his life around in such a short time.

~

Minneapolis, Minnesota

At one time, Robert "Bobby" Collins had a promising career as a police officer in his hometown of Minneapolis. But that was two years ago, the day before his life suddenly changed forever.

On a beautiful but ordinary Saturday morning, Karen Collins took their two young sons to visit their grandparents. Bobby couldn't go because he had to take care of some long-overdue yard work. Karen and the kids were supposed to return by 6:00 p.m. for a family dinner. But Karen, Jonathan, and David never pulled into the driveway. A few hours later, at 10:00 p.m., someone knocked at Bobby's front door. It was the knock no one ever wants to hear.

When Bobby opened the door, he saw John Higgins with tears in his eyes. John wasn't just a fellow officer. He was also Bobby's best friend. That's why John broke the news. He told Bobby that Karen and his two sons had perished in a horrific car accident.

Bobby collapsed into John's arms.

The loss spiraled Bobby into a deep depression. His only solace was a steady stream of anti-depressants. Within a month, he became dependent on drugs, lost his job, and became a loner. Even friends and family couldn't help because he was too far gone. The pain was unbearable. So, with nowhere else to turn to, Bobby convinced himself the only answer was to take his own life.

Bobby grabbed a handgun and walked through his backyard and into the woods. He circled the trees for 30 minutes, trying to summon the courage to end his life. When Bobby finally got the guts, he stopped, closed his eyes, and put the gun barrel to his head. But before Bobby pulled the trigger, someone intercepted his plans.

"Bang, Mr. Collins, you're dead."

Bobby opened his eyes. He put the handgun behind his back and looked to the side. Standing 20 yards away was a young boy from next door. "Little Mike" often played with Bobby's two young sons in those same woods. But today, Little Mike stared straight ahead, pointing his toy gun straight at Bobby.

"Mr. Collins, don't you know how to play cops and robbers?" Little Mike asked. "When I say bang with my gun, you have to fall down. Those are the rules."

Bobby didn't know what to say.

Little Mike came forward. Bobby had to act quickly. He found a hole in a nearby tree and hid his handgun. But Little Mike continued his pursuit and yelled out again, "Bang." This time Bobby cooperated and fell to the ground. Little Mike was ecstatic. He walked up to Bobby and said, "You're my prisoner now, and you have to come with me. Those are the rules."

"So, where is the jail?" Bobby asked.

"Don't be silly, Mr. Collins. Robbers don't have jails," Little Mike said. "Only good guys like you have jails for the bad guys."

"Why don't you pretend to be a cop instead of a robber? Then you can take me to jail," Bobby said.

"I never thought about it," Little Mike said. "I never got a chance because when I played with Johnny and Davy, they were always cops. It wasn't fair, but they said they had to be police officers because they wanted to be like their dad when they grew up."

Bobby got a little choked up, thinking about his sons.

"Mr. Collins, I know I can't play with Johnny and Davy anymore. But can you play cops and robbers with me now? Can you show me how to be a police officer?" Little Mike asked.

Fighting through tears, Bobby said, "I sure will, Mikey. You can count on me."

It wasn't a coincidence Little Mike was in the woods when Bobby's finger was on the trigger. Someone or something stepped in and prevented him from killing himself. He remained alive for a reason, and now he had to find out what it was. But first, he had to go away somewhere, kick his drug habit, and get his life in order.

Bobby heard of Project Diablo through a fellow addict. After a few interviews, he jumped at the chance and signed an agreement. That's how Bobby found his way to the town and went from a potential suicide victim to salvation.

Tümpisa, Wyoming

Bobby opened his eyes and took a deep breath. Before he got up from the bench, he reached into his wallet and pulled out a copy of a note, and read it to himself.

Little Mike:

I won't be able to play cops and robbers with you for a while. I'll be away for a year. My boss put me on a special double-secret investigation to catch bad guys. It's so secret I can't even tell you where I'm going or what I'm doing.

They told me those are the rules.

Don't let my absence stop you from playing cops and robbers. Play with the other kids in the neighborhood. I offer you an officer's promise, good as gold. I will return.

Mr. Collins

P.S. Jonathan and Davy gave me a message to pass along to you. They said that when you play cops and robbers, tell the other kids you're the police officer. If they ask, tell them you want to be like Uncle Bobby when you grow up.

Bobby read the Little Mike note every couple of days. The promise in the message wasn't only for Little Mike; the promise was also for himself. Bobby found a reason to live and something to look forward to. All he wanted was to play cops and robbers with Little Mike once again.

CHAPTER

33

Anniversary

Tümpisa, Wyoming

BOBBY WAS A DEPUTY and the town's longest-tenured officer. Each week he met with the Sheriff to review open issues from the prior week, events in the town, the schedule for the other officers, and how they would deploy resources. But one morning, a call interrupted their meeting. Bobby picked up the call and placed it on speakerphone.

"Good morning. This is Bobby. How can I help you?"

"Morning, fellas. This is James from the Main Street barbershop. We've got a situation here. Somebody came in for a haircut and walked out without paying. Can you meet me at Human Beans so we can confront him?"

"Sure," Bobby said.

The Sheriff looked at Bobby and asked, "Can you handle this?"

"I'm not sure," Bobby responded. "Sounds dangerous. Someone might assault me with an iced latte."

"You want me to tag along, don't you?" the Sheriff asked. "I wasn't born yesterday. You're up to something."

"Me? Have I ever done anything sneaky?"

"Aren't enough hours in the day to answer that question. Let's see what's going on. Maybe I can get a drink while you investigate."

The Sheriff and Bobby walked five blocks to Main Street. It was eerily quiet. Only a few people were on the street, and most businesses seemed closed. The two officers continued along the road toward Human Beans. James was waiting outside.

"Thanks for coming, guys," James said. "Let's confront this guy."

"How do we know who we need to talk to?" Bobby asked.

"It'll be the guy with the shortest hair," James quipped.

The Sheriff and Bobby peeked in the window and saw a crowd of people. That explained the mystery of the barren street. James pointed out the freeloader as they walked inside amongst 75 people. Everyone was milling around and preoccupied with conversation. After a few seconds, they all turned to the front of the coffee shop.

A few of them held up a big banner over their heads.

Happy Anniversary, Drake.

It was Drake Merino's first anniversary in the town.

~~

After Drake had his nervous breakdown in Tampa, he packed up the Range Rover and set out to travel across the country. Drake ran away with no destination in mind. All he knew was he just needed to get as far away from home as possible.

A few weeks into his trip, Drake found himself in an Oklahoma City bar. He sat next to a tall glass of beer after a long day of driving. Drake planned to spend the night in a cheap motel but needed a few beers to help him get to sleep.

After an hour at the bar, Drake noticed two men watching him. He avoided eye contact because he didn't want to bring attention to himself. Drake had a cache of guns and a money roll big enough to choke a horse in the Range Rover. But right before Drake left, the two men approached his table and sat without asking.

"Hello, sir. I'm Joe, and this is Chris, and you are?"

"I'm…uh…Mark, just passing through town," Drake said. He didn't want to reveal his real identity, and Mark was the first name that popped into his head. Drake let them know he worked at the FBI, thinking it would scare them off, but they didn't blink an eye.

The three men spoke for two hours. Joe and Chris turned out to be part of Project Diablo. They were traveling around the country looking for volunteers to fit specific needs for the town. One of the more critical positions on their wish list was law enforcement. They needed someone with the requisite experience. Drake fit the bill. Towards the end of the conversation, Joe and Chris asked Drake to join Project Diablo and become the town's first Sheriff. Drake thought about it for a minute and then accepted.

Drake never wanted to give up his career as an FBI special agent. It was still in his blood. It didn't work out at home in Tampa. Perhaps it would somewhere else.

~

Drake smiled at Bobby and said, "You planned this, didn't you?"

"Me? For as long as I've been here, have you ever seen me do anything like this?"

"Well, if you didn't, tell whoever planned this that I appreciate it," Drake said.

Human Beans emptied after an hour. But before Bobby and Drake left, a woman came up and introduced herself.

"Excuse me, I wanted to congratulate you, Drake," the woman said as she offered her hand.

"Well, thank you…and your name is?" Drake asked as he accepted her warm and friendly handshake.

"My name is Lynn. I've been here a while but haven't been out in public because I've been recovering from surgery. But here I am and thought I'd introduce myself."

"Where are you from?" Drake asked.

"A little bit of everywhere," Lynn said. "I grew up in Massachusetts and have lived in almost every state on the East coast. I was working my way west when I found out about Project Diablo. I needed an escape, and this seemed like an opportunity for a fresh start."

"Well, if you need anything, we're located right down the street," Bobby said. "You can also call us. Our number is posted on every phone in town. If you get voicemail, that most likely means we're out celebrating someone's birthday or anniversary."

"Pay no attention to Bobby," Drake said. "He's over-dramatizing. This town is as safe as any other town. There aren't many disagreements, almost no theft, and absolutely no violence. If you get voicemail, what it really means is that we're most likely in the back playing poker."

"I might have to stop by. I could use some extra cash," Lynn said as she laughed.

"We'll save you a seat at the table," Bobby said.

As Drake let go of Lynn's hand, she looked straight into his eyes. She gave an obvious wink as she walked away.

"Looks like someone has an admirer," Bobby said.

"You're jealous because she's got good taste."

Bobby laughed and said, "Looks more like desperation than good taste if you ask me."

CHAPTER

34

Grand Slam

Tümpisa, Wyoming

BOBBY WASN'T GOING TO LET DRAKE sit at home on his anniversary. He coaxed Drake out of the house and took him to the Bradford Inn, a popular bar named after Jameson in the middle of town. Bobby and Drake found a spot at the end of the bar and ordered a few beers.

Throughout the night, the locals stopped by to introduce themselves and congratulate him on his first anniversary. Some of them even bought him drinks. But there was one person in particular who caught his attention.

"This one is on me," Lynn said as she threw a ten-dollar bill at the bartender. "His money is no good here."

"Well, what brings you here this evening?" Drake asked.

"This is my first time out on the town," Lynn said. "Since the day I arrived, I've been in recovery mode and haven't had any fun."

"What was wrong, if I may ask?"

"I got a severe case of appendicitis, and the doctors removed my appendix," Lynn replied. "There were complications from the surgery, and it took a while for me to get back on my feet."

Drake felt at ease talking to Lynn, an attractive woman six feet tall with an athletic build. She was in Drake's age range but dressed as if she were ten years younger. He noticed something set her apart from the other women in the town. She had a gleam in her eye, which was a window into her soul. Drake sensed Lynn was holding onto a secret. He was intrigued and wanted to find out what it was.

"So, what brought you here, Drake?" Lynn asked as she took a swig of beer.

"The short story is I grew up in Florida, worked at the FBI for two years, and ended up here," Drake replied in a serious tone.

"You're right," Lynn responded. "That is a short story. But everybody in this town is here for a reason. So, what is yours?"

"I lost a bet with my brother," Drake said with a deadpan expression. "Project Diablo needed someone with experience to oversee law enforcement here in town."

"I'm not buying what you're selling," Lynn said. "You have a hidden secret, and I'm gonna find out what it is."

"You're gonna be looking for a long time," Drake responded, breaking into a smile.

Now he turned the tables and asked her the same question.

"So, let me ask you. What's your short story?" Drake asked, taking a swig of beer.

"I grew up in New York, worked in local government for some years, and then ended up here."

"That is a short story. So, what's your reason for being here?"

"I lost a bet with my sister. Project Diablo needed someone with experience to keep tabs on law enforcement here in town."

"Touché," Drake said, as they shared a hearty laugh. Drake and Lynn improvised the back-and-forth exchange as if it were a planned skit. They had a similar sense of humor, which made them feel comfortable with each other. Drake and Lynn talked for an hour but stopped short of sharing too much information. Both had secrets and weren't completely honest about who they were and why they were in the town. They would find out soon enough.

~

The next day, the ring of Drake's alarm clock was taken over by a much louder sound.

Bang, Bang, Bang.

He jumped out of bed, grabbed his throbbing head, and peeked at his watch. It was 9:00 a.m. He was late in reporting to the office. Drake gathered himself and opened the front door with his eyes still half-closed.

"Overslept now, did we?" Bobby asked.

"I...guess so," Drake responded. "I don't remember too much. Did I do anything last night that I should regret this morning?"

"Yeah. You said you were going to double my salary retroactive to the beginning of the year," Bobby quipped.

"I have no control over what Project Diablo is paying you," Drake responded. "You get nothing from me. So, what about last night?"

"No, you were in complete control the entire night," Bobby said. "We were all impressed someone could drink so much and still be in control of their faculties."

"It's all a ruse," Drake said. "I may have been in control the night before, but I'm belligerent and incoherent the next day."

"Just checking in on you to make sure you were okay," Bobby said. "Take the day off and relax. Nothing is going on. I can handle everything at the office."

"Thanks, Bobby. I'll check in later," Drake said.

Drake closed the front door, turned off the lights, and fell on the couch. He stayed in the living room all day, only moving to get something to eat and use the restroom.

At 6:00 p.m., the sun started its descent when he heard something.

Knock, Knock, Knock.

Lynn was outside with a bag of groceries.

"So, what brings you here?" Drake asked.

"I stopped by the office around noon," Lynn said. "Bobby said you stayed home today and weren't feeling well. So, I thought I'd bring you over something to eat. I always heard the way to reach a man's soul is through his stomach."

Drake laughed and said, "Only works if the man has a soul." He pointed towards the kitchen. "What did you bring us this evening?"

"Nothing fancy. I'm not much of a cook. Got some antipasto, bread, and a bottle of red wine. It's about the best I can do on short notice."

After putting everything away, they walked back into the living room. Drake and Lynn ended up talking for hours. Having someone else to talk to made him feel a lot better. Drake took a break to bring the food into the living room while Lynn poured each of them a healthy glass of red wine. They knocked off the bottle in record time.

Lynn then took matters into her own hands. She sat next to Drake on the couch, straddled his body, and then started a sensual kiss. Lynn's actions didn't surprise Drake in the least bit. He knew what would happen from the moment Lynn knocked on his front door. Drake picked Lynn up and brought her to the bedroom, and laid her down. They both continued exploring for a few more minutes. Lynn stopped and put her index finger on Drake's lips.

"I need to confess something, Sheriff," Lynn said in a high-pitched voice.

"What would it be?"

"I've been a bad girl," Lynn said with a smile.

"How bad? Do I need to call for reinforcements?"

"I've been very bad. But you don't need backup. I'm sure you can handle it yourself."

Drake ran his hand up and down her body.

"Sheriff, am I under arrest?"

"Yes, you are. You're in my custody now."

"Sheriff, you better make sure I don't get away," Lynn said as she pointed towards something lying on top of the bedroom dresser.

Drake smiled as he got up to retrieve the item. Lynn laid down on her back, put her hands overhead, and Drake handcuffed her to a bedpost.

"I'm sorry, Sheriff, I didn't mean to hurt anybody," Lynn said as she begged for forgiveness. "But every one of them deserved what they got. I couldn't help myself. I was out of control."

Drake stopped and asked, "What would you like your punishment to be?"

Lynn looked at Drake straight into his eyes and said, "I'm your prisoner. I don't control my punishment. Do with me as you wish."

The next morning, Drake walked into the kitchen to make a pot of coffee. He sat down and took a few sips and realized he didn't have a nightmare for the first time in a long time. Lynn came up from behind and caressed his head.

"Are you feeling better today?" Lynn asked.

"Sure do," Drake said, "I haven't felt this good in a long time."

"Have you ever handcuffed a girl in bed before?"

"Never. Anyone in law enforcement always thinks about it. If they tell you they don't, they're lying. But last night, it seemed right. I'm guessing you've done it before?"

"Yes. It's a big turn-on for me. I've had a thing for law enforcement officers my whole life. It comes down to control. Sometimes I want to be in control, and other times I don't."

Drake recalled what Lynn said at the Bradford Inn.

"Everyone in this town is here for a reason."

Now he wanted to know her reason more than ever.

CHAPTER

35

Abnormal

Tümpisa, Wyoming

THE TOWN HAD ITS SHARE OF MUSICIANS, and it didn't take too long for them to get to know each other. Every Saturday night, they got together at the Bradford Inn to play for the bar crowd. It was therapy for the volunteers. The music let them escape and forget their problems for a few hours.

One Saturday, Drake was at the bar with Lynn and a few friends waiting for the music to start. Everyone was enjoying the relaxed atmosphere. But that changed when Bobby suddenly came in through the front door.

"Drake," Bobby yelled as he pointed outside the bar.

Drake bolted from his barstool with another fellow officer. When they got outside, a middle-aged man was screaming at the top of his lungs as he broke car windows one by one.

"Drake, how do you want to handle this?" Bobby asked.

"Let me talk to him first before we do anything," Drake said.

Drake asked the crowd outside, "Does anyone know his name?"

Someone in the crowd yelled out, "I think it's David."

Drake walked closer to the man. He could smell the alcohol on his breath from six feet away.

"David...are you, David?" Drake asked.

The man stopped swinging and looked over his shoulder back at Drake and said, "Why the fuck do you want to know?"

"David, I'm trying to find out why you have a grudge against car windows?" Drake asked. "Did they do anything to piss you off?"

"You're a funny man with a badge," David said. "Mind your own business and go back inside."

David turned around and continued his assault on car windows. Drake got a little closer. He wanted to try one more time to calm David down.

"David, drop the bat and let's talk," Drake pleaded.

David stopped what he was doing and strolled over to Drake. The tirade appeared over. As Drake reached for his handcuffs, David lunged out at the last second. He cracked the bat across Drake's leg, forcing him to the ground. David spat on Drake.

"Ain't so funny now, is it?" David said.

Bobby and the other officer ran over to help, as David dropped his bat and ran away. Lynn helped Drake get to his feet. He was lucky he didn't break anything. All he had was a severe bruise, which would take a week to heal and go away.

"Drake, do you want us to go after David?" Bobby asked.

"Yes, but be careful," Drake said. "Alcohol can make men think they're ten feet tall and bulletproof. At 5 1/2 feet, you're at a significant disadvantage, my friend."

"Hilarious," Bobby said. "Let's get you home first, and then we'll go looking for him."

~

The following day, Drake woke up with a swollen leg. He realized he wasn't going anywhere for a while. He couldn't stay in bed all day, so he hopped over to the living room couch next to the front door. Drake stayed there until Bobby stopped by around 10:00 a.m.

"Mornin,' Drake," Bobby said. "How are you feeling?"

"Not too good," Drake responded. "I'll be limping around town for a while. Did you find David?"

"No, we didn't," Bobby said. "We went to his house, and there was no sign he ever returned home."

"Considering how drunk he was, he most likely passed out in a field somewhere. Keep your eyes and ears open. If you must, enlist people in the town to go on a search expedition."

A week later, Drake was back in the office, albeit with a slight limp. He was in the middle of his regular weekly meeting with Bobby when the phone rang. It was one of the search parties. They found David, and it wasn't pretty.

Drake and Bobby drove to the outskirts of town to a remote area. After walking with the search team through the brush for a hundred yards, they came upon David's body.

David had signs of blunt force trauma to the back of his head, causing his death. Someone tore off his shirt and used a Bowie knife to carve a diamond into his chest.

Underneath, someone attached a note to David's body.

NEVER HIT A MAN WITH A SHIELD,
BECAUSE YOU'LL END UP DEAD IN A FIELD—JACK

After seeing Jack's message, Drake began hyperventilating and ran back to the car. Meanwhile, Bobby picked up his phone and called Project Headquarters to update Glenn Norris.

"Glenn, we've had a murder on the outskirts of the town near the boundary," Bobby said.

"Oh, my God. Who was it?" Glenn asked.

"His name is David Williams from Ridgewood, New Jersey," Bobby said.

"Where's Drake?" Glenn asked.

"He is in the car," Bobby said. "He had a bad reaction when he saw the body. I'm not sure why."

"I'm on my way into the town," Glenn said. "Sit tight."

Bobby made his way back to the car. Drake was in the front seat, staring straight ahead into space. It looked as if he were contemplating something. Bobby thought it was strange Drake had such an adverse reaction. He was sure Drake had seen far worse situations in the FBI.

"Are you okay?" Bobby asked.

"I'm all right," Drake responded. "Don't know why I reacted that way. Not the first time I've seen a dead body."

Jerry Foster, the Director of Volunteer Data Collection, was fast asleep when his phone woke him with an urgent message.

I'm Falling off the Wagon.

The message came from Jack. Jerry responded.

Call you in 15 minutes.

Jerry jumped out of bed and made his way to the SODA conference room. He turned on the television and selected Channel 23. All he saw was an empty room for a minute, and then someone sat in front of a computer to start a conversation.

"Something is wrong with me," Jack said.

"What are the symptoms?" Jerry asked.

"I feel normal," Jack replied.

"I don't understand," Jerry said. "Normal is not a symptom."

"It is when you are someone like me," Jack said. "When I first came here, I knew who I was. But after a month, something changed. For once, I had a clear mind and forgot about the past. My violent behavior and thirst for control faded away. I became normal."

"Sounds like that is an improvement," Jerry said.

"Not when you're someone like me," Jack said.

"On the weekends, I went out in public and met people. Then I started a relationship with someone. I had always been an antisocial person. To go from a lonely caterpillar to a social butterfly was too much for me. "

"Why did you send me the urgent message tonight?" Jerry asked.

"Someone triggered my old feelings," Jack said. "It reminded me of who I am."

"Who would that be?" Jerry asked.

"I'm the person who decides who lives and dies."

CHAPTER

36

Missing Persons

Tümpisa, Wyoming

EACH WEEKEND, the regulars at Human Beans showed up by 9:00 a.m. to place their usual orders. After picking up their drink of choice, they retreated to a familiar spot somewhere in the corners of the coffee shop. Human Beans was a favorite spot because it was a hub of activity and a front-row seat to everything going on in the town.

Jordyn Michaels was the manager and head barista. She left Los Angeles and volunteered for Project Diablo, hoping it would help her deal with depression. Jordyn became a recluse and rarely went outside of her house. Working at Human Beans helped her forget about a past filled with failed relationships and physical abuse.

There were a dozen regulars who stayed at Human Beans for hours. Most preferred mornings, but a few people slept in and spent the afternoons. In between discussions, stories, and gossip, the regulars wrote in diaries or read books. To them, it was their home away from home.

Some regulars skipped a weekend every once in a while. But they always returned to reclaim their territory. But that would change. Over the past month, something strange happened. Some regulars went missing and never returned.

Ray Nichols, one of the first regulars, strode up to the bar. Ray placed his morning order with Jordyn as he shook his head.

"What's bugging you?" Jordyn asked.

"Notice anything different?" Ray asked as he turned around to face the crowd of human beans.

"Sure, you woke up on the wrong side of the bed this morning."

"No, silly, out there," Ray said as he pointed behind his back to the other human beans.

"You're right. Something is different, but I'm not sure what it is."

"We lost a few of the regulars. Is there a bug going around?"

"Not that I know of," Jordyn said as she poured a cup of joe.

A line of anxious caffeine addicts waited behind Ray.

"Maybe you can get Sheriff Merino to investigate," Ray said with a wink. Jordyn blushed because she had a crush on Drake.

Ray stepped aside and let the other patrons place their orders one by one. But he continued the conversation with Jordyn.

"Are you going to go through your whole life afraid to pursue what you want?"

Jordyn helped each customer while she prepared her answer.

"It's not as easy as you think. Drake has a relationship with a woman in town. I don't want to make a fool of myself."

"Better to take a chance and be a fool now," Ray said. "It might make you feel uncomfortable, but at least you'll know the answer. Otherwise, you'll go through life second-guessing yourself."

Ray knew Jordyn would take the easy way out, which was to do nothing. She lacked self-confidence and needed a swift kick in the pants. Ray wanted to open Jordyn's eyes and give her a sense of hope so that she would take a chance.

"I've got sources inside the law enforcement office who know Drake well," Ray said. "They say he's not committed to this woman you speak of. She keeps throwing herself at him, but the truth is he's leading her around until he finds what he wants."

"What does he want?" Jordyn asked.

"Someone like you," Ray said. "You're better looking than the slut he's hanging with. You've got a good head on your shoulders and can carry on a conversation about anything. Plus, you have an eclectic sense of humor. I almost forgot. You also have a secret weapon."

"Secret weapon?" Jordyn asked as she laughed.

"You're a beautiful young woman," Ray said. "You've got a leg up on that tramp. Use it to your advantage."

Ray made the entire story up and even threw in some harsh descriptors to boost Jordyn's confidence. Later on, he would learn that stretching the truth has its consequences.

As Ray turned around, he bumped into another patron, following a little closer than she should have been. Ray spilled coffee on her. As he apologized, he noticed the patron's eyes staring straight at him, filled with rage. He apologized again and left the coffee shop.

Jordyn passed a bunch of napkins over to the woman to help clean up the mess and said, "That was my fault, so this one's on the house. What would you like this morning?"

"I'll take a Rocky Mountain Brew."

"And what name shall I put on your cup?" Jordyn asked.

"Lynn."

A few weeks passed, and the list of missing regulars increased. Ray and Jordyn were the only ones who seemed to be interested in what was going on. Everyone else in the coffee shop wore blinders. But their guts told them something was wrong. They invited Drake and Bobby to Human Beans after hours to voice their concerns.

"When did you first notice people were missing?" Drake asked as he took a sip of his ice coffee.

"Been about three weeks," Ray said. "I've been coming here every day since I arrived in town. I mind my business and keep to myself, but my gut told me something was wrong. After checking their homes, I became concerned and mentioned it to Jordyn."

"Do you remember the last conversation you had with any of them?" Bobby asked. "Perhaps there's a clue somewhere."

"No, nothing out of the ordinary," Ray responded. "If anything were odd, I would've been all over it."

"Drake, any ideas what is going on here?" Jordyn asked. "There has to be a reasonable explanation. Do you expect foul play?"

Drake looked like he was in deep thought. He took another sip of ice coffee and responded.

"There're two possibilities," Drake said. "First is someone from Project Diablo Headquarters is removing people from the town without us knowing."

Everyone nodded their heads and agreed.

"What is the other possibility?" Bobby asked.

Drake swallowed hard before he responded.

"The second explanation is more ominous," Drake said.

"How so?" Jordyn asked.

"None of us are perfect. We have our demons to deal with," Drake said. "We would like to think we know our neighbors, but the truth is we don't. That also goes for us sitting at this table. We all came here for a reason. We're all running from something. It's possible these people were tired of fighting their demons."

"Are you saying they could have taken their own life?" Ray asked.

"It's the only other explanation," Drake said. "Probably unlikely. This town is small enough that if someone committed suicide, we would know about it by now."

After two hours of brainstorming, the foursome didn't get much farther. Drake's hypotheses seemed to be the only two logical answers. They agreed to assemble three separate search teams in the morning and knock on doors. Drake also said he'd put in a call to Glenn Norris at Project Diablo Headquarters.

When the meeting wrapped up, it was near 10:00 p.m. Jordyn didn't live too far away from Human Beans, but considering the circumstances, she felt a little nervous about walking home by herself.

"Can one of you guys walk Jordyn home?" Drake asked.

Both Bobby and Ray were standing behind Jordyn, who was facing Drake.

"I can't," Bobby said. "I still have to go home and do laundry. Trust me. You don't want me to show up commando tomorrow."

"Sorry," Ray said. "But I need to get home quick to write in my diary before I forget what happened today. My short-term memory isn't what it used to be."

"Those are the two lamest excuses I've heard in a long time," Drake said. "Let's hit the road, Jordyn."

Drake walked out the front door, followed by Jordyn. She smiled and gave a thumbs up to Bobby and Ray. Jordyn got what she wanted.

It should've taken 20 minutes to get to Jordyn's apartment. When they arrived, Jordyn invited Drake in for a nightcap.

"Not sure it's the wisest of ideas," Drake said.

"There's nothing to be afraid of. I don't bite," Jordyn said with a smile, "but I can if you want me to."

An hour later, Drake emerged from Jordyn's apartment. Drake didn't live too far away, so he walked. His house sat by itself on a cul-de-sac, surrounded by three other vacant lots in various stages of construction.

As Drake walked through the darkness, he heard a loud sound, like someone had dropped something on the ground. He turned around and looked at the tree line next to his house. It was pitch dark, and all Drake could make out was the faint outline of someone staring at him. As he walked over, the mysterious person took off running. Someone was following Drake, and it made him feel uneasy.

Inside his house, he read for a bit before going to bed. Just as he closed his eyes to go to sleep, his cell phone awakened him.

Bringgg, Bringgg, Buzzz, Bringgg, Bringgg, Buzzz

"Where've you been, Sheriff?" Lynn said in a childlike voice. "I'm all alone, and I've been scared all night."

"I had a meeting at Human Beans," Drake said. "There was an issue with some residents that Bobby and I had to deal with."

"I know it's late, but if I come over, will you protect me?" Lynn said, this time more seductively.

"Not tonight, Lynn," Drake said. "I'm too tired, and I've got to wake up early. Let's re-schedule."

"Okay, fine by me," Lynn said in her normal voice before breaking off the call.

Drake stared at his phone for a minute. The way Lynn acted was entirely out of character, which made him think twice about their relationship. Drake liked Lynn and enjoyed her company, but he wasn't ready for any sort of commitment. In his eyes, they were two lonely sailboats in the same ocean that sailed together. Nothing more than that.

Drake had to reset expectations to make sure they were on the same page. Little did he know, Lynn was way ahead of him and was already on to the next chapter.

The next morning, Bobby received an urgent call at around 7:00 a.m. It was Michael Crowder, and he was talking a mile a minute.

"Bobby," Michael yelled. "Someone has been murdered in my store. Come quick."

Bobby took two officers with him and walked to Crowder's Convenience Store on Main Street. Michael was standing outside in front of a locked door, pacing back and forth. He was in a state of shock, and tears were rolling down his face.

"Bobby, Bobby, Bobby," Michael cried. "I can't believe this has happened. It's so terrible."

"Michael, calm down and tell me what happened," Bobby said.

"I got to the store this morning around 6:45 a.m. I entered through the back door and walked into the stockroom. A body was hanging from the ceiling. Blood was everywhere. I ran out and locked the door and called you at once."

"Okay, Michael," Bobby said. "We'll take a look."

Bobby took one of his officers and unlocked the back door. When they walked inside the stockroom, everything on the shelves was on the floor. It appeared someone was looking for prescription drugs and sedatives. Bobby peeked around the corner and saw a bloody message on the wall.

THE DEVIL WAS WITH YOU WHEN YOU TOLD A LIE,
NOW YOU MUST PAY THE PRICE AND DIE—JACK

Bobby felt chills up and down his spine. He couldn't look at the corpse anymore, and his eyes wandered down to the floor. He noticed a wallet underneath the hanging body. Bobby pulled out a driver's license and realized who it was—Ray Nichols.

~

In the last week of September, Lynn invited Drake over to her apartment. He had been there only twice and appreciated the change of scenery. As usual, they had dinner and talked for a while. Lynn then grabbed Drake by the hand and led him to her bedroom.

As they embraced in a sensual kiss, Lynn whispered into Drake's ear, "Did you bring them?"

Drake smiled as he reached into his pocket and pulled out his trusty handcuffs. They both laid down on the bed, and Drake tried to put his handcuffs on her. Lynn stopped him.

"Do you remember what I told you the first night about control?" Lynn asked.

Drake shook his head because he couldn't remember. Lynn put her finger on Drake's lips.

"Sometimes, I like others to be in control. But tonight, I want to be the one in control."

While in the heat of passion, Drake gave up his handcuffs to Lynn and stretched out on the bed. He swung his arms above his head, and she handcuffed them to the bedpost. Lynn told Drake to close his eyes and enjoy the show. There was a good two feet between the bedpost and the wall, enabling Lynn to walk back and forth from one side of the bed to the other without Drake seeing her.

There was a long moment of silence. Drake then felt a pinch on the back of his neck. He immediately lost consciousness, and there was nothing he could do about it.

As he drifted away, Drake had a strange thought.

Now I'm going to be one of the missing.

He wondered if anyone would come looking for him.

~

When Drake woke up, he wasn't in Lynn's bed. Instead, he found himself in an unfamiliar room. Someone had chained his wrists and ankles to the bedposts. There was no sign of Lynn or anybody else. Drake was all alone and didn't know where he was.

After three hours, a stranger walked into the room dressed in black from head to toe, wearing a mask, hoodie, and baggy pants. All Drake could see were a pair of empty eyes.

"Who the fuck are you?" Drake screamed. "Where is Lynn? What am I doing here? Goddamn it, take these chains off me."

The stranger sat in a folding chair facing Drake and didn't say a word. He continued his barrage of questions for 20 minutes without eliciting a single response. Drake was on the verge of losing his strength but mustered enough for one last question.

"Who...the hell...are you?" Drake screamed.

The stranger got up and walked to a desk where there was a quart-sized jar and a paintbrush. The stranger dipped the brush and wrote on the wall in big red letters.

ONLY GOD CAN GRANT LIFE,

BUT ANY MAN CAN IMPOSE DEATH.

~

Three times each day, the stranger spoon-fed Drake food and water. It was just enough to keep him alive. He was weak from being chained up and could barely talk. But every few minutes, he kept asking the same question. He wasn't going to stop until he got an answer.

"Who…are…you?" Drake whispered.

The stranger walked to another wall and wrote the following bloody message.

This is the Toughest Decision to Make,
Do I Kill or Spare a Man Named Drake?

"Who…are…you?" Drake whispered.

The stranger stopped for a few seconds, and without turning around, added a signature to unveil their identity.

Jack + Lynn = Jacklynn

The signature confused Drake. He wasn't sure what it meant. The stranger then turned around and untied the hoodie, revealing long, dark, flowing hair. It was Lynn.

Jacklynn pulled up a chair and looked Drake straight in the eyes.

"What the fuck is going on here?" Drake screamed.

"Quite the surprise, isn't it?" Jacklynn asked.

"Jack, Lynn, and Jacklynn. Which one are you?" Drake asked.

Jacklynn stood and paced back and forth in front of Drake.

"I was born Jacklynn Matthews on June 30, 1965. My father was Dr. Carter Mathews, Ph.D., a well-known psychologist. Dad always wanted a boy, so when I was born, he nicknamed me Jack. At first, I didn't like it, but the name became an advantage as I grew older. If I wanted, I could assume different personalities using parts of my name. Something attracted you to Lynn, but you didn't know I was also Jack. That was my dirty little secret."

"Why did you seek me out?" Drake asked. "You must have had an agenda. What did you want from me?"

"I came to Project Diablo to escape the public eye," Jacklynn said. "After my arrival, I learned they set me up and brought here me on purpose. Project Diablo needed a test subject for a new drug that would change human behavior. But the researchers became impatient and wanted to test the drug on the most extreme behavior they could find. They wanted a serial killer and got me."

"Why a serial killer?"

"Pharmatech thought if they could get a serial killer to stop killing, then they could make anyone else do whatever they wanted. The drug worked for a few months. During that time, I felt better about myself. Killing became unimportant. I became a normal person. It gave me the confidence to pursue you."

"Why did you pursue me?"

"When I first introduced myself to you at Human Beans on your anniversary, I had an ulterior motive. I knew you were the Sheriff. To keep killing, I needed inside information on what was going on in the town. Who better to get it from than you? Then the drugs kicked in, and something unexpected happened. I grew fond of you."

"But you didn't stop killing?"

"I stopped for a period," Jacklynn said. "But I found out something the researchers didn't think of that made the drug useless."

"What was that?"

"Love," Jacklynn said as her voice cracked. "I loved you, Drake, and I couldn't stand to see anyone come between us. I killed David after he attacked you at the Town Hall. I killed Ray after he said horrible things about our relationship, and now it's Jordyn's turn."

"Are you planning to kill me too?" Drake asked.

"Perhaps. I was saving you for last because, deep down, I was hoping things would change," Jacklynn said. "It would be the moment of truth. If you didn't love me, then you would be guilty, and I would have to carry out the sentence."

"What is the sentence?"

"Death...it's always death," Jacklynn responded.

"Why do you kill?"

"Someone murdered my parents when I was ten years old," Jacklynn said. "I couldn't understand how God could let it happen. Any faith I had at the time flew out the window. With it went any feelings of love and affection. From that day forward, I didn't care about anything or anyone anymore. All I wanted was the power God didn't have. I wanted to be the one to decide who lived and died."

Jacklynn stopped walking and looked straight into Drake's eyes.

"At first, you were a means to an end. I planned to kill you a while ago, but I couldn't bring myself to do it. I kill those who deserve to die. But I also kill those who disrespect me."

"I never disrespected you," Drake said.

Jacklynn got upset and yelled, "You did. Admit it."

Drake looked down at the floor, not because he felt guilty, but because he was tired and weak.

"Silence speaks a thousand words," Jacklynn said.

"When will you decide my fate?" Drake asked.

"Soon," Jacklynn responded. "I need one other person here."

"Who would that be?" Drake asked.

"Jordyn," Jacklynn said. "I want her to admit in front of us what she did. Then you'll see her suffer the consequences. Based on how it goes, I'll make my decision on whether you live or die."

CHAPTER

37

Reservations

Tümpisa, Wyoming

DOMINIC WAS IN SAN FRANCISCO for the beginning of a two-week coast-to-coast tour of FBI field offices. After landing, he navigated his way through baggage claim and walked towards the rental car counter. A man appeared out of nowhere, holding an 8x10 placard with "Dominic Merino" written in bold letters.

"Are you looking for Dominic Merino?"

The man looked at his placard and said, "Yes. I'm here to take you to your hotel."

Dominic looked at the man's placard and rubbed his forehead.

"I didn't order car service," Dominic muttered.

The man pulled out an FBI badge and showed it to Dominic.

"Special Agent Merino, my name is Special Agent Richard Owens, but everybody calls me by my last name. Travis told me you were coming to visit the office, and I offered to pick you up."

"Well, that's very much appreciated," Dominic said.

"Follow me," Owens said as he motioned towards the exit.

Owens led Dominic to the parking garage. Once they were out of the public eye, Owens hesitated for a second. He had something to say to Dominic.

"I'm sorry. Travis didn't tell me anything," Owens said. "I found out through someone else you were coming to San Francisco. Special Agent Merino, there is something you need to know."

"I'm all ears."

"We found Jack, the serial killer you are looking for," Owens blurted out.

Dominic tried to wrap his mind around what he had just heard.

"What…What did you say?" Dominic responded as his voice trailed off. "Are you sure? You found Jack?"

"Yes, we did," Owens responded. "That's the good news."

"Okay, I see the bad news coming around the corner," Dominic said. "Hit me with it."

"The bad news is we no longer have Jack in our possession," Owens said.

"Did you lose last week's winning lottery ticket, too?" Dominic quipped.

"I know you're trying to be funny," Owens said. "But let me explain."

"The floor is yours."

"We responded to a call of suspicious activity on Pier 54," Owens said. "Right before we arrived, someone murdered two people. There were indications the killer was still in the vicinity, so we checked all the buildings on the pier and apprehended the suspect."

"How did you know it was Jack?"

"The crime scene was horrific," Owens said. "The killer posed the bodies and wrote a cryptic message on the wall. I knew those were Jack's calling cards. The suspect also confirmed their identity."

"Why didn't Travis call me?"

"I think he had eight million reasons not to call you," Owens said.

"What are you talking about?"

"Travis had a deal with someone," Owens said. "He was going to sell Jack to someone in Wyoming. I don't know the name of the person or the company. There's a market for serial killers. Who knew?"

"How did you find all this out?"

"I've got a recording where Travis met with someone and talked about his asking price," Owens replied. "The meeting took place in the back of a restaurant Travis frequents."

"Why did you record the conversation?"

"I didn't record it. Someone else did," Owens said. "I can't tell you his name right now. Let's call him Charlie for the time being."

"Okay. Tell me about Charlie."

"Travis had a meeting in a private room in the back of Charlie's restaurant," Owens said. "He paid Charlie a monthly fee to reserve the space for business. However, Charlie didn't trust Travis, so he recorded the meetings in his restaurant to protect himself. It's a good thing he did because Travis stiffed him."

"What happened?'

"On one recording, he overheard Travis offering to give Jack to someone for $8 million," Owens said. "Travis gave didn't give Charlie a single penny, citing that the FBI confiscated the money. Charlie wasn't happy because he knew it was going into Travis' pocket.

"But how did you end up getting the recording from Charlie?"

"Charlie approached me because he knew I was close with Travis," Owens said. "He wanted to find out what was going on. Charlie didn't know I was in the same boat. I was also shortchanged."

"What were you promised?"

"I was with Travis the night we captured Jack," Owens said. "Travis told me we all stood to make money, and I'd get a good chunk of change. But I got nothing."

"So, you and Charlie were singing from the same sheet music."

"Yes," Owens replied. "Charlie and I teamed up to get revenge. When I found out you were coming to San Francisco, I asked Charlie for a copy of the recording. I wanted evidence, so I could prove to you everything I was telling you was the truth."

"But you realize, now that you told me what happened, you may be considered an accomplice to extortion."

"I know," Owens responded. "But Travis can't get away with this. He needs to be held accountable for his actions."

The two men hopped in a car and continued the conversation. When they arrived at the hotel, Dominic got out of the car and turned back towards Owens.

"Thanks for the information. You did the right thing," Dominic said. "I'll figure out a way to approach this with Travis in the morning. In the meantime, I'll see what I can do legally for both you and Charlie. You'll get something out of this. I just can't promise you anything at this point."

"I understand," Owens said.

Owens handed Dominic a business card for Vincent's Italian Bistro.

"You didn't get that from me," Owens said as he winked at Dominic and drove away.

That evening, Dominic laid in bed as a montage of crime scenes flashed before his eyes. Alden Moore, Taylor Brooks, Danny's Dinner Club, Madison Street Sports, and a host of others. He suffered through three years of hard work, personal sacrifice, and mental anguish. Dominic remembered every failed lead, piece of evidence, and witness interview. Now, with that in the past, Dominic was on the verge of finding the root cause of the carnage.

Dominic grabbed his cell phone and called Norman Jacobson. He spoke with the doctor at least once a month to pick his brain about Jack. Now that Dominic was getting ready for the stretch run, the frequency of the calls increased to a couple of times each week.

"Hello, Dr. Jacobson," Dominic said. "How's the weather in Miami Beach in the fall?"

"Can't complain," Norman responded. "Not used to the warm weather this time of year. That's the upside of retirement."

"What's the downside?" Dominic asked.

"When people retire and move to Miami, something unexpected happens," Norman said. "Suddenly, you find yourself surrounded by others in their late seventies or mid-eighties. That's when reality hits, and you realize you're getting old."

"Age is just a number," Dominic said. "What matters is how you feel inside. But you know that already. You're the psychologist."

"Perhaps," Norman said as he chuckled. "So, what's going on in your neck of the woods?"

"I'm in San Francisco," Dominic said. "I've thought about what you said, 'Death isn't always the answer.' Those words stuck in the back of my mind."

"Why do you think that is?" Norman asked.

"Maybe it's because I'm getting closer to finding Jack," Dominic said. "To take Jack alive will be difficult. No one understands Jack's mind better than you. Why don't you join me?"

"Dominic, I wish I could," Norman said. "If Jack sees me, my life will be in danger. I can't take the chance. But if you have questions or need to talk, I'm just a phone call away."

"Doctor Jacobson," Dominic said. "I don't give up easily. I'm going to keep asking until you say yes."

"Agent Merino," Norman said. "Maybe you don't give up easily, but you're dealing with a stubborn old man. I'll keep it under consideration, but I can't make any promises."

The next day, Dominic showed up at the FBI San Francisco field office by 11:00 a.m. He met with various agents, saving Travis for the last interview. When Dominic got to Travis' office, he stuck his head in the doorway. Travis waved for him to enter. The two special agents shook hands and sat opposite each other, with a small conference room table between them.

"So, what brings you here to the bay?" Travis asked.

"The orders were to get out of the office for a while and go visit all the field offices," Dominic said. "I'm racking up airline miles, so no complaints here."

Dominic talked about a myriad of topics. Much of the conversation dealt with office protocol and compliance with FBI standards. But it was a means to an end. Dominic saved the best for last.

"We've been tracking Jack's whereabouts across the country," Dominic said. "Have you seen or heard anything out on the street?"

"No," Travis responded. "Jack is on the agenda at every staff meeting, but we haven't seen a single crime with any links or similarities."

"Are you sure?"

"Yes, I'm sure. If I came across anything, you would be the first person I'd call."

"Good," Dominic said. "Hey, I didn't eat lunch today. Let's get dinner courtesy of Uncle Sam."

Travis didn't say yes right away, but Dominic applied pressure and forced him to accept.

"Okay, let's get some dinner," Travis said. "Any urges?"

"I was out earlier today and came across a restaurant. The menu was interesting, so I reserved a dinner table for myself. I'll call and make it for two," Dominic said.

Dominic picked up his cell phone and switched on the speaker. He dialed a number, and someone familiar answered.

"Hello, Vincent's Italian Bistro. How can I help you?"

"Hi, this is Dominic Merino. I was in earlier today and reserved a table for one. Can you make it for two?"

Dominic looked straight ahead and waited for confirmation. Travis turned pale, and beads of sweat appeared on his forehead.

"Not a problem, Mr. Merino. Got a nice table towards the back right next to the kitchen."

"Thanks, see you in half an hour."

Travis wasn't dumb. He looked straight at Dominic and figured he was onto something.

"Okay, Merino, what do you want?" Travis asked.

"I want you to be truthful," Dominic said.

"But I have been truthful."

"You have? Well, I've come across three things that make it hard for me to believe you. First, I know Jack has been to San Francisco recently. Second, I found out about the suspicious murders down by Pier 54."

Dominic hesitated for a moment, hoping Travis would come clean. But he didn't.

"You left one out. What's the third thing?" Travis asked.

"I know you captured Jack," Dominic said.

Dominic caught Travis with his proverbial pants on the ground.

"What else is in your crystal ball?" Travis asked.

"Let's cut to the chase here," Dominic said, leaning forward in his chair. "I've got hard evidence. You sold Jack to someone for a chunk of change. Travis, you're in a lot of trouble here, so ask yourself a question."

"What?" Travis asked.

"How much trouble do you want to be in?" Dominic asked.

Travis buckled under the pressure.

"Okay. I'll tell you," Travis said, "but time is of the essence. I'm not sure how much longer Jack will be alive."

Travis got Glenn Norris on the phone, and the two men chatted for 30 minutes. He did it on purpose because he wanted Dominic to listen to the back and forth to show him he was telling the truth.

After he ended the call, Travis said, "Glenn Norris is the person you need to talk to. He knows where Jack is."

"Where is Glenn Norris?"

"He works for a company called Pharmatech in Wyoming. Let me give you his contact information,' Travis said as he jotted down an address and phone number and handed it to Dominic. Travis got his money, so he didn't care if he threw Glenn under the bus. He just needed to figure out how to disappear so he could avoid prison.

Dominic headed for the door, not realizing he was leaving Travis on his own. All he could think about was getting Jack and forgot that Travis had committed multiple offenses. Dominic should have taken Travis into custody.

Once Dominic left the office, Travis had a big smile on his face because Dominic inadvertently allowed Travis to escape prosecution. He immediately called his wife, Diana.

"Honey, time to switch to Plan B," Travis said. "Grab the kids and pack. I'll be home within the hour."

"What's going on?" Diana asked.

"Retirement is here sooner than expected," Travis responded. "We have to leave right away. A plane will wait for us at Sonoma Valley airport."

Travis prepared a contingency plan in case his transgressions caught up with him. No matter what happened, he would not serve his time in a jail cell in federal prison. Instead, he was going to serve his time on a secluded island with his family and 8 million of his closest friends.

~

Cody, Wyoming

Harrison received an email in his office from Wind River Power.

Harrison:

Pharmatech currently has outstanding invoices totaling $1.5 million, which remain unpaid. We reached out to your team but have not received a response. As a result, that leaves us with no choice but to shut off the electrical grid for the town immediately.

Wind River Power is grateful for our relationship with Pharmatech. Our doors are always open for discussion.

Let's talk soon.

Charles Sawyer, CFO - Wind River Power

Never in his wildest dreams did Harrison think he'd look forward to receiving a complaint letter from a vendor. The wheels were in motion, and now all hell was about to break loose.

Harrison placed a call to Dominic.

"Dominic, I received confirmation the electrical grid is shutting down. In a few hours, people will realize what's happening. Not sure how long until Jameson finds out."

"So, go ahead with our plan?" Dominic asked.

"Sure, send the guys here and have them wait outside. I'll call you when the action starts," Harrison said.

Glenn, Dominic, and Bobby sent out a false message to all the volunteers that Project Diablo was over and that everyone was free to leave. They also didn't have to worry about being tracked because, without power, the system was inoperable. Simultaneously, Glenn sent a message to security to stand down and prohibited them from using force.

Two hours later, Harrison received an urgent email from Jameson.

WHAT THE FUCK IS GOING ON?
COME DOWN HERE IMMEDIATELY.

Jameson Bradford's world was unraveling in front of his eyes. No one on The Project Diablo Executive Team was returning his calls. If he wanted to find out what was happening in the town, he had to rely on information from lower-level management.

Harrison strolled into Jameson's office as if it were another financial update meeting. He peeked out the window to give the impression he was looking for something. Harrison then turned to Jameson, who was red in the face and about to burst. Something upset him, and he felt Harrison knew more than what he was letting on.

"What happened, Harry? Why didn't we pay Wind River?" Jameson asked.

"It was the only way to shut down Project Diablo," Harrison said.

"Why would you want to do that?" Jameson asked.

"For two reasons," Harrison said. "First, innocent people have died, and their blood is on your hands. It had to stop. Second, your end vision was dangerous, not just to the country, but to the world."

"I'll fix this right now," Jameson said as he walked to his desk and picked up the phone.

"Not the wisest of decisions," Harrison said. "Look out the window first."

Jameson walked to the window and looked down at the Pharmatech entrance. A dozen FBI special agents were milling around by the front doors.

"Those special agents are coming for you," Harrison said. "They're waiting to get a signal from me to barge in and put you under arrest for multiple counts of murder."

At that moment, Jameson realized it was all over. He stepped back to the window and looked out at Mount Washburn.

"Harry, remember when I asked what you saw outside the window?" Jameson asked.

"Yes. I told you it was a large, majestic mountain overlooking everything within its domain," Harrison responded.

"And what did I say to you afterward?" Jameson asked.

"You said the mountain is Pharmatech, and our domain is the world."

Jameson walked back over to his desk and opened the drawer. He pulled out a small handgun.

"Harry, I envisioned myself on top of the mountain. I wanted more power than any man," Jameson said. "It was my dream, and now it's come crashing down thanks to you, my only son."

Jameson walked in front of his desk within ten feet of Harrison.

"I never wanted children," Jameson said. "I buckled under the pressure and gave your mother a son. She died during childbirth, and I never got over it. I've regretted that decision my whole life, but never more than right now."

Jameson pointed the handgun at Harrison, who couldn't move or breathe. He was waiting for the end to come.

"It wasn't meant for both of us to be on this earth together," Jameson said. "I'm sorry, Harry, but there's only one way to resolve this."

Jameson looked right into Harrison's eyes. He pointed the gun at Harrison with a tense grip for what seemed like an eternity.

After a brief smile, Jameson's body relaxed. Harrison held his breath and remained still.

"If you want to know where to find me, I'll be on top of the mountain," Jameson said.

Jameson smiled one last time, pressed the handgun barrel to his temple, and pulled the trigger. Harrison was in shock.

Harrison recalled Glenn's words from a while back.

> When you're as rich as Jameson, you become desensitized. You can go anywhere and do anything you want. Money and relationships don't mean as much anymore. The only thing you want to attain is the unattainable.

Jameson got his wish and finally had the absolute power and control he was looking for. But it wasn't over his domain. It was over his own life.

CHAPTER

38

Mushrooms

Riverton, Wyoming

THE PHONE RANG at the Super 8 Motel in Riverton.

"Hello, Super 8, where the rooms are great. I'm Wyatt. How can I help you?"

"I'd like to make a reservation," Bobby said. "We need 30 rooms starting this evening. Not sure how long we'll stay. I have a credit card if you need it."

The Super 8 barely sold 30 rooms in a month, let alone in a single day. Wyatt put Bobby on hold and ran to find Liam.

"Mr. Jones, you won't believe this," Wyatt said, out of breath with excitement. "Someone wants to reserve 30 rooms starting tonight. Can we make it happen?"

Liam looked up, "I have a question for you son, do you know what today is?"

"Uh, April 1st," Wyatt responded.

"Correct. Now one more question. You have a bunch of nicknames, but which one do I use most often?" Liam asked.

"Einstein, pinhead, meatball, numbskull?" Wyatt responded.

"Getting closer, try one more," Liam said.

"Oh...I almost forgot. You always call me a fool," Wyatt said.

"Correct. Now put together the answers to those two questions and think about the reservation," Liam said.

"April ...fool," Wyatt asked. "It's April fool's day?"

"Your correct, son," Liam replied.

Wyatt walked out the door. Liam stopped him at the last second.

"Son, remember the person who has a lot of nicknames also has a lot of friends. It's all fun and games."

Wyatt flashed a smile and went back to the front desk and got back on the call with Bobby.

"Sorry to keep you holding, sir. We can take your reservation," Wyatt said. "But I must ask. Is this some kind of April fool's joke?"

"Would I be giving you my AMEX number over the phone if it was?"

The two shared a short laugh as Wyatt reserved the rooms. Soon after, the calls poured in, and others made reservations. An hour later, the Super 8 in Riverton was sold out for the entire month of April.

To celebrate, Liam took Wyatt out for a quick steak dinner. Upon their return, they went to the small hill overlooking the Riverton Regional Airport. The vantage point also gave them an unobstructed view of downtown Riverton and U.S. Highway 26.

When they got to the hill, they shifted their attention from the airport to the highway. A convoy of cars stretched for as far as they could see. Both Liam and Wyatt couldn't figure it out.

"Over the past few years, all these transients didn't contribute two cents to our local economy," Liam said. "Now it seems they're gonna try to make up for it in a month."

"Good for the Super 8," Wyatt exclaimed.

"No, son, it's good for us," Liam responded.

The mass exodus from the town increased the population of Riverton overnight by 25 percent. Some transients were passing through, but many other people had nowhere else to go. Every motel in town quickly sold out for months, so the town reconfigured schools and auditoriums as temporary housing to take care of the overflow. Riverton became a national story. But everyone had the same question.

Who were all these people, and where did they come from?

~

Harrison and Glenn set up a command post with adjacent rooms on the Super 8's top floor. They became the face of what was going on in Riverton. They were the ones the press and public looked to for answers. To this point, their sole focus was ending Project Diablo and evacuating the town. However, they never stopped to think about what would take place in the days that followed.

"Riverton is going viral. People are sprouting up like mushrooms after a rainstorm. What do we tell the public?" Harrison asked.

"We can tell them only so much," Glenn said.

There was a knock on the door. It was Liam Jones.

"Guys, I counted over 50 reporters downstairs. I'm doing my best to hold them off. They're demanding a statement," Liam said.

Glenn and Harrison looked at each other.

"Tell them we'll be down within the hour," Glenn said.

"Guys, can you throw in a plug for the Super 8?" Liam asked.

"Can't promise it, but we'll try," Harrison said.

For the next 45 minutes, Harrison and Glenn put their heads together and came up with a brief statement. It would state the obvious but leave many open questions. Harrison would deliver the message. After all, who better to provide the message than the man who threw the Hail Mary to the end zone.

~

They held the press conference right in front of the Super 8 Motel. Harrison stepped up to the podium amongst a crowd of microphones overlooking a sea of reporters. Behind him were Mayor Joshua Williams of Riverton and Wyoming Governor Robert Anderson. Harrison felt like a lone goldfish amongst a herd of sharks.

> Hello, my name is Harrison Bradford, CFO of Pharmatech based in Cody. Behind me are Glenn Norris, SVP of Operations, and Bobby Collins, the town Law Enforcement Office deputy. Before we leave, we'll pass it off to Mayor Williams and Governor Anderson.
>
> There are a lot of questions circulating regarding the influx of transients in Riverton. However, because there is an ongoing investigation, I cannot answer many of those questions. So, I'll provide a brief statement and give you as much information as I can.
>
> Pharmatech is the largest pharmaceutical company in the world. Companies like ours continuously use research and development projects to identify new drugs to treat diseases and conditions. We created a town just north of Riverton for one of those research and development projects. Pharmatech recruited volunteers to take part. However, because of circumstances beyond our control, the town had to be shut down. As the volunteers left, the first town they came across was Riverton.
>
> Again, because the situation is under investigation, I can't give you any details regarding the project Pharmatech was working on or why the town was shut down. We will provide more information as we can in the coming weeks.
>
> Thanks for your time.

Right before Harrison concluded, Liam and Wyatt appeared behind him wearing Super 8 Motel t-shirts. Harrison looked behind his back and chuckled. He winked at the two of them, which was a sign a plug was on the way.

"One more thing. While we're in Riverton, we've set up shop at the Super 8 Motel, next to the airport," Harrison said. "If you're ever around these parts, stay here. Liam and Wyatt are gracious hosts."

Liam and Wyatt were beaming with pride.

As Harrison walked off, reporters shouted questions. Harrison ignored the media as he did with the runny scrambled eggs on Super 8's breakfast buffet.

Harrison didn't answer a single reporter but heard every question.

"Where is Jameson Bradford?"

"What was your role in the secret project?"

"Were people left behind? Are they alive?"

"How long will the transients be in Riverton?"

"Is it true Jack was in the town?"

Meanwhile, in Miami Beach, Norman was in his recliner watching everything unfold on cable news. He saw Harrison's news conference from the Super 8 in Riverton. At the end, he heard something he couldn't believe. To make sure it wasn't his imagination, Norman replayed the spot a second time. It was the last question from the press pool that sent a chill up and down his spine.

What was Jack doing in Wyoming?

Cody, Wyoming

Harrison was resolute in his feelings about Jameson's passing. It didn't bother him the least bit because Jameson had so much public disdain for his only son. For Harrison, there was no mourning period and no tears. The day after Jameson committed suicide was just an ordinary day. That's all anyone needed to know about how Harrison felt about his departed father.

But there was still an issue of what to do with Pharmatech, and Harrison had three options. First, shut the company down. Second, sell the company to a competitor. Third, take on the challenge and help the company rise from the ashes. Harrison would wait awhile before deciding on Pharmatech's fate. Much depended on what happened in the ongoing investigation and how he wanted to deal with his estranged and departed father's memory.

Harrison drove back to Cody and stopped at Pharmatech before heading home. It was late on a Friday, and almost everyone was out of the building. Harrison walked up to his office and sat down for a few minutes to reflect on everything that had happened. He stayed for about an hour, then packed up his laptop and some personal items. As he walked out, a familiar face appeared in the doorway.

"Harrison, what are you doing here?" Brandon said.

"Picking up a few things and then heading home," Harrison said.

"Sorry about your dad. Are you doing okay?"

"Sure, I'm fine," Harrison responded.

"What's going to happen to the company without Jameson?"

"I'm not sure, Brandon," Harrison replied. "This could be the end of the road. We'll know in the coming weeks."

"Hey, can you stick around for 30 minutes? I want to walk out with you." Brandon said.

Harrison wasn't sure if he would ever return to Pharmatech, so it only seemed fitting to walk out with his black knight. When Brandon returned, they both headed out the front door. When they got outside, Harrison stopped in his tracks. He blinked his eyes a few times and smiled from ear to ear. Brandon had cleaned the tires on Harrison's car and applied Armor All.

"Now, why did you do that?" Harrison said with a big smile.

"It's Friday. I know you like shiny tires," Brandon responded.

"Thanks, Brandon. This may be my last day at Pharmatech. If it is, I will remember this forever."

The two shook hands and parted ways. Harrison then yelled one last piece of advice towards Brandon.

"Hey, Brandon, when you get home, make sure you pay your power bill."

Harrison and Brandon both smiled, got in their vehicles, and drove off into the sunset.

CHAPTER

39

Found & Lost

Cody, Wyoming

A VISIT TO PHARMATECH HEADQUARTERS begins with a long wait in a large reception area. It's what you would expect when dealing with one of the largest companies in the world. But throw a top-secret project into the mix, and it takes the waiting game to a whole new level.

Security at Pharmatech is paramount. Each visitor is posed a series of questions to verify their identity and confirm meeting details. Afterward, a metal detector scans each person while a guard searches through personal items. If everything checks out, it's onward to the reception desk for further scrutiny and directions.

As Dominic waited in the security area, he noticed passersby looking at him as if he had two heads on his shoulders. People scratched their temples, trying to figure out where they had seen Dominic before. There must have been something tipping them off he was an FBI special agent. He just didn't know what it was.

Dominic waited half an hour in the reception area before someone called his name. He strode up to the reception desk and met a young girl named Aria.

"Good afternoon. My name is Dominic Merino. I'm with the FBI. I'm here to see Glenn Norris."

"Hi, Mr. Merino," Aria said. "I can check to see if he is available. Was he expecting you?"

"I don't have an appointment or meeting. But I need to ask Glenn a few questions about a particular case we're working on back in Washington."

"No problem," Aria said. "Please take a seat on the couch, and I'll see if I can track him down."

Aria took his contact information and called Glenn, who then made a phone call to Harrison.

"Harrison, I received a message from Aria," Glenn said. "Someone from the FBI is in your office looking for me. Does anyone else know what's going on?"

"I can't see how," Harrison responded. "The two of us are the only ones. But maybe we should speak to him. Perhaps the FBI can help us."

"I agree. Let's meet with the agent," Glenn said. "But let's do it here in Riverton, so we're near the town."

"Okay," Harrison said. "I'll have Aria set up the meeting," Harrison said.

Riverton, Wyoming

Three days later, Dominic met Harrison and Glenn at the Riverton Regional Airport. He drove from Cody the night before while Harrison flew in the morning of the meeting. Glenn commandeered one of the black SUVs used to transport volunteers from the airport to the town. It was spacious and private enough for their meeting.

Dominic parked his rental car and jumped into the back seat of the SUV. Glenn and Harrison were already sitting in front. After introductions, Dominic explained his quest to find Jack and how it led him to Pharmatech. When it was Glenn and Harrison's turn, they told Dominic the entire story of Pharmatech and Project Diablo, which included why Jameson needed Jack in the town. They shared their plans to end Project Diablo and their quest to stop Jameson.

"Dominic, we need your help," Glenn said.

"Why get the FBI involved?" Dominic asked.

"The odds are against us," Glenn said. "We're not sure if we can get a thousand volunteers through armed security."

"We're working with local law enforcement inside the town to build a small team to lead the charge from the inside," Harrisons said. "But with the help of the FBI, we stand a better chance of succeeding."

"Did you say there is law enforcement inside the town?" Dominic asked.

"Yes," Glenn said. "The Sheriff is someone...Hey, this is an odd coincidence. He has the same last name as you, Merino."

"Is it Drake...Merino?" Dominic asked as he watched both Glenn and Harrison nod their heads in agreement.

Dominic always thought the pursuit of Jack would lead him back to his brother. He closed his eyes to collect himself. It was too good to be true. Dominic thought his mind was playing tricks on him, or perhaps he was dreaming. But when he opened his eyes, neither was the case. A few tears trickled from the corners of his eyes.

"Guys...Drake...is my brother," Dominic said as he tried to catch his breath. "He has been missing for a long time, and I've been trying to track him down."

"Oh, my Lord," Harrison said.

"Unbelievable," Glenn exclaimed.

"I've got to get to the town as soon as possible," Dominic said. "I've got to find Jack and save my brother before it's too late."

"Dominic, you can't walk into the town on your own free will," Glenn said. "Nobody can suspect anything. Harrison, what's the date and time when the town will go dark?"

"Not sure yet. Wind River hasn't given us any sign if or when the electrical grid will shut down," Harrison said. "Once we get payment notices and other correspondence, then we'll have a better idea."

"How do we get Dominic inside the town without looking suspicious?" Glenn asked. "Let's set up a call with the town. We must coordinate together to pull this off."

The next morning, everyone dialed in. Harrison was back in Cody while Glenn and Dominic returned to the Riverton Regional Airport. Meanwhile, no one called in from the town. Then ten minutes later, they heard Bobby's voice on the speakerphone.

"Hello, this is Bobby from the town's law enforcement office. I'm here with the entire team, except Drake, who hasn't shown up today. We're not sure where he is. We're trying to track him down."

"Bobby, we can't continue with this call without Drake," Glenn said. "Go find him, and I'll schedule a call for later today. We can't afford to waste any more time."

"Will do," Bobby responded. "I'll give you an update later."

Bobby called later in the afternoon and told Glenn that Drake wasn't at home and remained missing. Everyone was concerned.

Something happened to Drake.

They had to find him before it was too late.

Tümpisa, Wyoming

Once the turboprop landed at Riverton Regional Airport at 1:00 p.m., Andrew Morgan stepped onto the tarmac. He panned the majestic mountains in the background and took a deep breath of brisk Wyoming air.

A convoy of SUVs appeared out of nowhere and took Drew, Larry, and the other volunteers to Project Diablo Headquarters. When they arrived, Janet Barnes greeted everyone, and the orientation process began. Over three days, Drew sat through the meetings and interviews and endured physical and mental tests. The last stop was at the dentist. After the dental hygienist cleaned Drew's teeth and took x-rays, he waited for a half-hour in the chair until the doctor came into the room.

"Hello, Andrew, I'm Dr. Thomas. There's root decay on one of your premolars. But don't worry. We'll take care of it."

Drew squinted his eyes. He knew his teeth were fine. In fact, he couldn't remember the last time he had as much as a cavity.

"Hey, doc," Drew responded. "How were you able to determine what was wrong without peeking into my mouth?"

Dr. Thomas hesitated for a second and said, "The...uh...x-rays told me everything I needed to know. Let's numb you up and take care of this."

The hygienist handed Dr. Thomas a syringe filled with lidocaine, which he injected at different spots in Drew's mouth.

"I'll be back in 15 minutes. That's enough time for the area to get good and numb," Dr. Thomas said.

Drew didn't understand why Dr. Thomas numbed his entire jaw and tongue when the root decay was confined to the left side of his mouth. Drew thought it was suspicious. Something was going on.

There's no need for that much lidocaine. I think I got a parting gift.

Afterward, Drew boarded a converted school bus with nine others to head back to town. The bus pulled onto Main Street and let off the volunteers at a small apartment building, their temporary home, until someone assigned permanent housing.

Drew checked in and wasted no time dropping off his belongings in his room. He then ran out and headed straight for the law enforcement office. On the way, many of the town's residents stared at Drew as if he were from another planet. They had seen him before. They just weren't sure from where.

When Drew arrived, he stopped outside to catch his breath. Staring at the building, Drew was shaking with anticipation because his search was almost over. After taking a deep breath, he both walked inside. Two officers greeted and escorted him to Bobby's office.

"The infamous Andrew Morgan," Bobby said, offering an outstretched hand.

"I'm Andrew Morgan to some people," Drew said, "but my mama calls me Dominic."

Dominic Merino put his Andrew Morgan persona to rest and sat down across from the lobby.

A thousand thoughts ran through Dominic's mind. But foremost, he had the one question he was afraid to ask.

"Do you know where Drake is?" Dominic asked.

"I haven't seen him in a week," Bobby said.

"What were the circumstances around his disappearance?" Dominic asked. "Was anything going on at the time he went missing?"

"Drake went missing around the same time others went missing in town. Search teams are trying to find them," Bobby said.

"We need to increase our efforts," Dominic said. "That means more people, even if they're not part of law enforcement. Map the territory and make sure we leave no stone unturned."

"Dominic, I understand what this means to you. We'll help as much as we can. We will find Drake," Bobby said as he put his hand on Dominic's shoulder.

"I've been looking for my brother for the longest time," Dominic said. "The only thing I can do is keep a positive outlook and assume he's alive. I've been there for him my entire life, and that's the way it will be to the end."

Dominic wiped away a tear from his eye and continued.

"Bobby, find recruits right away. We need at least five teams of five people," Dominic said. "In the meantime, I'll poke around the town and ask questions. I also have contacts at Pharmatech that might shed some light. Let's touch base every three hours by phone, starting at 9:00 a.m. every morning."

"Sure thing, Dominic."

Bobby cocked his head and stared at Dominic for a moment.

"What's wrong, Bobby?" Dominic asked.

"Hey, did you know if you got rid of that scraggly beard and lost the baseball cap, you could pass for Drake?"

"That's because he is my brother," Dominic chimed in. "But even though we look alike, I'm still the better-looking Merino."

Dominic went back to his apartment. After a long day, sleep was on the agenda. But when Dominic got back to the room, he couldn't fall asleep. His mind was preoccupied with thoughts that the search for his brother wouldn't end well.

An hour later, Glenn called Dominic to relay information he received from Harrison about Wind River. They were going to shut the electrical grid off within a week.

"I know the first thing on your mind is finding your brother this week," Glenn said, "but we can't lose sight of next week. When the power goes out, there will be chaos. The mass exodus will overwhelm the security team. We need to chip in and direct people to the exits."

"I understand, Glenn," Dominic responded. "The plan is to use the search teams we're assembling this week as support for next week. Don't worry. We'll be ready."

After the call, Dominic's eyelids became heavy, and he finally could go to sleep.

In the SODA room at Project Headquarters, there were 75 computer terminals. Each screen had four quadrants with live closed-circuit feeds. The video streamed from cameras placed throughout the town in high-security areas and remote locations. Towards the back of the room, thirty larger monitors tracked the higher-profile volunteers. Staff analyzed the incoming feeds. If they came across an issue, someone brought it to management's attention at once.

Glenn Norris stopped by the SODA room late Saturday night. Once he passed through security, he met Dr. Deborah Thornton and Jerry Foster. The three of them walked into a small theater accessible only by executive management. Inside was a large high definition television. The video started as they were sitting down.

"Thanks for coming. I know it's Saturday night, but there's something you need to see," Jerry said.

Jerry pointed to the screen, which showed an unconscious man chained to a bed. He was moving but was still alive. No one could make out who the man was except for Glenn. He bit his lip, swallowed hard, and took a deep breath.

"Jack is holding someone," Dr. Thornton said. "We're not sure who this man is."

"This video feed has monitored Jack from the beginning," Jerry said. "We know all the camera locations because we placed them ourselves at specific spots in the town. But no one is familiar with the room we see here on the screen. It's almost as if someone moved the camera to a different location."

"To complicate things further, the data from Jack's implanted chip is malfunctioning," Dr. Thornton said. "We're getting inconsistent metadata related to vital signs, body fluids, and brain chemicals. Even the GPS information is inaccurate. We're not sure what's happening. Jack could be anywhere."

Glenn sat in silence for a few moments and then responded.

"So, what you're telling me is a notorious serial killer is loose in a town with a thousand people. The killer has free rein to go anywhere and do anything. Then, to make matters worse, you've lost the ability to track the killer's whereabouts?"

"That about sums it up," Jerry said, as his voice cracked.

Jerry and Dr. Thornton slumped in their chairs in silence.

"We're not sure what to do, and we can't tell Jameson," Dr. Thornton said. "Any ideas?"

"You're right about one thing," Glenn said. "Jameson is the last person to tell. I wish I had an answer for you, but I don't."

At that moment, the lights flickered, and the power went out throughout the building. The three of them could hear staff outside scrambling for flashlights. Within minutes, generators kicked in to keep everything up and running. But the generators only had enough power for 24 hours. In the past, that would have been more than enough time for Wind River to fix any issues.

Both Jerry and Dr. Thornton still had blank faces when the lights came back on, but Glenn had a huge grin.

"I don't have an answer to your problem," Glenn said. "But if I were you, I wouldn't worry too much because, in two days, Jameson will have a much bigger problem on his hands."

Glenn walked to his car but, before leaving, texted Dominic a short message.

Drake is Alive.

CHAPTER

40

Pick Your Poison

Tümpisa, Wyoming

THE POPULATION IN THE TOWN dwindled from 1,000 to less than 50 people. With the volunteers liberated, Dominic could shift his focus on finding Jack.

Reports came in of suspicious activity in a remote area on the outskirts of town. Dominic and Bobby went to investigate. As they drove down Main Street, Dominic glanced inside Human Beans and saw Jordyn sitting by herself.

"Bobby. Pull over for a minute," Dominic said. "I want to go see Jordyn for a minute."

Bobby parked right outside Human Beans as Dominic got out of the car. He stopped in to see if she was okay.

"What are you still doing here?" Dominic asked. "You should evacuate like everybody else. It's time to go home."

Jordyn's eyes were red. She had been crying.

"I can't leave," Jordyn said. "This is my new home. The place where I learned a life lesson."

"What would that be?" Dominic asked.

"That nothing is more important than friends," Jordyn responded. "I've met so many people here at Human Beans. Each one of them became part of my family. Ray is dead and others are still missing. Their presence is within these four walls. It's hard to leave."

"Look, Jordyn, I understand your pain," Dominic said. "But you can't stay here much longer. The town has no power. You won't survive."

"I know," Jordyn said. "I'll leave at some point, but I'm not there yet."

"I've got to go, but I'm going to return before I leave the town," Dominic said. "We have two more places to check first. Promise me not to do anything stupid. Wait for me. When I come back, I want to see one last human bean."

"I'll be here," Jordyn responded with a smile.

~

Dominic and Bobby drove out to the same area where they discovered David Williams's body. When they got out of the car, they met Todd, who led one of the search parties. They walked through a wooded area along a narrow dirt path for two hundred yards until they came upon a small abandoned house.

"Hope you have a strong stomach," Todd said. "What you're about to see is hell on earth."

"Don't worry about me. I've already seen the work of the devil," Dominic responded.

There wasn't much to see when they walked in the front door, just a large family room with a couch and a couple of tables. The walls were barren, and the place looked as if it had been unoccupied for quite a long time. The family room branched off in two directions. A hallway on the left led to two bedrooms, while the entrance on the right led to the dining room. An extended galley kitchen connected the bedrooms and the dining room.

"Pick your poison. Do you want to go left or right?" Todd asked.

"Neither sounds like a desirable choice," Dominic said. "Let's go right to the dining room."

"To each his own, let's check out the last supper," Todd said.

In the dining room was a large rectangular table which sat six people. At three of the place settings were bodies in various stages of decomposition. There was one open spot at the head of the table. Dominic had an eerie feeling that someone was reserving the spot for somebody he knew. The group was silent as they walked from the dining room, through the kitchen, and to the two bedrooms.

"I like to refer to this scene as 'the unhappy ending.' The night started well for these two, but along the way, something went wrong," Todd said.

Dominic was tired of Todd's inappropriate use of humor.

They walked into the first bedroom. It was barren except for a bed, dresser, and night table. Sprawled out on the bed were two more bodies of a man and a woman in an embrace.

"Do we know who these people are?" Dominic asked.

"We recognize three or four. They are part of the missing we are looking for," Todd said. "Looks like we have a serial killer amongst us."

"Any more bodies?" Dominic asked.

"Don't think so, but you never know what might turn up when you're in a house of horrors," Todd said.

"What about the other bedroom?" Dominic asked. "Anything in there?"

"Just an empty room, but we can check it out," Todd said.

The group walked into the second bedroom. It was empty, with an 8x10-foot rug in the middle of the floor. Dominic looked at Todd, who gave him a strange facial expression.

"What are you waiting for?" Todd asked.

"A smart-aleck comment," Dominic responded. "You shouldn't take death so lightly. Respect the departed."

"Look, this isn't something you see every day," Todd said. "Humor is my defense mechanism. Without it, I'd have to face reality and most likely a nervous breakdown."

"Understood," Dominic said, "but it still isn't funny."

As Dominic walked around the room, he stepped on the rug and felt something uneven beneath his feet. Dominic rolled back the carpet to expose a trap door and stairs. They carefully walked down underground to an unfinished basement.

In the distance, there was a glimmer of light from another room. It reminded him of the light which emanated from the front door of Alden Moore's home. The only difference was that Dominic was hoping for a much better outcome.

With his heart in his throat, Dominic walked towards the faint light seeping underneath an unlocked door. A quick turn of the knob swung the door open. Tears rolled down Dominic's face.

"There you go, saving my life again," Drake said in a hushed tone. "How many times is this now?"

"Too many to count, Drake," Dominic said as he and the others tried to unchain Drake from the bed.

"Dom, you didn't follow instructions. I wrote in the letter you didn't have to look for me," Drake said.

"Yeah, but the letter also said we'd see each other again, somewhere, someday," Dominic responded. "Guess what? Today is the day."

"Good thing. I was on my last legs; I don't know how much longer I could have survived," Drake said. "Sometimes, in life, timing is everything."

"Timing isn't everything. It's the only thing," Dominic responded.

~

Jacklynn drove along Main Street dressed in traditional serial killer couture, a black outfit and matching hoodie. She parked across the street from Human Beans. As Jacklynn sat in the car, something didn't seem right. All the shops seemed lifeless, and vehicles headed in different directions. Something was going on. Jacklynn rolled down her window and flagged down a passerby named Landon.

"Excuse me, do you know what's going on here?" Jacklynn asked.

"Haven't you heard?" Landon replied.

"No. I've been stuck at home for a while," Jacklynn said.

"The news is there is no power in the town, and The Project is over," Landon said. "Law enforcement has ordered us to leave as soon as possible. It's time to go home."

"How can you leave? Security will stop you," Jacklynn said.

"Without power, nothing is holding us back," Landon said. "They can't stop us. I'm on my way to New York. Where are you from? Where is your home?"

"Since I was a child, I've been traveling around the country," Jacklynn responded. "I'm not from anywhere, and I don't have any place to call home."

As Landon walked away, Jacklynn sped off but didn't go back to her apartment. Instead, she drove to a boarded-up house in a wooded area. Jacklynn noticed a dozen men milling around. They found the house, so she assumed they had discovered what was inside.

Jacklynn couldn't kidnap Jordyn and bring her to the house, so she needed a backup plan. So, she drove back to her apartment, packed what she could, and returned to Main Street. She had another idea about how to deal with Drake and Jordyn.

~

Lynn parked across the street from Human Beans. It was early evening, and no one was in the coffee shop, except for Jordyn sitting at a table by the window, staring straight out into space.

"Are you still open?" Lynn asked as she stuck her head in the door.

"Yes, but we're limited in what we can serve with the power out," Jordyn said as she blew her nose.

"Are you okay?" Lynn asked. "Is something bothering you?"

"I'm okay," Jordyn said as she blew her nose again, "It's just a crazy time right now."

"How so?" Lynn asked. "What's going on?"

"I don't want to leave," Jordyn said.

"Why would you leave?" Lynn asked.

"Haven't you heard? Project Diablo is over. The power is out in the town," Jordyn said. "Law enforcement has ordered us to leave as soon as possible. They're telling us to go home."

"But security will stop you," Lynn said.

"Not anymore. Without power, headquarters can't track us, and there is no boundary," Jordyn said. "The residents outnumber security. Nothing can stop anyone from leaving."

"Why are you still here, then?" Lynn asked. "Why are you sitting in a dark coffee shop with no power?"

"I have friends that are missing, and I can't leave without knowing what happened to them," Jordyn said. "I'll leave at some point. Just not right now."

"Is anyone looking for them?" Lynn asked.

"Sheriff Merino and his team were searching, but now he has gone missing," Jordyn said as tears came to her eyes. "Drake is a special person. I can't leave without knowing he is okay."

"How well do you know him?" Lynn asked through clenched teeth.

"He came in here every day for coffee, and we knew each other casually," Jordyn said. "Sometimes, he would walk me home. I always hoped Drake would look at me differently, and it would turn into something. But he was in a relationship. I wish I had told him how I felt before he went missing. That's my biggest regret."

Lynn was boiling inside. Jordyn didn't know who she was talking to.

"I have a feeling you'll see Drake again," Lynn said with a fake smile.

Jordyn looked up with glassy eyes and smiled back.

"I'll check on you later to make sure you're okay," Lynn said.

"Thanks," Jordyn responded.

Lynn walked out of Human Beans with all the information she needed. Now she had to figure out what to do.

CHAPTER

41

The Verdict

Tümpisa, Wyoming

THE MERINO BROTHERS, Bobby, and Todd drove to Drake's house to plan their next steps. After Drake took a shower and changed into some fresh clothes, he trudged into the living room empty-handed.

"Sorry, guys," Drake said. "If I knew company was coming over, I would've ordered a couple of pizzas and a case of beer,"—Drake scratched his head—"But, now that I think of it, I couldn't anyway because my hands were tied."

Everyone looked up at Drake at the same time. They all had a "did he just say that" look on their face. Dominic flashed a glassy-eyed smile at his brother. Hearing Drake joke around after everything he had been through was priceless.

"I know we have serious business to discuss, but I couldn't help myself," Drake said.

"No worries," Dominic said. "Hearing your corny jokes is music to my ears."

"All jokes aside," Todd said. "I'm hungry. Do you have anything at all in this house?"

"Check the kitchen, but I doubt you'll find much," Drake said. "Anything in there is most likely spoiled."

Todd got up and went to investigate. Dominic's stomach rumbled, so he joined him. In the kitchen, they found two warm bottles of water and a half-empty box of Raisin Bran. As they reached in the box for a handful of dry cereal, something drew their eyes to the outside window. A napkin was taped to the window with a message.

To See Coffee Girl Alive,
Be at Human Beans at Five—Jack

"What does this mean?" Todd asked.

"Jacklynn has Jordyn," Dominic said. "She's trying to lure Drake to Human Beans."

"What should we do?" Todd asked. The two men stepped outside and made sure Drake and Bobby were out of earshot and couldn't hear them.

"Todd, I need to confront Jack by myself," Dominic said. "Drake is in no shape to do anything right now, and he'll get himself killed. But to do this, I need your help."

"How can I help?" Todd asked.

"We're staying here tonight," Dominic said. "I'll leave before dawn. If I'm not back by 6:00 a.m., go to Human Beans and look for me. In the meantime, play along for now. But promise me one thing. Don't tell Drake where I am until he wakes up."

"Are you sure you want to do this?" Todd asked.

"Yes," Dominic responded.

"Okay, I promise. I won't anything," Todd said.

They walked back into the living room.

"Guys, I got a call from FBI agents by the front gate near headquarters," Dominic said, even though it wasn't true. "They secured all the exits and, based on reports, they believe Jack is trapped in the town. Let's get some sleep and continue our search at daylight. We'll have a better chance in the morning."

Drake went to his bedroom and flopped on the bed while everyone else found a comfortable place to crash in the living room. At 4:00 a.m., Dominic got up, put on his shoes, grabbed his handgun, and headed for the door. As he was leaving, he saw Todd looking at him. Dominic flashed a "thumbs up," and Todd reciprocated.

At 6:30 a.m., Drake woke up and walked into the living room. After rubbing his eyes, he realized something was missing.

"Where's Dominic?" Drake asked.

"Dominic left early in the morning to go to Human Beans," Todd said. "He wanted to confront Jack and save Jordyn. He made me promise not to tell you. But it's been over two hours, and we haven't heard from him."

Without hesitation, Drake headed for the door and said, "Let's go." Todd and Bobby followed close behind.

~

When they arrived at Human Beans, they huddled together.

"Bobby, secure the back entrance," Drake said. "I'll go in through the front. Todd, you don't have a weapon, so it's not safe for you to go inside. I'll leave you my phone. If you see or hear any sign of trouble, speed dial #5, and it will automatically connect you with the nearest FBI special agent."

Drake checked his handgun to make sure it was loaded.

"Do you want me to go in through the back door?" Bobby asked.

"No need. I want Jack to think I'm by myself," Drake said. "I'll yell if I need you."

Drake worked his way to the front entrance with his gun drawn and noticed a gleam of light. It reminded Drake of the ominous words in the doorway when he walked into Alden Moore's house.

YOU MAY ARRIVE A VISITOR,
BUT YOU MAY LEAVE A VICTIM.

When Drake pushed the front door open, he smelled a trap. Inside, Human Beans was a minefield of cups, saucers, and dishes strewn around the store. Broken coffee pots and utensils were in odd places. Coffee stains were everywhere. All were signs that a struggle had taken place. Someone had fought for their life.

With the power out, the only light available came from two candles. In the back of the coffee shop, two chairs were facing towards the wall. As Drake got closer, he saw Jordyn tied to one chair and Dominic to the other. Their heads were pointed down towards their chest. Both had injuries and appeared drugged, floating in and out of consciousness. Drake heard footsteps as a shadowy figure emerged from the back of the store.

"Who is entering my chamber of justice?" Jacklynn asked.

"Drake Merino, the person you want to kill," Drake said.

"How can that be?" Jacklynn asked. "You're right here in the front row with your secret admirer awaiting your sentence."

"I'm Drake. The person in that chair is my twin brother Dominic."

"I'm not sure I should believe you. I think you're a figment of my imagination trying to disrupt the court."

Drake walked a little closer so Jacklynn could get a better look. Her eyes darted back and forth between Drake and Dominic.

"I'll admit there is an uncanny resemblance," Jacklynn said. "You do look like brothers, but you're a day late and a dollar short. The judge and jury have concluded the man in the chair is guilty."

"Guilty of what?" Drake asked. "Dominic has done nothing."

"You were late." Jacklynn said. "You missed the verdict."

"What is the sentence?"

"It's death…It's always death," Jacklynn responded.

"I'm Drake. Sentence me and not my brother."

Jacklynn paused for a few moments and once again looked at both Drake and Dominic. She wasn't sure if Drake was sitting or standing. Drake reached into his back pocket, pulled out a set of handcuffs, and threw them towards Jacklynn onto the floor.

"Remember these handcuffs?" Drake said. "You told me that sometimes you want to be in control, and other times you don't."

"Ah. So, you are telling the truth," Jacklynn said. "You are Drake,"—She kicked the handcuffs out of the way—"There is no need for these because I'm in control tonight."

"Let my brother go," Drake ordered. "Put me in that chair."

"I wish I could, but I can't," Jacklynn replied. "Your brother may not be guilty of your crimes, but he is considered collateral damage. He was in the wrong place at the wrong time."

Jacklynn moved next to Dominic, pulled out a knife, and put the blade against his throat.

"So Drake, I'll give you a chance to save your brother's life," Jacklynn said. "All you need to do is answer one question."

"What is the question?" Drake asked.

"It's the moment of truth," Jacklynn said. "Do you love me?"

Drake looked into Dominic's eyes. They were halfway shut, and he had little time left. Drake was about to fire his gun when suddenly…

Bang!

A single shot rang out, knocking Jacklynn and the knife to the ground. The gunshot came from Bobby, who emerged from the back of the store. He disregarded Drake's orders and snuck in to see what was going on. Bobby saw the situation and reacted. At that moment, Bobby heard Little Mike's voice in his head.

When I say bang with my gun, you have to fall down.

Bobby smiled and said out loud to himself, "Those are the rules."

~

Jacklynn writhed in pain. For a moment, Drake excused himself from rational behavior. He didn't hesitate as he had done in the past and knew what he had to do. There would be no arrest and no long drawn out trial. Drake would serve justice on the spot.

Drake walked up to Jacklyn and stood over her.

"Jacklynn, you thought you were the divinity, that you were second in command. You thought you were the one who could decide who lives and dies. Guess what? You were wrong. Now I get to play judge and jury, and the verdict is in. I never loved you and never will."

Drake pressed his handgun against Jacklynn's temple.

"You might wonder what the appropriate sentence is. I'll refer to your own words. It's death, always death."

When Drake pulled the trigger, time stood still. Even though it was only a fraction of a second, it seemed like a lifetime. The bullet traversed the chamber and made its way through Jacklynn's head. As blood flowed like a river onto the floor, Drake experienced a rush of emotions and temporarily lost consciousness.

When his eyes closed, his nightmare returned. Drake was a ten-year-old boy once again at the bottom of the pool. Someone tugged his arm and carried him to the surface. Only this time, it wasn't a headless Alden Moore that saved his life. It was his brother Dominic. Sonny turned out to be right after all.

Always be there for your brother,

because your brother will always be there for you.

CHAPTER

42

Call Me Charlie

Tampa, Florida

A MONTH LATER, after a quick investigation, the FBI reinstated Drake to full-time status. They concluded he acted within his authority in the death of Jacklynn Mathews. The FBI turned a blind eye. They could have charged Drake for murder. Instead, they let him escape prosecution so that he could get revenge for the death of his fiancé.

Drake walked in the front entrance to a warm reception filled with hugs and handshakes. Before Drake got to his desk, he passed by Dominic's office. It was dark, empty, and lifeless. That's because his brother wasn't there. Dominic was still in the hospital, recovering from his injuries.

Dominic sacrificed his life for Drake. It wasn't the first time, but hopefully, it was the last. Drake knew there weren't enough years remaining to repay his brother. But that didn't mean he wouldn't spend the rest of his life trying. So, he started by breathing life back into his brother's office. Drake turned on the lights, opened the blinds, and booted the computer. It was Drake's small gesture to pay tribute to his brother.

"Look who it is, Drake Merino," Special Agent Henry Tomlinson exclaimed as he walked in and shook hands. "Welcome back."

"It feels good to be in the office again," Drake said.

"If Dominic knew you were setting up shop here, he'd kick your ass," Henry said.

"You're right," Drake responded, "but I'll take my chances."

After Henry left, Drake cleaned up Dominic's desk and came across a sticky note with Dr. Jacobson's phone number.

Drake was intrigued and called the number. Norman didn't pick up, so Drake left a message. Norman returned the call later in the day.

Bringgg, Bringgg, Bringgg

"Special Agent Merino," Drake said.

"I've called, sent emails, and left messages without a response," Norman blurted out. "Not responding is disrespectful. So, tell me, Agent Merino, why have you been ignoring me?"

"Who am I speaking with?" Drake asked.

"Dr. Norman Jacobson."

"I haven't been ignoring you. I received no communications." Drake said. "How can I help you, doctor…did you say Jacobson?"

"You've already forgotten me? I'm Dr. Norman Jacobson. Jacklynn was my patient for years. I gave you privileged information."

"I'm sorry, but I don't know you, Dr. Jacobson," Drake said. "This is the first time we've spoken."

"Son, are you losing your memory? I have your FBI card and entered your number into my cell phone. How did I get your number if we've never met before?"

"Dr. Jacobson, I don't have an answer," Drake responded.

Norman was about to have a fit.

"What kind of game do you think you're playing here? I may be close to my golden years, but my mind is as sharp as a tack. I'm a well-known psychologist, been on television, and written best sellers. I've treated some of the most famous people in the country. Be straight with me. Agent Merino, why are you lying?"

Drake put the phone down, switched on the speakerphone, and shook his head.

"Dr. Jacobson," Drake said. "I know what the problem is here."

"What is it?"

"I'm not Dominic Merino. I'm his twin brother, Drake. I moved into his office this morning and forgot where I was."

There was silence on the other end of the line.

"Well, pinch my ass and call me Charlie," Norman said, "I've never been so embarrassed in my life."

"No worries, it's not the first time, and it won't be the last," Drake said.

"What happened to your brother?" Norman asked.

"Dominic was injured when we confronted Jack. He is still in the hospital but will be out soon. I'm keeping his seat warm for him until he returns to active duty."

"Oh. What happened to Jacklynn?" Norman asked.

"Jacklynn was killed. She was moments away from killing Dominic and one other person. We used lethal force to save lives."

There was silence on the other end of the line.

"I knew this day would come," Norman said. "I always wondered how I'd feel about Jacklynn's death. Now I know. It's kind of strange. She deserved to die for all the crimes she committed. But Jacklynn was also my patient, and I saw another side of her the public wasn't aware of. She was a troubled human being."

"I understand where you're coming from, but her death brought closure to many people. It was the right ending to a terrifying story."

"How long have you worked for the FBI?" Norman asked.

"Interesting question," Drake said. "I became a special agent and worked alongside my brother. I had some issues. Jacklynn's crime scenes haunted me for a while. The FBI put me on medical leave to figure things out. But I had a nervous breakdown and ended up running away from all my problems. I was in Wyoming for two years."

"Did you ever go see a psychologist?" Norman asked.

"No," Drake said. "Guess I was too proud to get help."

"I'm retired, but if you're ever interested, I could help," Norman said. "Everyone has hidden demons. When you don't know where they are, they take over your mind. But the good news is you can learn how to avoid them."

"Drake, I can get rid of your demons."

"Thanks doctor," Drake responded. "I'll keep that in mind."

Drake woke up in his bed, screaming once again.

The nightmares returned, but now they were led by both Jacklynn Mathews and Alden Moore. A crowd comprising other crime scene victims followed close behind. Drake laid in bed for hours, wondering what to do. He then heard a voice in his head.

It was Norman Jacobson—*Drake, I can get rid of your demons.*

Drake was sick and tired of running from his fears. Whether he won or lost, the battle didn't matter. All he knew was that it had to stop. Drake called Norman to get help.

"Hello, Dr. Jacobson, this is Drake Merino."

"Are you sure?" Norman joked. "Last time we talked, you had an identity issue."

"Not anymore. It's me, Drake. Is your offer still on the table? I need to talk to somebody."

"It sure is. I'd be more than happy to help. Monday is open. Let's meet at your house. It might take a few sessions, but I'm confident we'll find the underlying cause of your nightmares."

"I sure hope so, because I can't live the rest of my life like this. Do me a favor, please keep this private. I don't want anyone to think I've regressed."

"No need to worry. There's a physician-patient privilege. Anything you disclose stays between us."

"Didn't you break physician-patient privilege by telling the FBI about Jacklynn?"

"Yes, but it was the only time I did so in my entire career. It was an extraordinary set of circumstances. There's nothing to worry about unless you plan to go on a murder spree."

As Drake resumed his life, there was a fear he would have a relapse. He tried to be strong but struggled without Dominic by his side to look out for him. Kurt saw the kinks in Drake's armor and tried to assume Dominic's role until he returned. He watched out for his neighbor and friend.

Kurt visited Drake as often as possible without being too intrusive. Everything seemed normal until a strange visitor started appearing. For two straight days, an older man parked in front of Drake's house and walked inside. Each time, the man stayed for the entire afternoon. Kurt was curious, so on the third day, he enlisted Jacques to help him find out who the man was . Kurt opened his back door and pointed towards Drake's house.

"Go on over and see Uncle Drake, Jacques," Kurt said. "You know you want to. I'll stop by to pick you up soon."

Jacques, armed with marching orders, meowed as he trotted next door. Kurt watched from a distance as Jacques climbed on Drake's deck and scratched at the back door. It took about ten minutes for Drake to let his furry friend inside.

Kurt waited half an hour before walking over to Drake's house to reclaim his cat. He was hoping his innocent plan would force Drake to introduce him to his visitor. Kurt followed Jacques's exact path and climbed on the deck. But instead of scratching the back door, he opted for a more conventional method.

Knock, Knock, Knock.

Drake opened the door.

"Jacques is missing. Is he here?" Kurt asked.

"Yeah, he's here," Drake responded.

Kurt spotted the man in the living room behind Drake and yelled out a friendly, "Hello!" The man responded in kind.

Drake grabbed Jacques, handed the feline to Kurt, and walked outside. He knew Kurt was wondering who the man was.

"Who's your visitor?" Kurt asked.

"Kurt, the man is a doctor, helping me get through a few things," Drake responded. "I'm okay, just getting therapy. Please do me a favor and keep this between us. I want no one to find out. People might think I'm headed downhill again."

"Don't worry, your secret is safe with me," Kurt said. "Just checking up on you. Making sure everything is in order. If you need anything, you know where to find me."

"Thanks, Kurt," Drake said.

As Drake closed the door, he walked back into the living room.

"Neighbor?" Norman asked.

"Yeah, Kurt Schwartz from next door," Drake said, "He knows I've been through a lot and is checking up on me."

"How does it make you feel?" Norman asked.

"On one hand, I appreciate he's concerned and wants to see me get back to normal," Drake said. "But I don't like everyone thinking I'm weak-minded. I don't want to spend my life living in fear."

"Today, we'll see what we can do," Norman said. "It's time we climb Jacobson's Ladder."

Norman didn't have the luxury of spending a year with Drake to perform a myriad of tests. Instead, he used the first couple of days to accelerate the process. Norman took half an hour to explain Jacobson's Ladder to Drake and how it could help him. Drake was excited and felt he was on the verge of finally finding a solution to solve his issues.

Jacobson's Ladder was Drake's last hope. He had no choice but to confront his fears. He couldn't run away from it anymore. Because, for the first time in his life, there was nowhere else for him to run.

CHAPTER

43

The Deep End

Tampa, Florida

IN THE MID-1970S, the Merino family hopped into an early model station wagon every summer and drove from Jacksonville to Miami Beach to vacation on 'Motel Row.' It was a string of oceanfront luxury resorts replete with pristine beaches, eclectic food, and top-notch entertainment.

The Merinos had pleasant memories of their summers in Miami Beach. But for Drake Merino, those feelings were a stark reminder of a darker time. It was hard to remember the happiness of summer vacation. A single moment of terror overshadowed it all. A moment that left a deep scar on Drake's psyche that would never go away.

After all these years, Drake needed to figure out how to get rid of his demons once and for all. He was tired of running away from his fears. That's why he agreed to climb Jacobson's Ladder.

Drake's living room wasn't ideal for a therapy session, but it had to do under the current circumstances. Norman sat in a chair perpendicular to Drake, who was sitting opposite him on the couch. Norman induced his patient and began the session.

"Drake, are you feeling comfortable?" Norman asked.

"Yes," Drake responded. "I've never done this before, so if I fall asleep, let me know."

"Guess that means I need to stay awake, or we might be here for a long time," Norman said as he chuckled.

Norman set up his recording equipment.

"What are you doing?" Drake asked.

"There's a good chance we won't be able to recall what happens when we climb the ladder," Norman said. "Most likely, I'll have to rely on the recording to find out what happened."

"Okay."

"Let's start. Grab the first rung of the ladder and tell me the year."

"2009."

"Now, look along the ladder. What do you see?" Norman asked.

"The past."

"Good. Now grab the next rung and tell me the year again."

"2008."

"Grab the next rung."

"2007."

"Keep going until you reach the year where your story begins."

Drake stopped in 1975, almost three decades in the past.

A 43-year-old Drake Merino was in Miami Beach, standing outside the Colonial Inn. He was watching his family unpack the station wagon. The moment was both surreal and confusing. It was hard for Drake to wrap his mind around the fact he was in two places at the same time. Drake was once again a young boy, reliving the events of that day. But he also was an adult, seeing everything from a distance.

"How can this be?" Drake asked. "How is the past the present?"

A man standing next to him introduced himself and explained.

"Drake, it's me, Dr. Jacobson, by your side. We've traveled on the Ladder back in time. You stopped in 1975 on this day for a reason. Let's find out why."

"Dr. Jacobson, I know what is going to happen, and I'm afraid I might not survive. I'm not sure if I can go through with this."

"One step at a time. If you feel you can't go on, raise your right hand, and we can stop. But let's try to see how far we can go."

"Okay, but stay close."

"I will. Now let's walk through what happened."

Drake swallowed hard and started to sweat.

"The day began like any other," Drake said. "There were a lot of other kids my age. We spent most of the time on the beach or in the game room. But we also walked around exploring the resort and tried our best to stay out of trouble."

"Was there anything you were afraid of?" Norman asked.

"Yes, there was. The resort had an Olympic-sized swimming pool surrounded by thousands of sunbathing vacationers. I stayed as far away from it as possible."

"Why was that?" Norman asked.

"I never felt comfortable around water because I didn't know how to swim. Back home, everyone had a pool except for our family. My friends would invite me over to go swimming, but each time I had a convenient excuse. I kept avoiding the truth for years until the anxiety, insecurity, and self-consciousness became overwhelming."

"Okay, you were afraid of the water. You're not the only one," Norman said. "As long as you kept your distance from the pool, you were safe, correct?"

"Yes, but all that changed during this vacation," Drake said. "Mom surprised me with swimming lessons. She didn't know about my fear of the water. Suddenly I had a problem to solve."

"There were two choices. You could face your fear or run from them. My guess is you chose the latter."

"You're a smart man, Dr. Jacobson," Drake said. "When it came time for my daily swimming lesson, I said goodbye to Mom and walked to the opposite end of the resort. Once I was out of her sightline, I made a beeline for the game room. After an hour of ping pong and pinball, I jumped into the kiddie pool to make it seem like I had been in the water for a while. It was the perfect plan as long as you discount the fact it came from the mind of a ten-year-old."

"On the surface, it was a good plan," Norman said. "But not all plans are successful. As the saying goes, 'Sometimes the best-laid plans of mice and men often go awry.' True for most people, but even more so for ten-year-olds."

Drake laughed at Norman's little joke.

"You're also clairvoyant, Dr. Jacobson."

"The swimming instructor found out I was spending lessons behind the flippers of a pinball machine," Drake said. "He decided to teach me a lesson. So one day, the instructor marched up to the game room, grabbed me by the arm, and dragged me to the pool. I was kicking and screaming all the way."

"What was going through your mind?"

"As we got closer, I became desperate and clawed and grabbed onto strangers," Drake said. "I yelled at the top of my lungs and looked for someone to save my life. But all I got in return was a crowd filled with blank faces and deaf ears."

"What happened next?"

"The instructor took me to the deep end of the pool," Drake said. "My most prominent fear was right in front of me. I was crying because I knew what was about to happen. The instructor threw me into twenty feet of water, and I sank to the bottom like a rock. I tried my best to switch into survival mode but panicked instead. Within seconds I lost both consciousness and hope."

"You gave up and decided to die?"

"Yes, it was the easy way out," Drake said. "Wherever my next destination was, it had to be a better place. I didn't want to live in fear anymore. Ending my life was the only option."

"But something happened. You're still alive."

"You're an expert analyst, Dr. Jacobson," Drake said.

"Before passing out, I felt the tug of my right arm. Someone grabbed my limp body and brought it to the surface. After regaining consciousness, I opened my eyes and saw a welcome sight. Standing over me was my brother, Dominic. He saved my ten-year-old life."

"So, there was a happy ending," Noman said. "It looks like God intervened at the right time and sent someone to save you."

"That's one way to look at it," Drake said. "I was grateful to be alive, but it came with a significant cost. All I remember is the blank expression on people's faces. I wondered what was going through their minds. The more I screamed and pleaded for help. The more everyone ignored me. Why did they all sit by and do nothing?"

"There are three types of people in these situations," Norman said. "First, there are those who think it's not their business to get involved. Second, others assume somebody else will respond. Third, there are a few who will help."

"That may be true, but this crowd was different," Drake said. "The thousands of vacationers surrounding the pool were all judging me. I saw it in their eyes. It was as if they had collectively decided I was guilty of something and deserved what was coming."

"It looks as if the near-death experience and your perception of the surrounding crowd at the time was the genesis of your anxiety, insecurity, and self-consciousness," Norman said. "Perhaps that's why you're not strong-minded. That is why evil is winning in your mind. Evil knows where your weakness lies, and it takes advantage."

"But why?" Drake asked. "What does evil want from me?"

"Don't worry, Drake," Norman said. "We need to climb forward on the Ladder to find out. We'll find the underlying cause of this. Our session may take a while, but we'll find the answer."

"What if we don't find out? What if evil wins? Will God let that happen?" Drake asked.

"You know there's someone we both knew that had the same question," Norman said. "I had a patient who asked her grandmother, and she said that during our lifetime, sometimes evil wins. It's just a test of our faith. But be reassured to know even though evil may sometimes win the battle, God always wins the war."

"That sounds like one of Sonny's maxims," Drake said. "He always said the weak always have a chance to win the battle, but the strong always win the war."

"There is a reason those statements are so similar," Norman said.

"Why is that?" Drake asked.

"It's because both statements are true," Norman said.

Norman helped Drake off the ladder. When Drake was conscious, Norman provided some immediate feedback.

"Drake, we have accomplished quite a bit in a short period," Norman said. "I'll have to review the recording, but my gut tells me there is good news and bad news."

"I always like to start with the bad, so hit me with it, Dr. Jacobson," Drake said.

"The bad news is you need to address something that you've ignored your entire life," Norman said. "You'll have to do something difficult that you never thought you would ever have to do."

"Okay, now tell me the good, Dr. Jacobson," Drake said.

"The good news is I know how to get rid of your demons and your nightmares forever," Norman said.

CHAPTER

44

Old Routine

Tampa, Florida

DRAKE HAD ALREADY RETURNED TO WORK, but he didn't return to his usual routine. The shortest and most direct way for Drake to get to the FBI Tampa Field Office was to drive past Political Donuts. Seeing the donut shop brought back bad memories. It was the backdrop for the events which led to his nervous breakdown, forced him to run from his fears, and almost ended his life.

He purposely took a longer route to the office, to avoid Political Donuts, which added 15 minutes to his commute. After his sessions with Dr. Jacobson, Drake realized if he was going to move forward with his life, he needed closure. He got the strength to stop by Political Donuts. He wasn't sure what he would find when he got there. When Drake walked in, he saw Billy Walsh, who managed the store.

"Drake, it's been such a long time. How have you been?"

"Hi Billy, do you have a few minutes to talk?" Drake asked.

The two walked to the back office for some privacy.

"Billy, I want to apologize for what happened a couple of years ago," Drake said. "I should have prevented the robbery, but something terrible happened. I don't know if I'll ever get over it."

"No worries, Drake," Billy responded. "There's nothing to be sorry for. Things happen sometimes, and we must accept them. Haven't thought about it since, and you shouldn't either."

Drake then asked the one question burning inside of him. He wasn't sure if he could handle the answer but needed to know. He braced himself for the worst.

"On the day of the robbery, I had an opportunity to save Nikki and didn't," Drake said. "That night, I saw her in the hospital. She was on her deathbed. I ran away like a coward, so I wouldn't know what happened. If no one told me she died, then in my mind, she was still alive."

Tears trickled down Drake's face.

"But now everything is different. I can handle the truth. Billy, please tell me what happened to Nikki."

Billy paused for a few seconds and took a deep breath.

"Drake, you're right. Nikki was in bad shape. She lost a lot of blood and was in intensive care for a while," Billy said. "But there's nothing to worry about. She recovered and is alive."

The tears continued to trickle down Drake's face, but now they were tears of joy.

"Do you…do you know where she is?" Drake asked as he wiped his face.

"She never came back to work here," Billy said. "It was too traumatic for her. Over the past two years, she stopped in once or twice to say hello, but that's it. If she stops in again, I'll call you and let you know."

"Thanks, Billy. I appreciate it," Drake said.

"Drake, before you go, make me a promise," Billy said. "Next time you drive by, make sure you stop by here and pick up breakfast. From this point forward, it's on the house."

"Billy, there's no need—" Drake said before he was interrupted.

"Look, Nikki meant a lot to you, but you can't go through life avoiding places and situations because of what happened in the past," Billy said. "The sooner you face your fears, the sooner you'll heal. Move on with your life. I'm not asking you to stop by here for the free donuts and coffee; I'm asking you to stop by, so you can get over this and get back to normal."

Drake shook Billy's hand and promised he would stop next week. Billy watched Drake walk away and realized how important Nikki was to him. After all this time, Billy had thought Drake came to Political Donuts because of the donuts and coffee. He turned out to be wrong.

There was something else Drake liked.

The following Monday, Drake slipped back into his routine. He woke up early and went out on the back deck with a cup of coffee. Drake watched the sunrise. Then, after getting ready for work, he ran his usual errands.

His first stop was Race Trac to fill his gas tank and grab a newspaper. He walked in, picked up a Tampa Bay Times, and made his way to the cashier.

"Well, look who we have here," Brian exclaimed. "How are you doing, Drake?"

"Much better," Drake responded. "Thanks for asking."

"Hey, look at you. No more bags under the eyes," Brian said. "You don't look ten years older anymore."

"It doesn't make me look ten years younger?" Drake asked.

"I'm afraid not," Brian quipped. "You'll need some plastic surgery for your ugly mug."

I was hoping you would say 'yes' so I could start dating younger women," Drake said as he walked out the door.

~~

The next stop was Designer Cleaners to drop off and pick up dry cleaning. He flung a bag on the counter filled with shirts and pants.

"Hello, Mr. Drake," Luis said, as he turned to get Drake's clothes. "How are you doing this morning?"

Hearing Luis' voice again was comforting.

"I'm doing fine, just a little nervous."

"Did you see the Tampa Bay Devil Dogs last night? They made three home runs and beat the Yankees of New York 3 runs to 2."

Luis remembered the last time they spoke and wanted to steer the conversation as far away from work as possible. Luis's choice of topic wasn't his strongest suit. He knew as much about sports as Drake did about tying bait onto a fishing rod.

"Luis, I think you mean the Tampa Bay Devil Rays and the New York Yankees," Drake said.

"Oh, you're right, Mr. Drake. What do the kids say nowadays? Is it 'my very bad'?"

"No, dad, they say 'It's my bad'," Christopher said.

Drake laughed and said, "Close enough."

"Luis, it's about time you learn about the game of baseball. I'll pick up tickets, and I'll take you and Christopher to a game next week. My treat."

"Great, Mr. Drake. I was wanting to go to a baseball game."

"When we go to the game, I need a favor from you," Drake said.

"What's that?"

"Drop the Mr. part. My name is Drake."

"Sure, Mr. Drake…" Luis said. "I mean…Sure, Drake."

~

The final stop was Political Donuts. When Drake pulled into the parking lot, he shut the car off and took a deep breath. Drake looked into the rearview mirror and told himself that it was time to move on.

It was a beautiful day. There wasn't a single cloud in the sky. All Drake could see was a sea of bright blue stretching across the horizon from one end of the earth to the other. The sun was at its peak, and there was a light breeze.

As Drake drove to the donut shop, a Beatles song suddenly came on the radio. It was from *Abbey Road*, their final album. Only this time, the song wasn't "The End." It was "Here Comes the Sun."

The front doors of the donut shop were wide open to welcome in the good weather. When Drake walked in, there was only one customer in front of him. When he got to the counter, he saw Billy.

"I wasn't sure you were going to make it here this morning."

"Until now, I wasn't sure either. Just trying to live up to my promises. I thought about what you said. You were right. I need to come back here regularly and move on with my life."

Drake looked at the menu board.

"So, tell me what you have on the left and right side of the aisle this morning."

"Today is something special," Billy said. "The donut of choice is neither left nor right. It's something you've wanted for the longest time, an independent donut that stands on its own. We lost the recipe a few years ago, but we found it this week."

"That's awesome. What is it?"

Billy excused himself and walked in the back to get the donuts. Drake noticed no one else was in the shop and thought something seemed strange. It brought back memories of the day he stumbled upon a robbery in progress. After about a minute, someone walked out with the donuts.

It was Nikki.

Drake ran behind the counter to give Nikki a big hug. Billy worked overtime to track her down. He was relentless and didn't stop until he found her.

After Nikki recovered from her injuries, she knew Drake took it extremely hard and blamed himself for what happened. She tried to track Drake down, but he had run away and was impossible to find.

"Nikki, I can't tell you how much it means to see you," Drake said. "I wasn't sure if you would make it and couldn't accept the truth. I ran away because it was my fault."

"Drake, it wasn't your fault," Nikki said. "You didn't come into the donut shop with a knife. I've been depressed for the longest time because I thought I was the reason you left."

The two hugged again. It seemed like a dream.

"Let's get together and get reacquainted…without donuts," Drake said.

"Sure, let's go to dinner on Friday night," Nikki said.

"I won't look at another donut or pastry until then," Drake said.

The two laughed and hugged one last time.

Drake went to Political Donuts, only hoping to gain closure. But he never thought in his wildest dreams he would see Nikki again. Drake never felt more alive in his entire life.

As Drake left to go to work, he heard Taylor's voice in his head.

This is not the end. There goes the darkness.

It's only the beginning. Here comes the sun.

CHAPTER

45

Independence Day

Tampa, Florida

DRAKE CIRCLED SATURDAY, July 4th on his calendar.

The day commemorates the anniversary of the thirteen original colonies becoming the first states. But somewhere along the way, celebrating the birth of a country descended into the background of consciousness. Over time, Independence Day became a day of fireworks, small-town parades, family barbecues, beach trips, and afternoon baseball games. Independence Day means something different to every single citizen. It doesn't matter how people observe the holiday. The important thing is once each year they celebrate life, liberty, and the pursuit of happiness.

But for Drake, this Independence Day had an alternative meaning. As people around the country remember the nation's birth, Drake would celebrate a rebirth of mind, body, and soul. He would take his life back once and for all. Drake would gain independence from the anxiety, insecurity, and self-consciousness which haunted him. Drake realized if he wanted to rid himself of his demons, he couldn't do it by himself in his living room. He needed people, a few familiar faces, to witness his redemption.

Drake planned for a small Independence Day party with family and friends. The morning of July 4th, Drake kicked off the day by joining Kurt for a couple of hours fishing on the lake. He was on the dock early. Drake wanted to watch Kurt launch the boat. He took mental notes for later in the day.

Jacques started head-butting both Drake and Kurt. He was beside himself with excitement. Within half an hour, they were all out on the lake in Kurt's boat, enjoying a beautiful morning.

"Kurt, thank you for your advice," Drake said. "You were right. If you want to catch something, you have to use the right bait. That's how we tracked down Jacklynn and put an end to all the murders."

"No need to thank me. I'm just an old fisherman who knows a few things here and there," Kurt said. "You and your brother did all the work. You would've caught Jacklynn even without my advice."

"Perhaps, but you know what's funny about your advice?" Drake asked. Kurt shook his head.

"When you talk about the right bait, I never thought in my wildest dreams the bait would be me," Drake said.

Kurt put his hand on Drake's shoulder, and his rod shook. He hooked a fish, and it was a big one. It took a good five minutes to reel it in. Jacques jumped on the fish, and Kurt removed the hook.

"It's the first fish I've ever caught in this lake," Drake exclaimed.

"If you're going to wait your whole life to catch your first fish, it might as well be a big one," Kurt said. "It's a largemouth bass, probably 18 inches."

Drake grinned from ear to ear. It was a great sign of things to come.

~

Everyone showed up, including his parents Sonny and Mary, brother Dominic, and other friends and neighbors. Even Nikki showed up. But someone was missing. There was one person he needed there to make it all work. Finally, at 4:00 p.m., the face Drake was waiting for appeared.

"It's about time you got here," Drake said.

"There was more traffic than I thought," Norman said. "I know how important this day is to you. I wouldn't have missed it for the world. Are you ready?"

"Never more in my life, Dr. Jacobson," Drake said. "I'm ready to do something difficult, something I thought I would never do."

"Does anyone else know what's about to happen?" Norman asked.

"Not a soul," Drake said. "People will panic, but everything will turn out all right."

"Good luck, son," Norman said. "Godspeed. I'll be pulling for you."

At 6:30 p.m., about two hours before sunset, Drake slipped away from the crowd and made his way over to Kurt's dock. He pulled the boat 30 feet from land. Norman had his eyes on Drake and provided cover. Once he received a sign from Drake, Norman turned everyone's attention to the lake.

Drake was 50 yards from the dock, standing in Kurt's boat along with Jacques. He stood on the front part of the boat. Drake was about to do something he thought he would never do.

He jumped into the lake.

Back on land, everyone gasped.

Mary fainted as Sonny yelled, "The boy can't swim, he doesn't know how to swim, he's committing suicide."

People shrieked in horror. Neighbors scrambled for their boats to save him. It was as if Drake was saying goodbye to everyone all at the same time. Drake sank to the bottom of the lake. As he sat there, he felt at peace for the first time in his life. For once, he didn't need a tug from anyone. Drake was on his own.

Two boats arrived, and all they saw was Jacques sitting in the boat. They feared they were too late. Right before they jumped into the water, Drake's head popped up. He pulled himself onto the boat and smiled. Everyone was relieved.

Drake's family and friends were witnesses to his rebirth. He conquered his greatest fear and the genesis of his anxiety, insecurity, and self-consciousness.

It was his Independence Day.

~

When Drake returned to the boat dock, everyone welcomed him with warm towels and hugs. None lasted longer than the hugs received from Mom and Dad. But the question everyone wanted to ask was, "Why did you jump in the lake?"

Drake's answer was, "I just felt like it. I wanted to be the center of attention. After all, it's my party...I'll dive if I want to." Drake laughed at his little joke.

After drying off, Drake sought Kurt to apologize. "Sorry for stealing your boat, Kurt, but it was something I had to do," Drake said.

"I wasn't the least bit worried." Kurt said, "Jacques was with you. If something were wrong, he would have let me know. I knew you would be okay."

Norman walked up and gave Drake a big hug.

"You did it, Drake," Norman exclaimed. "You overcame what you thought was impossible. Now, anything is possible."

"Thanks, Dr. Jacobson," Drake responded. "I wouldn't have been able to do it without climbing the ladder."

Kurt was standing by and seemed confused.

"What does climbing a ladder have to do with jumping in the middle of a lake?" Kurt asked.

Drake and Norman looked at each other and said, "Everything."

~

Later that evening, there was a fireworks show in the distance. Afterward, everyone relaxed on the deck with beer and wine under the moonlight. The stars came out of hiding, and the night was sparkling. It was the end to a perfect day.

"Look at the moon. I've never seen it so big and bright. It's the most beautiful thing in the world," Drake said.

"Drake, what were you thinking? Why did you jump in the lake? Your mother almost had a heart attack." Sonny said.

"Dad, you always said for decisions. The head is adept, the heart is ardent, but the gut is absolute," Drake said. "I trusted my gut, and I am a better person for it."

"But that doesn't answer the question," Sonny said. "Why? Why did you do it?"

"Sometimes the obvious question can be the key to the ambiguous answer," Drake said. "Your question is simple, but it solved the unsolvable puzzle. Something was wrong with me."

"What was wrong with you?" Sonny asked.

"Ever since I was ten years old, I've lived in fear," Drake said. "I developed anxieties and insecurities and lost all my self-confidence. Something evil preyed on me. I was vulnerable. Evil saw my weakness and took advantage. Then, after Taylor's murder, the nightmares started, and I couldn't do my job. I felt like a total failure. I couldn't live with myself. The only choice was to run away from everything."

"Sonny, while working with your son over these past few months, he told me about something you taught your boys," Norman said. "The weak always have a chance to win the battle, but the strong always win the war. Tonight, Drake won the war."

"Enough already with the Sonny Merino greatest hits," Mary said. "I'm about to get nauseated over here."

Drake got up and said, "Mom, you forgot Dad's number one hit!" Drake walked over to Mary and sat in her lap as if he was ten years old again. He wrapped his arms around her in an uncomfortable but playful bear hug and said, "Always be there for your mother because your mother will always be there for you."

Drake kissed his mom on the face until she pushed him away. Everyone laughed at his shenanigans. But deep down, Drake meant what he said. He wouldn't be alive without her unconditional love and unceasing support.

Kurt leaned over to Norman and said, "Good thing Sonny wasn't a one-hit-wonder."

Norman replied, "Better to have one hit than none."

When he finally got to bed, Drake spent most of his time tossing and turning. He couldn't sleep as his mind raced a mile a minute, replaying the events of the past couple of years. Every few minutes, chills ran through his body. Drake realized he was losing the battle with his restless legs. So, he surrendered and got out of bed.

Drake walked outside onto his back deck and looked upwards towards the night sky. The moon hovered above, minding its own business. The sight was comforting and peaceful.

All of Drake's anxiety, insecurity, and self-consciousness were now in the past. His nightmares went gone forever. He no longer feared the water. There were no more visions of a headless Alden Moore or Jacklynn Mathews. He accepted Taylor's death, and he stopped feeling guilty about what happened to Nikki. The farther he got away from the past, the more at peace he was with himself.

Drake looked up at the night sky one last time.

Some people believe the moon's bright side is a sign of hope, and the moonlight is a subtle hint that the sun will rise the next day. But there are others who look at the moon's dark side and take a more ominous view. The truth is there is no dark side. At some point, both sides of the moon receive the radiance of the sun.

Drake then remembered when he was in Alden Moore's doorway and the words he heard that night emanating from the light.

YOU MAY ARRIVE A VISITOR,
BUT YOU MAY LEAVE A VICTIM.

On that night, the light in the doorway was right. Drake arrived as a visitor, and he left as a victim. But after all he had been through. Drake realized he had learned a valuable lesson.

IF YOU EVER BECOME A VICTIM,
IT DOESN'T MEAN YOU HAVE TO STAY ONE YOUR WHOLE LIFE.

Other Books by P.H. Figur

The New America

"A thriller with themes relevant to current events. If you're interested in politics or realistic fiction, this book is for you."

"Great to read about our heroes and their love of this country and their sacrifices. Makes you proud to be an American!"

"This book is a reminder of what is in most people's hearts and minds—real patriotism."

"An interesting take on WW3, how politicians operate, and society's response to the hardships a world war creates. Richly drawn characters makes this book a pleasure to read."

Killen

"Worthy of Ten Stars. Absolutely outstanding. Fast, exciting, and totally unputdownable. A definite must read."

"Well-crafted story told from multiple viewpoints with very rich and unique characters."

"The author has taken the ancient story of Cain and Abel and elevated it to a new level, one with unique twists and turns."

Afterword

Thank you for taking the time to read The Divinity Complex. This was my second novel, and it was a pleasure to write. Some may think it's unfortunate to find your passion later in life, but it's better than not finding it at all. I have plenty of books to write and many more stories to tell. So, jump on board. It's going to be a wild ride.

If you would like more information on my other novels and short stories or just want to know more about the author, visit my website at www.phfbooks.com or email me at peter@phfbooks.com.

Made in United States
North Haven, CT
26 October 2022

25965518R00186